THERE WAS A ~~FAINT SCRATCHY~~ SOUND ON THE OTHER END

Not breathing, it was too loud and ragged. Then, faintly, I heard my name. "Louise? Don't hang up. It's me." I stood stock-still. Suddenly I wasn't tired. "It's Tony."

I gasped. "What?..." I started, but he broke in. Still weakly. The scratchy sound went on. It was his breathing.

"Don't say anything," he whispered. "I know Volker..." Pause. "There."

"How?" I whispered back, but I got no answer. He was trying to say something else, there was a kind of hissing sound. "Hhhhee." Another pause. "Dangerous." Silence. Then a strange terrible sound. Something between a moan and a sob and a hiccup. Without thinking, I started to say, "What happened to you?" But with what must have been a surge of energy, Tony gasped. "Don't. Don't ask. He beat me. Wants...etui. Get away." And then there was a clatter. As if he had simply dropped the receiver.

──────────── ★ ────────────

"...a thrilling chase through Paris."
—*Publishers Weekly*

Fly By Night

CAROL McD. WALLACE

WORLDWIDE®

TORONTO • NEW YORK • LONDON
AMSTERDAM • PARIS • SYDNEY • HAMBURG
STOCKHOLM • ATHENS • TOKYO • MILAN
MADRID • WARSAW • BUDAPEST • AUCKLAND

FLY BY NIGHT

A Worldwide Mystery/May 1993

First published by St. Martin's Press, Incorporated.

ISBN 0-373-28004-1

Warmest thanks to: my agent Lynn Seligman for her perpetual perseverance and optimism; my editor Hope Dellon for meticulous care; my able research assistants, Emily Mikulewicz and Linda Ducruet, for improving my percentage of accuracy; and my mother for sending me to Paris at just the right age.

ONE

I HATE TO SAY IT, but it really wasn't the best of times. At least, not for me. Granted, it was spring, April in Paris. (Which is overrated; October is much sunnier.) I had a roof over my head and a decent job and plenty to eat and a pair of almost-new Maud Frizon shoes sitting in my closet. That was the plus side. On the minus side, I had just broken up with my boyfriend and—I know it sounds strange—I thought he was trying to drive me crazy. Literally.

I could have sworn I'd seen him behind me in line at a movie. That might have been coincidence. But a few days later I caught sight of him across the street, walking in the same direction. And on the second floor of Galeries Lafayette. Then I'd look again and he would have gone away. That was bad enough. Then I thought he was trying to get into my apartment when I wasn't there. Or maybe when I was. It was creepy. And it made me very nervous.

Of course, we had not exactly parted amicably. But my romantic experience had not, until then, run to being subtly harassed by a former mate. Sometimes I did think I was losing my mind. Other times I didn't want to do him the favor.

I guess Volker was an error of judgment right from the start. But you can never tell about these things, least of all at the start. We'd met casually; I got caught in an August downpour and ducked into the American bookstore, Shakespeare & Co. I usually avoided it, because it tended to be full of pretentious trust-fund poets, some of whom lived upstairs in exchange for work in the shop. There were always hushed conversations about Ezra Pound going on in corners, and more heated ones about who was going to buy milk at the desk up front. Still, I was wet, it was there, I went in.

And there was Volker. I'm not saying I fell in love at first sight. But in spite of everything, I have to admit he was easy to look at. He had the high cheekbones and brilliant blue eyes I think of as German, but chestnut-brown hair. I kept sneaking looks at him, just to admire, the way you'd look at anything beautiful. Anyway he struck up a conversation and we ended up going out for coffee and then we ended up going out.

We made a striking couple, I'll say that. Particularly on the dance floor. I am small, and Volker, though not exactly tall, was broad-shouldered, and strong enough to throw me around: toss me off his hips, turn me upside down. I have curly red hair, and I always wore it loose when we went dancing. We also shared an interest in clothes. I dressed like a Parisienne (protective coloration, maybe), but Volker had a kind of indefinable international chic. We did turn heads when we walked past crowded cafés. I enjoyed that. For a while.

He also read poetry to me. Hofmannsthal, Hölderlin, Goethe. He was deeply romantic, not just about romance, but about Life. He even had romantic politics: He spent a lot of time working for a group that wanted a united Germany free of American influence. I used to tease him about having an American girlfriend since he hated Americans so much, and he'd say he was getting to know the enemy. He might really have meant it; he had no sense of humor at all.

And then there was his temper. The first time he lost it I thought he might be an epileptic. Honestly. His face turned purple and his eyes bulged and he sputtered, then roared. He was so enraged that he couldn't even throw things—he saved that for when he was calmer. The funny thing was, he sort of enjoyed it. I saw him get really angry only a couple of times (which was still too many). He would lash himself into a frenzy that terrified me and anybody else around, but that he still controlled. It seemed to exhilarate him. And then he was tickled, afterward, at how much he'd scared people. I know, not attractive.

Anyway, he moved in on my life. My friends, my job. He became thick as thieves with my boss, Tony Geist. I worked at a junior-year-abroad program and he often picked me up at the office. I'd find him sitting in our courtyard chatting up the students. Then gradually, though he was still there—at my job, in my apartment—he was paying less attention to me. He spent endless hours on the phone, arguing about ideology and American imperialism. More than once he switched to German just as I walked into the room. And not the German of Goethe either. When we were with Tony, I might have been a shadow. He stood me up a few times and I found out afterward he'd been out with one of our female students. It got ugly. He accused me of jealousy...oh, well. Old story.

So I tried to get rid of him. It wasn't easy. Promises of reform. A pair of green kid gloves under my pillow. Protests that he didn't know what he'd do without me. Of course I waffled. I don't ever want to go through that kind of thing again. Tempests of tears, then a scary kind of exhilaration when things were going smoothly. Finally I put all of his things in a box and took it down to the concierge and told her not to let him in. And (since he did outweigh her by some hundred pounds) I changed my lock. And added another one.

Which was pure bravado, given the nature of my apartment. It had been built as an artist's studio on top of an apartment building on the boulevard St. Germain. To reach it you climbed the stairs to the top of the building and walked across the tarred roof. And since it was a studio, the entire north wall and part of the roof were glass. If Volker really wanted to get in he could.

The first time it happened, I had left and come back to get a heavier coat. As I walked out onto the roof from the stairwell, I thought I heard something scuffle, but there were sometimes cats on the roof. Then when I came out of the apartment, I noticed something different in the shape of the shadows behind the water tank. I called out, "Who's there?" but there was no answer. When I got downstairs Madame Cabrol was watching TV and said nobody had gone up. But she was a little deaf. I was uneasy going home that night but talked myself into climbing the stairs alone. The next day I noticed scratches around the new lock.

It went on like that. You know how, if you once spot a mouse in your kitchen, you keep whirling around each time something moves at the corner of your eye. And pretty soon you're whirling around a lot. I came home early one afternoon and found one of the tubs of geraniums by my door tipped over. No cat could do that. And why would a burglar? If he wanted to get in he had only to break a pane. By then

I was sure it was Volker. I started to hear sounds in the night; maybe the wind rattling a window blind, maybe not. Once you start to listen for those things, you'll hear them. I was not sleeping well. Did I see a face at the window? I hoped not. One night I even woke up from a dream in which someone was calling my name: "Louise, Louise," on a long sighing note. Was someone really calling? Or was I going picturesquely mad?

As I said, not the best of times. By the time my father arrived for his annual spring visit, I was feeling pretty overwrought. And even Daddy, who doesn't see me all that often, said I looked haggard. Thanks, Dad.

Five years ago he came over to make sure the roof over my head didn't leak, and he enjoyed himself so much that he has made an annual event of it. Nothing if not methodical, my father. Actually, I think that's why he liked Paris so much. He stayed at the Hotel St. Simon where they treated him with a formality he relished. And he roamed around studying eighteenth-century furniture. One year he'd be specializing in ormolu, the next he'd be working on marble. *Fleur-de-pêche, verde antico, brèche d' Alep.* Mind you, he didn't really like French furniture. He'd go on and on about the superior integrity of American craftsmanship. But he loved to think he had mastered a body of information.

So he'd come every year in the spring and haunt the musée des Arts Decoratifs and the musée Nissim de Camondo while I was at work. He'd come up to Passy to take me out to lunch with Tony. I found it amusing (though he didn't) that the school whose Paris program I worked for, Winfield College, was his mother's alma mater. In spite of Winfield's pretensions, it hadn't changed a whole lot from those quasi-finishing-school days.

Lunch with Daddy and Tony was a strange experience. Daddy had very smooth manners, but they were Boston lawyerish manners. Tony, unless you knew him well, was frankly heavy sledding. For the first year at my job I'd been scared of him because he had this brusque, arrogant way of making pronouncements instead of making conversation. And then bit by bit other facets of him appeared. He loved to putter, for instance. One day after he'd heard me complaining about how I could never get my front door shut, he came over and fixed it. Of course he did tell me witheringly that "It only needed to be planed," as if it was something any idiot could have figured out. But then he whipped it off the hinges and planed it—which had nothing to do with aircraft, naturally—and fixed my bureau drawer that stuck and rehung a couple of pictures. And the whole time he would sing these side-splitting music hall songs. He couldn't really sing very well but the lyrics were hilarious.

Of course with Daddy things were different. Tony had to prove how smart he was. So Daddy was always asking Tony thoughtful questions about relations between Winfield College and the University of Paris (which could be hair-raising), and Tony would respond by quoting Heidegger. At a given point the conversation would always get onto opera, their only common ground. At that point, I more or less checked out and daydreamed while they traded opinions of the latest recording of *Lakmé* and Renata Scotto's upper register. I'd sat through enough *Traviatas* with Daddy to know opera wasn't my cup of tea. In fact, what he and Tony saw in it was always a mystery to me.

Not the only mystery about Tony, I have to say. For instance, why did he wear only khaki pants and blue shirts ordered in multiples from L.L. Bean? (I think it simplified his life.) Why did his curly hair always stay exactly the same length? (Constant trims with nail scissors?) What about his love life? He was impervious to the charms of our nubile girl students, which I was glad of because that could have made my life really complicated. But he was also impervious to the charms of the boys, and of our constantly changing secretarial staff, some of whom were real beauties. I thought he was saving himself for Maria Callas.

For that matter, I wasn't quite sure what he was doing running Winfield College's junior-year-abroad program since he was, as I've said, smart. He spoke French perfectly and I know he also spoke Italian and German. I had also gathered, though he never talked about it directly the way some people would have, that he had a Ph.D. from the University of Michigan and had even done a fellowship at the American Academy in Rome. But I assumed that, like me, he just wasn't very ambitious. Why bother to be, when you could live perfectly pleasantly in Paris, indulging in the things you really cared about, like shoes and food? Or opera and well, opera?

Anyway, that was the status the day the whole thing started in earnest. It was a lovely spring day, I remember that. Since Daddy had come, I'd been sleeping fine and I was wondering if my imagination wasn't overheated. There had been no noises I couldn't explain, nothing moving out of the corner of my eye, my little cast-iron chairs had not shifted a millimeter since I set them out on the roof. And on this gorgeous morning there were chestnut blossoms, café tables outside, all the clichés. Strawberries in the market for the first time. I noticed that as I walked up to work from putting Daddy on the bus to the airport. I had people coming to dinner and though I had planned on a lemon tart, I thought I'd pick up berries instead on my way home if they still looked all right.

When I got to work, Tony was already there. It occurred to me, as I looked at the back of his head, that he was starting to go bald. The curls were definitely thinning. He didn't seem to have moved since the previous evening, though the date on his newspaper was current, so at least he'd been outside. That was another one of Tony's peculiarities. He read three newspapers a day, the way most people eat three meals. He started with the *International Herald Tribune,* reading the reviews and doing the crossword puzzle. At lunchtime, he read the pompous gray *Le Monde.* And as I was leaving (Tony always stayed late in the office for no obvious reason), he would be reading the gossip rag *Le Quotidien de Paris.* He said this way he got a balanced view.

"Your father got off all right?" he asked as I peered over his shoulder.

"Yes," I said, looking at the clues.

"What's this one?" He pointed to a five-letter gap with a *q* in the middle.

"Queen Mary's hat," I read the clue. "Toque."

"For Christ's sake," he said disgustedly, and scribbled it in. "Oh, guess what? Sago struck again."

"Really?" I said, amused. "Who did he pick on this time?" Mr. Sago played sort of a walk-on part in *Winfield Abroad.* He was an American in his seventies, a dapper gent who haunted the Louvre and had a habit of picking up our students there. He would sidle up to them in front of, say, the Winged Victory of Samothrace, and compare it to, say, Delacroix's *Liberty Leading the People*. If they were interested he'd take them on a tour of the museum, and sometimes to lunch afterward.

"Serena. He told her she looked like the Madonna of the Rocks, and offered to show her the painting. She thought he was 'some kind of pervert.'" Tony raised his voice, perfectly rendering Serena's whiny Long Island accent.

I was silent for a minute imagining what I would have done in her place. Mr. Sago did radiate peculiarity. He was even a little unsavory; I'd seen him once at the opera in a dinner jacket with braid on the lapels that had to be as old as he was, and might not have been cleaned since its birth. "She probably thought he was going to make a pass at her."

"She always does think so." It was true. Serena tended to overestimate her charms. "Also Madame Boguet is coming in today to see you," he added as I turned to leave his office. "She called after you'd left yesterday afternoon. Something about '*punaises.*'"

I sighed. Living in Paris was heavenly. But sometimes my job was just glorified baby-sitting. And sometimes it was like running the complaint department of an unreliable railroad. The Parisian housewives with whom we lodged our students never stopped griping about them. "She thinks Gabriel brought bedbugs in because of her long hair, I bet. She's going to want us to buy her a new mattress."

Tony looked up at me and grinned maliciously. "Of course we couldn't possibly afford to do that," he said.

"Of course not," I agreed, and walked away.

We were lucky enough to have our own building, unlike many of the American college programs that shared a big building on the Left Bank. A rich child-less alumna had left Winfield her nineteenth-century house in one of the nicest Parisian neighborhoods. Nice meaning expensive. Fortunately she had also left a lavish endowment for the junior-year-abroad pro-gram so we didn't have to worry about raising money. Tony would have made a lousy fund-raiser.

As it was he did a reasonably good job. He handled all the external things: enticing French professors to come and teach courses in our building; arranging for our students to take courses in the byzantine Paris university system; haggling over grades and transfers of credits; and dealing with the City of Paris to han-dle taxes and assessments and that kind of thing. You might have thought these jobs demanded a certain tact that Tony certainly didn't have. But somehow his in-tellectual arrogance (and a hide like a rhinoceros) was even more effective than diplomacy in dealing with the Paris bureaucracy.

Diplomacy was my department. From September to November, I dealt with the kids' culture shock. No, they could not have their parents ship them all their food. No, they would not get diseases from shower-ing only once a week. No, it was not a good idea to wear a miniskirt and black fishnet stockings in cer-tain neighborhoods. In the middle of the winter there were usually a few months of calm except for the in-evitable cases of mild bronchitis from the bone-chilling Parisian damp. Then in the spring the housewives (who got paid pretty well for their boarders; we had to compete with all the other colleges) started to grouse. About loud music, too much use of the hot water, or *punaises.* In a month or two I'd be dealing with "I've run out of money" or "I'm in love with François and I think I'm pregnant" or students simply going AWOL and announcing, when they got back, that they'd been to Venice.

But it was still *punaise* season. So that was something to look forward to, I thought, as I flipped through the mail. My office was in a little room right by the front door, probably the room where, a hundred years ago, unwanted visitors were left cooling their heels. Tony occupied the old butler's pantry at the back of the house. The ranks of glass-fronted cupboards were full of books and papers that looked like they'd fall on your head if you dared open a cupboard door. It was very inefficient, having us so far apart. But I guess it worked the way he wanted it to because he hid out in back and I screened all the walk-in traffic. And if I spent hours every day trotting back and forth between his office and mine, well, that wasn't his problem, was it? I could always call him on the intercom, which was this peculiar contraption rigged up for Winfield in the early '70s by some electronics-wizard student. It mostly functioned normally; you could turn it on or off, have your calls switched to any phone in the building, and so on. But every now and then the thing went bonkers. All incoming calls would be routed to one phone, or else they'd ring on all phones and you'd have a mass conference call, or the intercom would suddenly come to life and a private conversation would be broadcast in all the offices. Naturally no French technician could control the contraption. So Tony would have to call the former student who'd put it together (a computer millionaire in Silicon Valley, naturally) and he'd talk

Tony through the repairs. I thought the whole system was ridiculous, but Tony was secretly proud of it.

Aside from the looming threat of the shrewish Madame Boguet, it was a routine day. Students drifted in for a class, I paid bills, I had lunch in the courtyard. Gabriel of the offending long hair came and perched on my desk to protest his innocence, and offered to show me the bug bites on his stomach.

"Oh, Louise, I know you want to see them." He pulled his work shirt out of his jeans.

"You just want to ripple your muscles at me," I said, and tried to pull a file folder out from under him.

"Can I show you my tattoo, then?" The tattoo was on his upper thigh. After he'd had it done (on a weekend in Morocco) he'd dropped his trousers to show me. When Tony came in Gabriel wasn't at all embarrassed. Gabriel was one of those brash amiable free spirits who are completely impervious to other people's opinions. He had been flirting with me all year in a heavy-handed jocular way; harmless but enjoyable. He got on Tony's nerves.

He was pretending to draw a tattoo on the inside of my wrist when the phone rang, and it took me a moment to register that it was my father.

"I'm only allowed the one call, Louise," he was saying, "so pay attention."

"What?" I said foggily, letting my hand go limp in Gabriel's grasp and watching blankly as he started to draw a dragon. Daddy was supposed to be happily ensconced in the Goring Hotel in London by now. "But...allowed? Wait, where are you?"

"Do you have something to write on?" he continued in a steely tone. It was the voice he had always used when something went wrong and he was trying to maintain control, like the time our brakes failed on the Massachusetts Turnpike. Or when my mother died. "I'm being held at Heathrow. Customs found a stolen illuminated missal in my briefcase and some packets of white powder that they tell me is cocaine." He went on, without inflection. "It wasn't my briefcase, of course. Identical on the outside but not mine. But I can't prove it. Call Nick Turner. I don't have his home number because my address book is in my real briefcase, wherever that is. You'll have to get the number from information. It's Brookline, remember. Are you writing this down?"

I wasn't. Gabriel was bent over my hand, adding flames to the dragon's mouth. When I yanked my hand away, the red pen scored a long line down my palm. He looked up in surprise, and I shook my head and made a shooing gesture as I took up a pen and started to write. "Okay, yes. Sorry."

"All right. Call Nick, tell him what's happened and that they'll probably let me post bail. I also want you to call the American Consulate in London. Tell them what's happened. Nick will get in touch with them once he gets here. All right? Now read back what you've written."

Any other time I would have resented being treated like a moron, but obediently I reread his instructions, then blurted out, "Isn't there something I can do? I mean, bring you anything? Or... are you going to be in jail?"

"Yes, Louise, it certainly looks that way," he said with chilling sarcasm. "And I don't want you to visit. Nick will keep you informed. I have to go now." And he hung up.

I could feel my face crumple as our connection was broken and a series of clicks was followed by the dial tone. I put the receiver down carefully on my desk and sank my head into my hands, as if I could scoop the tears back into my eyes.

"Hey! Are you all right? Here, wait, take this." Gabriel hadn't moved since I yanked my hand away, but now he untied the bandanna from around his neck and thrust it in my hand. He put a hand on my shoulder and patted awkwardly. "Is everything okay?"

I sat up straight and tried to stop crying. "Yes," I said, and took a deep breath. Shut my eyes. Took another breath. "I'll be all right. My father's in some trouble." I blotted my eyes and hung up the phone.

"Is he all right? I mean, he's not hurt or anything?"

"No." I swallowed hard and blew my nose. I couldn't think about Daddy in jail. "Excuse me, but I need to make some calls," I said, not looking at Gabriel.

"Sure. Sorry. Keep the..." He didn't finish, but sidled out. I picked up the phone and dialed Massachusetts information.

Nick Turner is my godfather. He tried to be reassuring, but it was obvious he was alarmed. "I'll take the shuttle and hope to catch the Concorde," he said, thinking out loud, "and he didn't say anything more specific about bail? No figure? All right. I'll call the consulate for you, I know somebody there."

That sounded like a good idea, since there was still a big lump in my throat and I could just imagine myself bursting into tears on the phone to the consul. "But what can I do?" I asked. "I want to go see him, but he said I shouldn't."

Uncle Nick's voice softened. "Weezie," he said, using my old nickname, "your father doesn't want you to see him in jail. You understand that. I know it's going to be hard just sitting and waiting, but I'll call you the instant I know anything. There's really nothing else for you to do."

There really wasn't. When I'd hung up the phone I could hear Gabriel out in the hall singing a snatch of "Eleanor Ribgy." I couldn't face him, or Madame Boguet and her mattresses. Or Tony, for that matter. I grabbed my purse, thrust Gabriel's damp bandanna into his hand on my way out, and left. No note, no excuse.

When I got outside the sun was still shining. Automatically I turned left, heading down toward the river. People were still sitting in cafés. I was thinking about Daddy in jail. Wondering if they put him in a separate cell. I tried to imagine what he looked like now, but my mind flinched away from it. Fastidious Daddy.

I walked home in a daze of worry, though I remember glaring at the driver of a Peugeot who tried to cut me off at a crosswalk. Madame Cabrol the concierge looked surprised to see me home so early, but I swept by her without stopping to chat. I marched up the six flights of stairs and across the tarred roof to the studio. I was greeted by the smell of the lamb marinade (red wine, rosemary, garlic). I opened all the windows as wide as I could and considered the lamb, sitting innocently in a bowl on Tony's ingeniously constructed kitchen counter. I'd never be able to eat it. So I picked up the bowl and ran downstairs and gave it to Madame Cabrol, explaining that I was ill and wouldn't be having my dinner guests and didn't want it to go to waste. She clucked and shook her head and offered me a *tisane* and called me her *"pauvre petite,"* but I finally got away. Then I called my guests and told them the same story. None of them called me *"pauvre petite,"* but they were all sympathetic. Then I put my answering machine on so I wouldn't have to talk to Tony, and gave myself up to worrying.

TWO

As the sun turned gold and the air turned chilly with twilight, I sat on a sofa and brooded. I got up every now and then to make a pot of tea, to change my clothes for a kimono, to splash water on my face. I plucked a few stray eyebrows. Sentimentally I dusted Lily and Elsie, the pair of Staffordshire china pugs that my father had given me as a belated birthday gift. Lily was slightly cross-eyed, which Daddy had said made her more valuable. Mostly I fretted, picking at my hangnails until they bled, wandering out onto the roof and peering over the parapet onto the street below. I knew I was only making myself miserable. I should have left, gone for a walk or something. But I wanted to be there, just in case someone called.

Finally I decided to do something useful and make asparagus soup out of what would have been the first course of dinner. Midway through the second chopped onion, someone rang the handbell hung outside the door.

My heart sank. To familial disaster, I was about to add social disaster. Without even putting down my butcher knife I padded barefoot to the door, knowing what I would find. My guests were to have been the usual mixed bag: some French, some American, some old friends, some new acquaintances, and the inevitable friend of a friend who had been given my phone number as someone to call in Paris. That evening's friend of a friend was Edward Cole, an American lawyer who had just been transferred over here. And whom I had forgotten to call to say that dinner was canceled.

I opened the door and leaned against the frame. I suddenly felt very tired.

There was a very tall man standing by the parapet, looking down at the traffic. Boring lawyer's suit (I was an expert in those, from Daddy). Pretty good shoes, not polished often enough. In his left hand, a huge bouquet wrapped in the paper of the expensive florist around the corner in the rue du Bac. Biggish ears. Then he turned around. For a moment he leaned back against the parapet, taking me in, I supposed. There I stood in all my glory: barefoot, kimono-clad, hair knotted on top of my head with a couple of chopsticks thrust through, holding a butcher knife. Not an inspiring sight.

He pushed himself off the parapet and walked over with two long strides. *"Pardonnez-moi, mademoiselle, sans doute je me suis trompé..."* he began, in perfect French.

Automatically I started to answer him in the same language, then abruptly switched. *"Non, non, monsieur...* No, I'm sorry," I said, my voice dropping out of the polite Parisian singsong. "You must be Edward Cole. You're in the right place and everything. It's my fault, I canceled the party and I just..." I paused and, with an embarrassed flourish of the knife, finished: "forgot to call you."

He just stood there, easily six four, one hand in his pocket, head a little cocked, looking quizzical. Then he thrust out the hand with the bouquet and said, "Well, you should have these anyway."

I backed up a step or two, over the threshold.
"Thank you, that's awfully kind, I-I..." I stuttered
myself into silence. He just looked at me calmly. I felt
awful. For a moment I stood there staring at him, my
mind blank. Then I heard myself say, "Look, would
you like a drink anyway? I was just about to open a
bottle of wine." Then I realized it was true. A glass of
wine sounded like a good idea.

His expression didn't change. "If you like. Or I'll
just vanish quietly."

"No, no," I said, and tried to smile warmly. I put
down the knife too. "I'm not sick or anything, and
you're here and you brought these nice flowers." I
stopped myself, and looked up at him. I am five three
if you don't mash my hair down. It was like looking at
the steeple of a church.

He said, "Well, then, yes, thank you," and prof-
fered the flowers again with a tiny smile. This time I
took them.

As I opened the wine and took two glasses off the
table to fill, he stood in the center of the room, with
his hands behind his back, and looked around. Daddy
liked to refer to it as my "garret," and it did have a
stagey air, with its wall of windows, the pair of long
Second Empire couches draped in paisley shawls, the
painted tin trunk set between them, the tattered Ori-
ental rugs. Cole studied the table, set with mismatched faience, the pine dresser and the lacquered
screen and the bright red door that closed off the narrow hall to the bathroom and bedroom. "Thank
you," he said as I handed him his glass. "It's quite a
room. Did you, um, furnish it?"

"No," I said, and explained that I sublet from an
Italian illustrator. I had gone back to the flowers and

was cutting the paper off them. Apricot-colored tulips, with petals ruffled at the edges. A sophisticated
choice, particularly for a man who looked so staid. He
was older than I'd expected, in his late thirties or even
forty. Brown hair going gray, but not thinning. Strong
eyebrows that would probably get bushy when he was
older. I kicked a little stepstool over to the cupboard
where a cut-glass bowl sat on the top shelf. As I got
down, bowl in hand, he had turned to watch me.

"Can I help?" he asked.

"No, thank you, it's done. The flowers are lovely,
thank you."

He watched me trim the stems and place the flowers in the bowl. Of course they wouldn't cooperate and
kept flopping back onto the counter. I swore and went
back to the stool, but Cole forestalled me. "Here, let
me." He put his glass down and peered up at the top
shelf. I decided he must have trouble with a lot of
doors. "There's a sort of jug up here, is that what you
want?"

"There is? Can I see it?" He stretched a bit and
brought down a blue-and-white beaker I'd never seen
before. "Is there anything else up there?" I asked in
astonishment. He patted the top shelf and brought
forward a tiny shot glass, only about three inches high.

"I don't know how you've lived without this," he
remarked mildly, handing it to me, then rinsing his
hands in the sink.

"Sorry. I don't dust up there too often," I said, ex-
amining the shot glass. It was faceted, and a small
medallion was set in its narrow base. When you peered
through the bottom of the glass, you could see a pansy
painted on the inside of the medallion. I gave him a

towel to dry his hands. "Look; it has a flower in it." I showed him the glass.

He took it gently and turned it around. "My great-grandmother had a set of these," he said. "A different flower in each one. We used to take our cough medicine from them." He gave it back to me. "Do you want to finish what you were doing when I rang the bell?" He eyed the pile of asparagus on the chopping block.

"Yes, I might as well," I said. "Why don't you sit at the table. Just push one of those places aside."

He folded up onto one of the dining chairs, and carefully pushed cutlery and napkin aside. I picked up my knife and started chopping, and there was a little silence. I remembered about Daddy.

"You're probably wondering why..." I started.

"How long have you lived..." he began at the same time. We both stopped, took a breath, and started again.

"Go ahead," he said. "What were you going to say?"

"I was going to explain why I canceled dinner," I said. "I told everyone else I had the flu, but it's actually some family trouble." I glanced at him. There he sat, holding his glass by the stem like a serious wine drinker, looking at me deadpan. I knew I shouldn't say anything more. I knew next to nothing about him; only that he had gone to Yale Law School with my old friend Matthew Steele. He seemed polite and no guest with manners would press for details of what was, after all, private. And something I should probably keep private.

But there was something restful about him. He seemed unshockable, as if he wouldn't cluck or fuss.

Impulsively I said, "My father was arrested at Heath-row this afternoon for smuggling a stolen missal and some cocaine. They were in his briefcase, only it wasn't his."

Cole didn't twitch. But he kept his eyes on me. "And he's in custody now? No wonder you didn't want a dinner party. What's being done?"

I put my knife down and rubbed my forehead. "His lawyer's flying over and he's called the American Consulate. The lawyer seemed to think they would let him post bail." I sighed. "I'm sure it will all work out fine, but I *worry* about him. And his lawyer's great at trusts and estates but probably doesn't know a thing about criminal law. Let alone English criminal law."

"Mmm." Cole reached for a fork and flicked the tines with the tip of his finger. "Do you know how much cocaine it was?"

"He just said 'some packets.'"

"He doesn't use it himself," Cole stated, but it was a question.

"He's a Christian Scientist. Won't even take an aspirin."

"I see. And a stolen missal?"

"Yes. Illuminated. Daddy hates the Middle Ages. He thinks Western civilization began with Martin Luther." I thought of something. "Anyway, how do they know it's stolen?"

"Interpol bulletins. Once they'd stopped your father and found it, they'd check the listings of stolen objects. Why did they stop him?"

"I can't imagine," I answered, shaking my head. Cole was sitting upright now, still calm, but concentrating.

"I wonder... It must have been a very thorough search. Presumably the missal was pretty carefully wrapped. And you say it wasn't his briefcase?" I nodded. "So meanwhile he is protesting ignorance of it all." He raised his eyebrows. "Very peculiar."

"What?"

"The combination. A little of this, a little of that. So casually placed. It's obviously not a professional job. I think actually your father's chances of getting bailed out are good, particularly once they dust the contents of the case for his fingerprints. Assuming they won't find any." He looked up at me. "What do you think happened? You know your father. Any ideas?"

I started chopping asparagus again. "If I wanted to get something through customs without a search, I'd give it to Daddy. Well, I mean I have. Clothes and things. He's so respectable-looking. I thought maybe somebody had planted it on him. I don't know how they'd get it back but—pickpockets? It couldn't be too hard."

"It's a little unusual. Usually couriers know what they're carrying. And are paid. But usually they're carrying large quantities. Here it seems almost as if the cocaine had been an afterthought." He frowned, bouncing the fork.

"Why do you know so much about this?" I asked. "I know you're a lawyer too but I thought... you're with some corporation, aren't you?"

"No." This time the smile was wry. "I'm with the government. The U.S. Attorney's office."

"But this is Paris."

"Right."

"So..."

"I'm setting up an investigation here. That's really all I can tell you."

"But you know a lot about drug smuggling."

"Not really."

I sighed. "Well, more than I know. This is just going to *destroy* Daddy." I chopped for a moment in silence, trying to think hard about asparagus and not my father in a jail cell.

Cole pushed his chair back and stood up. "You know, I just might be able to get some information. Someone I know slightly in London. I'll go back to the office and make a couple of calls."

I gaped at him. "But...you hardly know me.... It's a lot of trouble." I felt my eyes welling up, the way they always do when somebody's extra nice. I put the knife down and pressed the heels of my hands against my eyes. They were oniony. It only made it worse.

When I looked up, Cole was standing in front of me. He put a hand on each of my shoulders and said, "Don't worry. At the very worst, your father will be bailed out tomorrow. I'll call you later, whether or not I find anything out. You'll be all right alone?"

By then, of course, tears were pouring down my face. He was the second man that day to give me a handkerchief; his was regulation white. He took it from his pocket and put it in my hand, then turned and left.

I burst into sobs the instant the door closed, and the handkerchief was drenched (and streaked with mascara) by the time I was done. Actually, I felt better. Partly because of crying. Also partly because of Edward Cole.

True to his word, he called. Though I've had a lot of experience with guys who say they will and don't, I hadn't doubted him for an instant.

"Louise?" He had a great voice for the phone, deep and resonant.

"Hi. Listen, I have to apologize for behaving like that, I'm so embarrassed—"

"Louise," he said again, cutting me off. "Don't. It's natural. You probably felt a lot better afterward. Anyway, I have a little news. Apparently there was a tip-off about a bombing at some state banquet for the King of Jordan. Anyone entering England today was searched very thoroughly. So that explains why your father was stopped. And I'm told he will be released on bail as soon as his lawyer appears. And if it can be proved that it wasn't his briefcase, they'll drop the charges."

"How will they prove it?"

"As I said, fingerprints, the contents; they may call you for a list of what he usually carried."

I could feel my eyes getting all hot again. "Thank God," I said.

"And they've tried to make him fairly comfortable. He's in a cell by himself," Cole added. "It's still jail, but it could be worse."

He wouldn't listen to my thanks. He just said it was late, and told me to call him when I heard anything.

IT HAPPENED THE WAY he had said it would. Early the next morning, Daddy called.

"I've been sprung," he said, clearly jubilant. I thought he was also a little punchy, but that was his prerogative. Evidently his prints weren't on anything in the briefcase, and the papers had been a lot of bro-

chures for travel to California, instead of Daddy's
notes on marble and ormolu (which he was furious
about losing). The charges were dropped. He and
Uncle Nick were flying right home. Daddy said he was
so mad at the Brits he didn't want to spend any money
in their country. That sounded like Daddy.

Then Uncle Nick got on the phone. "I wanted your
father to keep this little episode quiet but he's rather
pleased with himself. I think he's going to dine out on
the story for years. But you won't talk about it, will
you? And I just wanted to ask you if you can think of
any time when the briefcase could have been
switched."

"It has to have been at the airport," I said. "Don't
you think?"

"I would have said so. But he swears not. Says nobody got close enough to him. It's very odd. I mean,
we still don't know if it was a mistake, or if somebody planted the case on your father on purpose. Give
it some thought, okay, Weezie?" And before I could
thank him (or burst into tears again) he hung up.

I went out onto the roof and looked down. Just another busy spring morning in Paris. Cars honking,
clumsy buses, and a glowing light streaming down the
boulevard St. Germain from the east. Daddy winging
back to the States. I suddenly felt a little lonely. Boston was pretty far away.

Of course the briefcase switch must have been a
mistake. It seemed impossible that somebody could
have gone to the airport, waiting for a passenger with
exactly the same briefcase to get on a plane to London. If you wanted to transport a stolen missal and
some cocaine to London, why not just dress up as a
lawyer and carry them yourself?

Because then if you got caught you might go to jail. While if somebody else got caught, he would go to jail.

It made me mad, and I shook myself like a dog shaking off water and looked at my watch. It wasn't even nine o'clock. I dressed in a hurry and wrapped half the tulips to take to work. If I rode my Mobylette I wouldn't even be late.

As I wheeled it into the courtyard of the building in Passy, it seemed hard to believe that I had only been gone for an afternoon. Even though nothing had changed, I felt as if it should have. But there was Tony, in exactly the same spot where I had left him. Wearing the blue shirt and khakis. Doing the crossword puzzle.

He looked up and frowned. "Damn it, where were you yesterday afternoon? Madame Boguet came in breathing fire and there wasn't anybody to talk to her."

"Except you," I said. "Did you promise her the new mattress?"

"Yes. She's an incredible harridan. Can't you find someone else with a spare bedroom? It seems to me that ninety percent of these people are more trouble than they're worth."

I rolled my eyes. He didn't know the half of it. To soothe him I said, "You're right, I'll see about finding some new landladies. And it isn't as if I was just out playing around. Daddy got arrested."

I don't know what kind of reaction I had expected. Surprise, maybe incredulity. Instead, he stared up from the paper and, for a moment, I thought I saw fear behind his black-framed glasses. Pure, frozen alarm. Then he blinked, and I realized I must have been wrong. "What? That's nonsense, Louise. What a stupid excuse." He unfolded the newspaper and ostentatiously spread it out on his desk.

I was dumbfounded. "It's not an excuse. It's true. Daddy was arrested at Heathrow for smuggling a stolen missal and some cocaine."

I looked down. Tony was still staring at his newspaper, but his shoulders were rigid. Then he looked up. This time he was incredulous. "You're not kidding, are you?"

"No, Tony, I'm *not*. When customs opened Daddy's suitcase they found an illuminated medieval missal. And some packets of cocaine."

"Cocaine? Your father? That's ridiculous." With much rustling he folded his newspaper up and then glared up at me. Then it dawned on me that for some reason Tony was furious. Maybe it was because I'd left and he'd had to deal with, heaven help him, a problem. But he certainly was overreacting.

"Fine," I said airily. "If you'd rather believe I was out shopping for shoes, go ahead," and I turned smartly and stalked back to my own office.

Tony's social skills were seldom his strong suit. It wasn't until I had put the tulips in water, sorted the mail, written three letters, and answered innumerable phone calls that he came and apologized. Of course he didn't actually apologize.

"Are you serious?" He no longer looked mad or scared. Just intent.

I looked back at him with my best I-may-only-be-five-three-but-don't-mess-with-me look. "Perfectly," I said, and turned back to the typewriter.

"But your father's so...straight."

"I didn't say it was his. Besides, he'd never steal a missal. First of all he wouldn't steal and second he couldn't care less about prayerbooks. The stuff wasn't his. The briefcase wasn't even his. Somehow somebody must have switched with him.''

Tony's reaction was to give me another one of those inscrutable looks and walk away.

Edward Cole called later that morning to see what had happened, and I thanked him profusely though he pointed out that he really hadn't done anything. And then before I could say anything about a repeat invitation, he excused himself and put a hand over the receiver of the phone. When he came back on he said he had to go and that he would call me. This time I wondered if he would.

The tulips lasted all week.

THREE

THE WEATHER TURNED sour over the weekend, so I spent most of Saturday and Sunday refinishing the chest of drawers in my bedroom. It was sort of unfortunate, because the sanding and varnishing left my mind free. And of course I brooded. What set me off was finding a pair of Volker's socks stuck behind one of the drawers when I pulled them out. Blue-gray cable-knit cashmere. Typical Volker. For all his political ardor, he was fanatical about his own comfort.

I couldn't decide quite what to do with the socks; they were too expensive to throw away, but I sort of felt like I should touch them with tongs. I ended up using them as rags for the refinishing. It seemed appropriate.

He had started messing with the phone. At least I had assumed it was he when the phone rang at four that morning and there was nobody there, just crackling. I took the phone off the hook and buried it under my duvet and tried to get back to sleep but it was hard. It always is when you wake up with your heart pounding. And when you have the conviction that somebody is watching your every movement. While my father was visiting, coming and going every day, Volker had left me alone. And now that Daddy was gone, he'd resumed his campaign.

What I thought about until 6 A.M., when I finally got back to sleep, was moving out. And as I sanded the long side of the bureau, I thought about it some more.

I didn't want to. I liked my apartment and housing was hard to find in Paris. But what else was I going to do? I could just imagine the reaction if I went to the Paris police—it was probably perfectly legal in France for a man to harass his ex-girlfriend. I wished I knew what Volker wanted from me. Assuming he wanted anything concrete.

I sighed and turned the bureau upright, then sat back on my heels. I didn't even know whom to ask for advice. I'd thought of mentioning the situation to Daddy but we had never, even when I was living at home, been on the kind of terms that included my talking to him about boyfriends. There was Tony; but that was a terrible idea. Not only was Tony a friend of Volker's, but I was beginning to think that maybe he was not the kind of guy to count on in a crunch. Well, not in an emotional crunch, anyway. He'd always been brilliant in practical emergencies, and faithful (once we were friends) about things like picking me up at the airport. There was no one in the world I'd rather go to the movies with. But his behavior on Friday about Daddy had been frankly weird.

As I pried open a can of varnish I ran over the scene in my mind, telling Tony about Daddy and seeing his reaction. *Had* he looked frightened? It made no sense; but then nothing about the whole episode did. How could Daddy have ended up with this other briefcase that looked exactly like his? Granted, it was a fairly ordinary one, scuffed oil-finished calf. But ordinary for America, not for France. And if somebody switched cases with Daddy on the assumption that customs wouldn't stop him, how could they guarantee that he wouldn't just open the case and discover it wasn't his? It could have been locked, I supposed. I'd have to ask Daddy.

But still. Even without considering what would have happened in London (would somebody switch back? would he be the victim of a prearranged mugging?), he said nobody had come close enough to him to have exchanged briefcases. I tended to believe him. So then, when had it been done? He had gone to the airport bus from my apartment.

I had too much varnish on the brush and a big drop splashed on the floor. So much for not paying attention to what you're doing. After that I tried to keep my mind on the job, but it kept drifting. Volker, Tony, moving, getting a new phone number. I tried to concentrate on how angry Volker made me. I didn't want to think about the other side of the problem, which was that I was getting scared. Phone calls, visitations—what would be next?

By Monday the chest was finished, the drawers re-lined, the clothes arranged in them, the socks, now stiff with varnish and sawdust, consigned to whatever fate the City of Paris determined for its garbage. And I was still uneasy. My concern about Daddy and the briefcase had receded from the near-obsession level it reached over the weekend, but I still didn't know what to do about Volker. That was the problem with man-ual labor, I thought as I unchained my Mobylette. It gave you too much time to think. As I stuffed my purse in the saddlebag it occurred to me that the Mo-bylette could use a paint job (and I'd always hated the pale blue anyway). And that it was just going to have to wait, rust or no rust.

My phone was ringing when I walked in the front door at Passy and I dashed for it, wondering who, in the city of casual working hours, was calling at 9 A.M.

That deep voice again—Edward. "I was wondering if you'd have dinner with me some time this week." Oh. Fine. Yes, I was free Wednesday. "Would you mind the Closerie des Lilas? It's sort of a sentimental favorite of mine." No, lovely. "Shall I pick you up, or do you want to meet there?" Wow. A real date. I said I could get there on my own. "Okay. Is eight-thirty all right?" Fine, fine. "Good. I'll look forward to seeing you then." *Click-click, buzz.*

I sat back and ruminated. Usually, a guy asks you out on a date if he finds you attractive and entertains some notions of a romantic and/or sexual (I should probably put that the other way around) liaison. Or he asks you on a date if he has some other agenda and old-fashioned manners. If, for instance, he is trying to cultivate you for business reasons. Or if he is new in town and has been told to look you up.

Given our first meeting and the impression I must have left (a knife-wielding hysteric?), I guessed that this evening fell into the last category and Edward hadn't considered the possibility of, say, a drink after a movie. Which would at least have given us something to talk about. Still. It was a kindly gesture and I'd do my best to make it a pleasant evening.

When Wednesday came I decided that, since Edward was being so formal and polite about dinner, I might as well meet him halfway. It wasn't that I wanted to vamp him. For one thing, I wasn't ready to think about other men yet. I still hadn't gotten Volker out of my system. And Edward Cole was not my type at all. All the same I went home Wednesday night and washed my hair, changed my clothes, put on perfume. Even put on heels, remembering his height.

He was there when I got there, and I have to admit, my heart sank a little. When I spotted him sitting at the table, he looked so boring. But when he saw me and stood up, he said, "No knife?" in that sexy voice.

"No knife. And I've brought back your handkerchief, and I have shoes on," I said, sitting down. From then on, it was clear sailing.

He never stopped being polite, but I realized it wasn't an effort he was making, he was just naturally courteous. For instance, he asked my opinion about the wine. "You probably know French wines better than I do," he said. No man had ever done that before.

And he asked tons of questions. About living in Paris, why I was there, what my life was like, the people I met. I kept thinking I should try to change the subject, but he seemed so interested. He couldn't hear enough about Tony. It was a little funny, the way he wanted to dwell on him.

"I wonder," Edward mused between courses, "what the career path is for somebody like Tony."

"Well," I said, a little defensive (after all, what is the career path for somebody like me?), "not everybody is ambitious."

"No, of course," he said instantly. "But with those credentials, a Ph.D. and a fancy fellowship, he could be teaching anywhere."

"I think he'd be a lousy teacher. He's very difficult. Besides, I've wondered sometimes about the credentials. He's not the most truthful person ever."

Edward pulled the bottle of Graves (thank heaven, I'd chosen well) from the wine bucket and refilled my glass. "In what sense?"

"Well—he's just unreliable. I think sometimes he tells lies just to stir things up. Or because he thinks he's so smart that he can make things be true if he wants them to be."

"Such as?"

I tried to think of an example. "Oh, once the president of Winfield was here to check us out (though I think he really just wanted a vacation) and Tony said he'd get Bernard Henri-Levy—you know, the philosopher with the long hair; Mel Gibson for intellectuals—to give a lecture. Now, Henri-Levy is just about the most fashionable person in Paris. And of course he wouldn't come. But right up to the very day of the supposed lecture, Tony kept saying he would. And then he pretended he'd canceled."

"Was anybody fooled?"

"Yes. Actually, everybody was except me, and the only reason I knew the truth was that because of our stupid intercom I heard Tony call Henri-Levy and get turned down." Just then the waiter brought our main courses, but when he'd left, I said, poking at my sweetbreads, "The thing about Tony is, he's deeply, deeply insecure. So in a way he's always pushing himself to prove that the rules don't apply to him because he's special." I paused, thinking about what I'd said. It had never occurred to me before, but it was true. "Like once he got out of paying an assessment for new sidewalks because we were an educational institution. It wasn't really the money, because Winfield is loaded. I think he just wanted to take on the French bureaucracy. He really relished it. Does that make sense?"

"Yes, but it's dangerous," said Edward. "Disruption of the social contract. If you'll excuse the lawyer's point of view."

"No, I agree completely. It makes me furious." And then we were launched on a discussion of the social contract, and from there I finally got Edward to talk a little bit about himself. It turned out that his French was so good because he'd done a Fulbright in Montpellier a dozen years earlier, studying sixteenth-century Provençal paintings. And then hadn't been able to get a teaching job he wanted, and had gone to law school, which he enjoyed, to his surprise. He liked his government work because it was varied. But he wouldn't say anything else about it.

At some point during the evening, I realized that I wanted to make a good impression on Edward. I really liked him. Enjoyed him. He had a nice sense of humor: Well, actually, he laughed whenever I said something I thought was funny. And it also became clear that I didn't have to try to make an impression. He was having fun too.

And I'd changed my mind about why we were having this date. I wasn't sure it *was* just good manners. Believe me, I was cautious. With my psychic bruises from Volker so fresh, I wasn't about to make any new mistakes. But Edward seemed very...interested. He watched me. He seemed to be studying me sometimes. Complimented me in the most matter-of-fact way. I usually take compliments with a grain of salt. But, for instance, we were talking about exploring the city and he said, "The men don't bother you? I've often thought it might be hard to be a pretty woman in a Latin city." Of course I pointed out that you don't have to be pretty for a lowlife to make awful noises at you. But a comment like that made me feel, well, appreciated.

I was surprised at how late it was when we left. I hadn't noticed, but there were only a few people in the bar, and the garden and dining room were empty. It was a little cool when we got outside, but pleasant. Edward said he'd walk me home, and we ambled slowly along the rue d'Assas. I had on a silk shirt and I was a little chilly so I was hugging my elbows unconsciously, when Edward stopped. "Here, you're cold," he said, and took off his jacket, dropping it over my shoulders. I burst out laughing; when I put my arms in the sleeves, my hands didn't even reach the ends. But I was grateful.

I must have rolled up the sleeves without thinking, because when we got to the front door of my building and I gave him back the coat he had to roll them down. I told him I'd had a wonderful evening. "So have I," he said, with a contented little smile. Actually, I had been wondering since we left the restaurant how to say good night. I'd made up my mind to kiss him on the cheek, but he got there first. Deliberately, with his hands on my waist, he kissed both of my cheeks. And said, "Good night. *Beaux rêves.*" Then he stood there for an instant, just looking down. I had the sense, somehow, that he might be trying to make up his mind. Anyway he kissed me lightly on the lips, and turned and left.

The phone was ringing when I got to the top of the stairs. It rang steadily for three minutes, then I took it off the hook. I tossed and turned a lot that night, but each time I woke up completely, it was Edward I was thinking about.

WE HAD sort of expected bits and pieces from Daddy's briefcase to surface; if it had just been stolen,
maybe his address book would be thrown into a gutter, that kind of thing. But by Saturday, when I called
him in Boston, he'd heard nothing. I asked him, just
out of curiosity, if he'd even tried to open the other
briefcase on his trip, but he hadn't. Had his tickets and
a murder mystery in his pocket. He also swore, again,
that nobody had come close enough to him on the
plane or in the airport to make the switch. And then
he said he was tired of talking about it and he didn't
want to run up my bill so he'd say good-bye.

I was a little depressed after that. Sometimes weekends did stretch out a little. It was an iffy day, warm
but with a high cloud cover. Not really nice enough to
encourage leaving town. I went, instead, to the
Louvre.

I hadn't been there in months and noodled around
aimlessly for a while. And ended up in a gallery I'd
never visited before, full of sixteenth-century paintings. Some were portraits, some were religious. One in
particular (a "Lamentation," according to the terse
label), painted in Provence, was pretty staggering.
Gold background, tiny city on the horizon, Jesus being taken down from the cross. Very stark; very moving.

Of course I was thinking of Edward. Basically, I was
curious to see what it was he'd studied on his Fulbright. Maybe I hoped that somehow I'd get a reading on his character. (Of course studying Goethe had
not exactly done me much good with Volker.) You
know: Does he tell fibs? Is he kind to bores? What it
really came down to was, can I trust him? When I was

with him, he had seemed so solid, so reliable. But the feeling had faded.

And I really wanted to know. He'd actually written me a postcard thanking *me* for dinner. I called, and invited him to come for dinner on Tuesday. I would have to say he was coming on pretty strong and in spite of all my reservations I was…well, here I was in front of those paintings, looking for answers. You know how it is, you swear you won't be susceptible and try to save yourself pain. You look for any clue that a man might be trouble. And you try very hard to maintain your defenses. But there was something about Edward that undermined my resolve.

In the next room there was a group of Holbein drawings, mostly portraits. They were amazingly modern-looking, straightforward and detailed. I was thinking that maybe Edward could explain why they looked so current when I heard a soft voice virtually in my ear.

"Quite extraordinary, aren't they, Miss Gerard?" I jumped about a mile even though I knew the instant I heard him that it was Mr. Sago.

As I said hello, I reflected that, living in America with a normal job and normal friends, you wouldn't even look twice at a guy like this. You might see him in his fusty old suits and pince-nez at the public library and never give him a second thought. But in a funny way, Mr. Sago was a staple character in my Paris life. I ran into him every few months at a cultural event, he picked up our students, Tony saw him occasionally at the opera. He had even lectured at Winfield once, when one of our art history professors called in sick, but it wasn't a success.

And there he was, staring at a drawing of Edward VI with me. It *was* extraordinary, especially if you'd ever seen the Disney version of *The Prince and the Pauper*. I didn't think Mr. Sago had.

"I like to compare these drawings to the Clouet miniatures," he said in his pedantic way. "Similar composition, similar subject, but the execution...worlds apart," he said. "Would you like to see?"

It was, as I said, not the best weather. I didn't have any plans for the rest of the weekend. I was pretty eager to avoid sitting at home and brooding. And I was curious about Mr. Sago. After all, I'd known about him for so long, and I wondered just what he was telling our students. So off we went. He trotted through the galleries, stopping here and there to rhapsodize about a canvas, greeting a number of guards by name, telling a couple of witty anecdotes at the expense of the Minister of Culture. By the time we fetched up in front of the Clouets, I was genuinely impressed. And when he asked me to have lunch with him, it sounded like a great idea.

So we went to the Restaurant des Arts, where he was known by name. He told me that he lived in a house near the musée Rodin where Proust had gone to garden parties. (I think Proust must have had a double to visit all the houses he was supposed to have gone to.) He said he spent a few months every winter in Venice, where they referred to him as "Il Professore" because he was so knowledgeable. He said I had a wonderful eye, based on my reaction to Titian's *Man with a Glove*. It was probably exactly the line he used on our students (and whomever else he might pick up at the Louvre) but it was pleasant, and we walked the few blocks home very amicably. We were standing outside my building and he was saying "We must do this again some time" and I found myself inviting him to come to dinner on the same night as Edward. He was very pleased, began to twitter, and after a bit of fussing and patting of pockets gave me a large engraved calling card on which he wrote his phone number "in case there should be any change."

When I got upstairs I was sort of irritated at myself. It wasn't that I necessarily wanted a tête-á-tête dinner with Edward. It might be a little easier to have other people around. But Mr. Sago was such an oddity that it promised a pretty sticky evening. So I called Gisele, a ravishing Frenchwoman who worked for the Alliance Française. And at the last minute Tony came too because his stove broke and he was tired of eating out. Which was unfortunate in more ways than one.

FOUR

IT WAS A lovely day, and I hauled some extra chairs and a little table outside so we could have drinks on the roof. Tony arrived early with a brand-new balloon whisk for me because he thought my old one looked rusty. Then he paced up and down drinking a Stella Artois out of the bottle and acting out for me a scene he'd witnessed at a recital the night before when in the middle of some quiet passage a grande dame in a long dress started screaming because a mouse was climbing up the inside of her skirt. He was doing all the voices: the lady, her husband, the house manager, and the soprano who refused to come back onstage for twenty minutes afterward. I was laughing so hard there were tears in my eyes and I couldn't see so I finally gave Tony a pair of scissors and put him to work cutting the thorny tips off the leaves of the artichokes.

Mr. Sago came next, on the dot of eight. I wondered if he had been walking around the block to arrive so precisely. He had brought a box of chocolates from Debauve & Gallais, reputedly Proust's favorite *confiseur*. He was explaining this to me when Edward Cole arrived, and there was a little confusing moment of accepting Edward's flowers and getting them introduced. Tony had vanished to make a phone call and reappeared at the bedroom door just as I was saying "and Mr. Cole works for the U.S. Attorney's office. Oh, and I think you know Mr. Geist," I said, gesturing to Tony and wondering if we were going to call each other "Mr." and "Miss" all night.

Tony hesitated at the bedroom door for an instant, then came forward. He nodded to Edward but barely glanced at Mr. Sago. I remember thinking his greeting was typical of his lack of finesse. He came back behind the kitchen counter to work on his artichokes, but I shooed him outside with the other two, promising to bring their drinks after them.

I unwrapped the flowers first. They were lilies of the valley. On May 1, there's an old tradition of selling bunches of lily of the valley on Paris streets. I bent down to smell them, shutting my eyes to drink in that heady sweetness. When I opened them, Edward was standing in the doorway, with his little wry smile. I felt myself blushing.

"Can I help?" he asked.

I picked up the flowers in both hands. "They're lovely. Did you smell them?"

He came over and I held them up. "It's nice, isn't it. Even though it's not quite Mayday." He touched one of the small white bells. "And you may not want this strong a scent on your table."

"Please," I said, moving over to the cupboard. "I'm not the Tour d'Argent."

"Here, let me," he said, forestalling me. "The top shelf?"

"Yes, there should be a little pitcher up there," I said. "Thank you. Did you have a nice weekend?"

"Weekend? Oh, no, not really. I had to go back to the States." He handed me the pitcher and propped himself against the sink. "You know, I was thinking about your father. Has he thought of anything else? How the briefcase might have been changed?"

"Excuse me," I said, "you're . . ." I gestured at the tap and the empty pitcher. Instead of moving, he took the pitcher and filled it, then gave it back. "Thanks. Here, why don't you open the wine?" I put the corkscrew in his hand and pointed to the wine bottles sitting on the windowsill. "No. I talked to him on Saturday," I began, "but he was kind of testy." I looked up from the flowers. Gisele had arrived, and through the window I could see Mr. Sago bowing to her. "Excuse me," I said to Edward. "Another guest."

Gisele turned out to be the perfect addition. While I clattered around in the kitchen (Tony's presence meant I had to do some fancy carving of my four baby chickens), she told a few funny stories. She listened deferentially to Mr. Sago, who flirted with her in an elaborately mannered way. She asked Tony about a currently famous historian who claimed that François I had signed a secret pact with Henry VIII, agreeing to make France Protestant. And she flirted with Edward, who didn't exactly flirt back, but played straight with a slight twinkle.

I had cleared the table and served the soufflé (whipped up with my new balloon whisk: Tony in his thoughtful mode was often uncannily on target) when she started telling Edward some of her stories about foreign students at large in Paris. Since the Alliance Française attracts them from all over the world, the array of culture shock Gisele deals with makes my job look like a piece of cake. Some of her tales were mildly alarming, like the one about the girl who decided to stow away on a train to Vienna that turned out to be full of recently discharged and naturally drunken soldiers. (They hid her from the ticket collector.) Others were simply funny, like the one about the Arab millionaire's son who was supposed to buy art for his father and invested in a piece that involved six television sets, a hundred yards of plastic tubing, and some turtles that Kuwaiti Customs wouldn't let into the country because of some turtle disease.

We always had customs stories. Even the kids who didn't indulge in illicit substances didn't want to declare their new clothes, or had some antihistamines that they didn't have a prescription for, or couldn't explain why they needed a Bowie knife to go camping. And sometimes we had actual trouble.

"We had a kid last fall," I said, "when was it, Tony? I know, November, because he was meeting his parents for Thanksgiving. He had been a pain right from the start. You know, a really spoiled boy, can't stay just anywhere, has to have his own apartment, the courses aren't very interesting, his stereo is stolen. Why he needs an expensive stereo in an apartment he's going to be in for eight months is beyond me. Anyway, he was going to meet his parents in Italy for Thanksgiving. They were going to that famous hotel near Positano, you know." I appealed again to Tony. He was poking at his soufflé and didn't look up.

"The San Pietro," supplied Mr. Sago. "Exquisite; built into the cliff."

"That's it. Well, he decided to drive down, so he rented an Alfa Romeo from Hertz and apparently made record time to the Swiss border. Where he's stopped, and in a carton of books—and I'll swear he's never opened a book since he read the Hardy Boys—the customs agents find 600,000 francs, in neat stacks. He claims never to have seen the books, which I believe because apparently they were volumes from the

Encyclopedie de l'Homme. So his father comes tearing up from Positano and makes a stink, and George's fingerprints aren't on the money or the books so they let him go. But he didn't come back here. I had to clean out his apartment and send the stuff home. I did *not* try to send the porno magazines."

"Do you think he was trying to smuggle?" Gisele asked.

I hesitated. "I wouldn't have put it past him, because he really did seem unscrupulous. But where would he get 600,000 francs to smuggle? And why bother? He was already rich."

"Was that all that was in the car?" Edward asked.

"What do you mean? He had his luggage and some presents for his family," I said.

"Well," he said, "it's just that there are other things people try to get across borders. I wondered how carefully the car was searched."

"I don't know, Tony, do you?"

"They didn't find anything else," he said curtly. "And I don't think it's a good idea to talk about our internal business in front of strangers."

I raised my eyebrows, but I remembered that at the time Tony had worked very hard to keep it out of the papers. "Okay," I said. "But then there's Daddy." I must have had a little too much wine to even consider launching on the story, remembering my concern for Daddy's reputation. But in that company, it seemed too good to resist. Daddy the model citizen, opening his briefcase for British Customs to find that it contained a bunch of travel brochures and a little bundle that turned out, unwrapped, to be a hot missal.

Mr. Sago reacted admirably. "What!" he squeaked in astonishment.

"That's right. A medieval missal, illuminated I gather. And some packets of cocaine tucked in, like a gift card or something."

"Cocaine?" said Mr. Sago, looking flustered. It occurred to me that maybe he was so sheltered that he never heard about people who used drugs.

"Well, of course it wasn't Daddy's. He's a Christian Scientist. The whole briefcase wasn't his. But can you imagine? If you *knew* my father!"

"Whose briefcase was it?" Gisele asked.

"We don't know. It looked just like Daddy's, though. Let's have coffee outside."

Gisele helped me clear and when we took the coffee tray outside Edward was explaining to Tony why the U.S. Attorney felt he wanted an office in Paris.

"It's just a temporary part of an ongoing investigation," he said. "Normally I'm based in Washington."

"And what are you investigating?" Tony asked, leaning a little closer.

Edward looked up as I held the tray in front of him. "It's international. That's really all I can say."

"But you seem to know a lot about smuggling," Tony persisted, pouring his coffee without taking his eyes off Edward.

"No," Edward demurred, "just war stories people tell. Like Louise and Gisele tonight."

Mr. Sago was sitting a little apart, and I pulled up a chair next to him. He seemed nervous all of a sudden, and he kept watching Tony. I passed him his plate of chocolates and asked him about Proust's famous maid, which seemed to cheer him up a little bit.

Tony fiddled with his cup and spoon for a while, then got up and took them inside. Mr. Sago was still keeping an eye on him for some reason, like a dog who doesn't want his master to go too far out of his sight. I excused myself and went back inside to make a little more coffee. I put the flame on under the kettle and went into the bedroom. I was surprised to find Tony there, sitting on my bed with a book in his hand.

"Bored?" I asked, watching him in the mirror as I brushed my hair.

"What?" he asked, leafing through the pages.

"You must be bored if you're reading a Georgette Heyer, Tony. Why don't you just go home?"

He turned over the book and looked at the cover as if it were in a foreign language.

"Do you really read this kind of thing, Louise?" he said, and put it back on my bedside table. "You've got a better mind than that." Then he walked out of the room.

As I poured water on the coffee grounds I wondered what Tony had been doing in the bedroom anyway. Then I saw, out the window, that Tony was leaving with Mr. Sago hot on his heels. I stepped outside, but they were both gone. Tony's behavior, since he was often unintentionally rude, I could understand, but for Mr. Sago not to say good-bye to the hostess struck me as very strange.

Gisele and Edward were still sitting down, but as I came over, they both got up. "Mr. Sago told me to say good-bye for him. He said he felt ill suddenly and had to go home. What a funny little creature!"

"Yes, he is odd," I said, looking toward the stairwell. I shrugged. "Well, there's more coffee. Would you like some?"

But Gisele had to leave too. Through all of this—getting her coat, saying good-bye—Edward stood politely, shook hands with her, but made no mention of leaving. When she had walked across the roof he put his cup down gently on the chair where Tony had been sitting.

"You see, I'm persistent," he said. "I still want to know what your father said. Let me help you do the dishes."

I hesitated. I hate doing dishes. He smiled. "You know, you have a completely transparent face. You hate doing dishes, but you don't think it's polite to let me do them." He bent down to pick up the coffee tray. "And you're deeply embarrassed that I figured it out. Come on. I'll enjoy it."

He took off his jacket (another boring lawyer suit) and rolled up his sleeves and looked around him. The entire kitchen area was stacked with dishes and glasses. Without any fuss, he got to work. As I went back and forth clearing the table and drying the plates, he stacked and washed and rinsed. And asked me about Daddy.

I explained that nothing had turned up from the real briefcase, and that Daddy hadn't tried to open what I thought of as the "fake" one until he got to British Customs.

"So when was the last time he looked into it?"

"The night before, as he packed," I said. "But he swears nobody came close enough to him to switch it after he got to the airport."

"On the plane?"

"Very empty flight," I answered, edging around him to take the saucepans off the stove.

"Where was he the night before he left?"

"Here."

He concentrated for a minute on the pan the chickens had cooked in. "What did you do that night?"

"Went out to dinner."

"Just the two of you?"

"Tony stopped in for a drink."

"Hmm." He handed me the pan. "This was nice, tonight," he said. "One of the things I was looking forward to about coming back here was the social fluidity. Meeting a broader range of people than I see in Washington."

I nodded. "It is wonderful. I have lots of friends here I wouldn't even know at home. Even Tony. Or Mr. Sago. He picked me up at the Louvre last week."

"And this week he's here for dinner." He turned off the water and dried his hands. "You're very intrepid, aren't you?"

"Not if you're talking about Mr. Sago!" I protested. "The man's seventy, and having him here with three other people is hardly intrepid."

He put down the dish towel. "No, that's not what I meant. At least"—he gestured toward the living room—"well, you're pretty vulnerable up here with all these windows. And I'm sure you're careful about the neighborhoods you go to..." He trailed off and looked at me. "Are you all right?"

"Yes, of course," I said, turning away from him to stack dessert plates in the cupboard.

"Well, you looked as if you'd seen a ghost," he persisted. My transparent face, no doubt, telegraphing my reaction to his talk about windows. I hadn't thought about Volker all evening. And come to think of it, the phone hadn't rung.

I turned back, trying to look cheerful. "Can't imagine why," I said. "I'll let the wineglasses dry overnight." I got a clean towel from a drawer and spread it out on the counter.

Edward was still watching my face. Then he said, "Okay," and turned back to the sink. He didn't actually shrug, but he might as well have.

Suddenly I was sorry. I could have told him, I thought. That was the moment, and it had passed. As little as I knew him he seemed like someone I could confide in. He might have had some good advice about getting rid of Volker.

But something had held me back, and I told myself it was probably a good thing. He already knew more about me than I was entirely comfortable with. No point in giving away everything. He might seem as safe as the Rock of Gibraltar. But I'd been disappointed by appearances before.

He rinsed a glass and, as he handed it to me, our hands touched. I placed the glass very carefully stem up on the dish towel, not daring to look up. It's a liability, a transparent face. Because it had occurred to me that I didn't want him to leave. At least not right away.

I edged past him again and went out to the roof to bring in the chairs. There was a siren down below, and I went to the parapet to look down. Three men arguing, a car slewed sideways, a police car with the lights flashing. Should I ask Edward to stay? On one level, I didn't want to. I didn't want to pursue him. I didn't want to make any mistakes about his intentions or his character. I didn't want to get into anything I wasn't ready for. Still. I didn't want him to go.

Edward came out and put his elbows on the edge. He had his suit jacket on. We stood there for a minute, elbows almost touching, looking down the street. I felt incredibly self-conscious. And shy and silly, like a thirteen-year-old. I turned around, so I was facing him with my back to the wall. Then I saw that he had put one of the lilies of the valley in the buttonhole of his jacket.

"Would you like a brandy?" I asked.

He nodded. "Thank you." He stayed there while I went in to collect the brandy bottle and two glasses from the dresser. When I came back out he had turned around and had his back to the wall, watching me. It made me feel even more awkward, especially when I brought a glass over to him. Would he touch my hand when he took the glass? Our fingers grazed, casually. I desperately tried to think of something to talk about. All I could think of were impossible openers like "Do you have any brothers or sisters?"

He rescued me. "Sago reminds me of a character out of Balzac," he said, turning his glass in his hand. "He's such a . . ."

"Relic?" I suggested.

"Relic. Exactly. I wonder how he deals with the parts of the modern world that he can't escape."

I considered it, with a corner of my mind relieved that we'd found a conversation that got my mind off Edward. "I don't know him well enough to be sure. But I bet he relishes them. As special treats, you know? Ooh, an airplane! Even though he flies all the time."

"Mmm. I can see that. He seems to take a great deal of pleasure in his life. He was very eloquent about you."

"Flattering the hostess." I dismissed it. "Why don't we sit?" I dragged two chairs together so I could use one as a footstool. "He doesn't really know me at all."

Edward put his glass on the table and folded his frame into a chair that suddenly looked tiny. "He said you had a brilliant eye."

"I'm sure he says that to everyone. You can't be comfortable in that chair. Do you want to bring out an armchair?"

He considered for a moment. "No, I don't think I will. Thank you, though. Sometimes other people's furniture is torture."

So we sat amicably for half an hour discussing the trials of our relative heights, and the French attitude toward physical comfort, and French mattresses and *punaises,* which he'd had as a student and the doctor at the American Hospital told him were "vermin" in a disgusted voice.

"I must let you get some sleep," he said, looking at his watch when he finished his story. He got up and helped me carry the furniture inside. And then stood by the counter, twisting the corkscrew, talking about nothing much. But still watching me. And I kept thinking about my transparent face and trying to concentrate on putting the glasses away or something prosaic. I suppose it didn't work, because he stopped in the middle of a sentence and picked up my hand in both of his, and kissed it. Then he drew me toward him and started kissing for real. I was practically hanging onto his lapels, it was so... effective. Very sweet, persuasive. He was wooing me with his lips and I was his. Then he lifted his head. He had that little smile again; really just a crinkling around the eyes. He ran a finger along my cheek and drew in a breath, as if he were going to say something. But stopped. And finally said, "Good night." And left.

Two minutes after he'd reached the stairs, the phone started to ring.

FIVE

LIGHTHEARTEDLY, I went into the bedroom to answer it and, without even putting it to my ear, shoved the receiver into the wastebasket, which happened to be full of crunched-up paper from the dry cleaner's. As I got ready for bed, I kicked the basket every time I walked past. I know it was childish but it gave me a lot of satisfaction.

Naturally I didn't sleep much that night. It was late when Edward left anyway, and I was all wound up. Then I kept dreaming. They weren't all pleasant dreams. In one of them Tony and Edward were together at a party and I was a waitress, trying to carry a tray of flaming meringues to a table, and they were in my way but wouldn't move and meanwhile the tray was getting heavier and heavier and I was about to drop it and get scalded.

The light looked pretty bright when I woke up. I decided I'd let somebody else do the driving, and take the bus to work. I think it was partly the brandy. The worst thing was I didn't want Tony to know, or rather to suspect anything about Edward, especially since I hadn't made up my mind about him. Tony was still giving me grief about "the Byron of the Black Forest"; I could just imagine what he'd find to mock about Edward.

Fortunately Tony left me alone. In fact he was back in his office, not taking calls all day. That was fine with me. We were in the middle of filing our annual report for Winfield, which was a long paper full of statistics about our finances and supposed comments from the students that, since I could never get them to fill out the forms, I had to make up. I never could figure out what Winfield did with the thing. I was almost done by six-thirty and decided to stay to finish up. Tony had rung me on the intercom at six to find out if I knew how to spell "portmanteau" so I assumed he was doing the crossword. It was a golden opportunity for peace and quiet.

I was out at the Xerox machine when I heard voices coming from the intercom. My first reaction was to figure out what time it was in California to see if we could call the mad inventor. I walked back to my office thinking we'd been pretty lucky because the system hadn't had a fit for almost six months. Then I started to really hear the voices on the intercom. And what they were saying.

"...end of it. Gross irresponsibility! I am aghast! I am appalled! Never again. That is all I can say, never again." It was Mr. Sago. Screaming, practically. Sounding as if he were about to burst.

Then Tony broke in. "Albert." I was thinking Albert was a perfect first name for Mr. Sago, and that I'd never heard Tony talk like that. He was almost whispering, but it was incredibly intense. "I think you'll change your mind. Remember exactly what it is I've been doing for you. And who approached whom. After all. And I have another project in hand that I'm sure you want to see to completion." Mr. Sago started to sputter, but Tony overrode him smoothly. "We'll talk it over, Albert. But not on the phone..."

Then I realized I was eavesdropping. And that I didn't like what I was hearing. I had no idea what it was all about. I didn't know that Tony knew Mr. Sago that well. It hadn't seemed that way last night. I couldn't imagine what their quarrel might be either. I wasn't even sure that it had anything to do with my dinner party. But I remembered Mr. Sago watching Tony like a hawk. And Tony slipping out. Without thinking I went back out to the Xerox machine and flung it open with a bang just so Tony could hear and remember I was there. And stop talking. In the morning I'd have to "discover" the broken phone system because I didn't want Tony to know I'd heard any of his conversation. It wasn't my business. And I didn't want it to be. I couldn't imagine why Mr. Sago should be mad at him, or why he should be using that voice to Mr. Sago. And I didn't want to know.

For good measure I went to the supply cupboard near Tony's office and slit the top off a carton of Xerox machine toner. He couldn't miss that. Sure enough. "Louise? You still here?" he called out.

"Just going," I said. "See you tomorrow."

"Right," he muttered. "Good night."

I was restless when I got home that evening. I might have been thinking about Tony and Mr. Sago. Or about Edward. Or it might have been the air. It had been one of those intoxicating days, warm and soft and bright. Nightfall had barely brought any cooling. I took a chair and a glass of wine out to the roof, but I kept getting up to look over the wall, to see what was going on. I tried calling Gisele, to see if she wanted to have dinner. No answer. I tried another couple of friends, but I knew I wouldn't get them. Nobody was home. So I gave up. I'd go out myself.

It was a great night to be out. You could just tell, everyone strolling along the boulevard St. Germain was in a mood to be pleased. I stopped in front of the church where the buskers were making a mint. Jugglers, mimes, sword swallowers, fire-eaters. There was even an audience for a pair of Swedes with a guitar and dirty hair, singing Abba songs in French. I bought a piece of coconut from one of the carts with the fountains to keep the coconut fresh. Not that I like coconut that much. But I love the fountains.

I ambled along, nibbling. Lots of lovers out, with hands in each other's back pockets. Cafés crammed to the gills, with waiters working up a sweat. A line at the Odéon movie theater; I considered going, but it was another farce starring the inevitable Gerard Depardieu. The whole quarter blazed with light: the streetlights, the car headlights, the shop windows. At Joseph Gibert a block down the boulevard St. Michel the doors were open, and I went in to browse, handling the tiny graph-paper notepads and translucent plastic folders as if I'd never seen them before. When I left I stood for a moment on the corner, looking up toward the river, where the spire of Ste. Chapelle was spotlit. Across from me the musée de Cluny squatted in its own bath of light. I decided to head over to the Ile St. Louis to get an ice cream cone. It seemed like the perfect goal so I crossed the Boul' Mich' and dove into the narrow streets right next to the river.

It wasn't my favorite neighborhood. The streets were incredibly congested, with a pretty rough element hanging around. I hung onto my purse and shouldered my way past the Moroccan bakeries with sticky yellow-orange cakes piled up in the windows. I came to the back of the church of St. Severin and followed its wall to get out to the wider rue St. Jacques. The doors of the church were open, and there was a little crowd standing by the steps. I could see why; the most heavenly music was coming out. It was a boys' choir, singing in Latin. A little poster tacked to the notice board told me it was a Palestrina mass, being sung by some American choir. It would cost me 5 francs to enter. I decided the ice cream could wait, and slipped in.

St. Severin has a double cloister, so there are two rows of columns marching around the nave. The Gothic arches aren't very high; it's not a lofty space, more a mysterious one. And the weaving, twining music seemed so perfectly suited to the rows of columns. I found a seat on the end of a row, on the side. Of course I couldn't see (I never can), but the sound was gorgeous. I looked at my watch and realized that, if the concert had started at eight, it must be close to finished.

It was just the right length for me, actually. About twenty minutes after I sat down, they started singing "Amen." And about five minutes after that, it was over. I picked up my purse and joined the crowd filing out, when someone touched my shoulder. I looked back. There, a few pews behind me, was Edward.

"Are you a fan of Palestrina?" he said as he reached me.

"No. I mean, I liked it. But I was just walking by and I came in because it sounded so pretty."

"It was nice, wasn't it. And nice in here. It's a wonderful space." We had reached the door of the church, and the exiting crowd was pushing us forward. "Are you... are you on your way somewhere?" he asked.

I looked up at him and grinned. "Just to get some ice cream. Want to come?"

He smiled back. "Are you going to Berthillon?" I nodded. "I haven't been there in years. What a good idea."

We turned to cross the rue St. Severin, and I leaned forward to see if there was anything coming. Suddenly a motorcycle shot toward me, and I jumped back, bumping into Edward.

"Are you all right?" he asked, with his hand on my shoulder.

"Sure. Fine," I said. Wondering about that hand. It stayed there until we were across the street, then dropped. But then we were jostled again, crossing the rue de la Huchette. He put it back.

"Look, let's go along the quai," Edward said. "I'm afraid I'm going to lose you in the crowd."

He guided me, like leading a dancing partner, across the Place du Petit Pont until we were safely on the river side of the Quai de Montebello. "There," he said, dropping his arm from my shoulder as we reached the sidewalk. He crossed behind me, to walk on the outer side of the pavement. I've always thought that was a nice gesture, protecting a lady from brigands or stuff dumped from windows. "I guess you're just the average size for a Frenchwoman," he said. "But you seem so..." He didn't finish the sentence.

"Small?" I offered helpfully. "Are all the women in your family tall?"

"Amazons," he agreed. "Maybe that's it. Doesn't it look just like a postcard?"

"It" was Notre Dame, looming, as he said, exactly like a postcard across the river from us. The spotlighting made all the ornament and the flying buttresses stand out almost more than three-dimen-

sionally, like some sci-fi movie you have to see with
special glasses. There was a *bateau mouche* going by,
and we could see all the people at their tables as the
loudspeaker instructed that this was "*la cathedrale de
Notre Dame.*" Then he said something in another
language that sounded Japanese.

"Have you ever done that?" asked Edward. "It's
actually more fun than it looks like."

"No, I always thought it would be awful. Bad food,
condescending guide. And very expensive."

"My parents took me when they came over for a
visit. They loved it. My mother thought the whole
thing was so wonderful; Notre Dame, the Eiffel
Tower, her son living in a garret . . ."

"Did you?"

"Not like yours. It didn't look like a set for *La
Bohème.*"

"That's what Tony says," I told him. "He even
calls me Mimi. But then he stopped after he saw the
production with Linda Ronstadt because he said it
would be an insult."

Edward stopped, and looked over the wall to the
water lapping below with the wake of the *bateau
mouche.* "That was a New York production, wasn't
it? I remember reading about it." His voice sounded
a little strained. Probably because he was leaning over.

"Yes. He flew over for it." I shook my head. "He
does that now and then."

"Flies around to see operas?"

"Yup. Always takes his vacation during La Scala's
season. Goes to Bayreuth, Glyndebourne. It's supposed to be hard to get tickets for some of these things,
but he manages. Gets them scalped, I guess. I need to
get that ice cream. I didn't have any dinner."

Of course there was a line at Berthillon, which is the best place for ice cream in the whole city of Paris. Possibly in the world. Edward insisted on paying for my cassis/praline cone. He had mocha and myrtille. We strolled up the quiet street, past the well-kept *hôtels particuliers,* some of them private, some real hotels.

"I don't even know where you live," I said as we reached the pont St. Louis. "I mean, am I taking you out of your way?"

"No. I'll walk you home. I'm in a sublet on the avenue de Friedland."

I raised my eyebrows. It was a stuffy neighborhood, and in spite of his clothes, I had decided that Edward wasn't stuffy. "I know," he answered. "I wanted to live in the Marais, actually. But in the end it wasn't my choice. Look, let's go back along the quais, if you don't mind. It's hard to talk to you in the crowds." He held out a hand, looking at me.

I put my hand in his. We strolled along the quais, like the other couples we met, out for a walk on a spring evening. We passed the Institut with its round dome and the long galleries of the Louvre on the opposite bank of the Seine. We were walking slower and slower, closer together. Then Edward stopped and put his hands on my shoulders and kissed me. Instantly I felt as if he'd lit a fire. I'd been waiting for his touch, it seemed, for so long. I put my arms up, around his shoulders. I was sure I'd stagger and fall if he didn't hold me up.

Then he picked me up, just lifted me as if I'd been a doll. And sat me on the wall toward the river, holding me in two hands. Now I was taller and I looked down into his face. There was an expression there I'll never forget. There was need and warmth and some kind of pleading: He was completely undefended emotionally.

"Louise," he said in a kind of muffled voice, "I don't want to rush things. But, God, I'm so... You make me feel...bewitched." He pulled my head down and kissed me again. In spite of a kind of flinching at what he'd said, I just gave up. Just...gave in. He could have dropped me over the wall into the river; I would have gone happily. I was so swept away.

It was all we could do to get home after that. We stumbled down the rue du Bac, which seemed surrealistically crowded. I felt as if it were 3 A.M. and the streets should be empty. When we had to stop at corners, we pressed together, yearning. Edward pulled me into a doorway just before we reached St. Germain. "I can't make it to your door," he whispered, and pulled me close. Then after a moment he lifted his head. "Louise, darling Louise," he said into my hair. "Will you always wear high heels when you're with me?"

I leaned back, against the wall, and smiled muzzily. "Yes, Edward, I will. Because I've been standing on tiptoe all this time."

He laughed and nuzzled my neck, then propelled me out of the doorway. Madame Cabrol was watching TV as I opened the big door. Edward walked past quiet as an Indian in the shadows while I called out, *"Bonsoir, Madame."* Not that she would care, I thought. Edward was ahead of me slinking up the stairs, moving incredibly quietly for a man of his height. On the third-floor landing he waited for me and took my hand. For some reason we both tiptoed and whispered, like children sneaking out of a house at night.

When we got to the roof, he took me in his arms again. But this time his kisses were gentle. Almost regretful. And he said very softly in my ear, almost moaning, "I can't do this. I can't stay." Though he didn't make a move to leave, but nuzzled the skin under my ear. "I must go." He sighed again and straightened up. "When can I see you again?" he asked. Soberly.

"I don't know, when can you?" I said, teasing.

"Tomorrow? Are you free?" I nodded. "Good. I should be able to get away from work by eight. Will that be all right?" I nodded again. "Damn work anyway," he muttered, and pulled me toward him almost roughly. In the tiny corner of my mind that was left to me, I wondered why he was leaving; there was such hunger in his touch. Finally he lifted his head and smoothed the hair back from my cheek. "About what I said earlier . . ." he began.

I shook my head. I didn't want to hear him.

"No, listen. It's not just a line."

"I wish you wouldn't say it, anyway," I said, irritated. "Can't you see? It's like a cheap movie. It makes me feel like you think I'm stupid."

"Oh, no," he said with a hand on my cheek. "Anything but stupid. I just wish you'd trust me." Then he kissed me quickly and left.

I shut my eyes. It was the last thing any man should ever say to a woman. Particularly if he means it.

SIX

WORK WAS PRETTY SLOW the next day, and it was warm. That, and a glass of wine at lunch meant I was moving pretty slowly by three in the afternoon. Nearly dozing, actually, when Tony called me on the intercom. He wanted to borrow my Mobylette for the evening.

"Fine," I said, trying not to yawn.

"I may be out late. Should I leave it at your house or just bring it to work?" Oh, God, a decision. For about two seconds I tried to decide what would be more convenient, then gave up. "Bring it home. You remember the combination for the front door?"

"Seventy-seven thirty-six. Leave the keys in the saddlebag?"

"Right. Why don't you come get them right now? I may be leaving a shade early today." Actually I wasn't. Edward was coming to fetch me, but I was hoping to avoid Tony's seeing him. In fact, I'd tried to arrange to meet him anywhere else—his apartment, a café, a bookstore. I even suggested a particular park bench. But his apartment was a mess, he didn't know when he'd get free, it might rain. He had an answer for everything, so I was expecting him around eight and hoping Tony would be safely out of sight.

It was actually a little earlier when I looked up from my desk and saw Edward leaning against the door frame. My heart (for want of a better word) did a funny little bump in my chest.

"How long have you been there?"

"A couple of minutes," he said, smiling.

"You're so quiet!" I answered, remembering how he'd crept up the stairs the night before.

"I was an Eagle Scout." He came over to my desk and bent down to kiss me.

"Excuse me," came Tony's voice from the door. "Sorry. Don't like interrupting tender moments," he said, coming in. "Louise, have you already replaced the Byron of the Black Forest? Good for you. Another notch in your lipstick case."

I looked at him with exasperation. Sometimes Tony had an amazing gift for sheer malice.

"I'm working my way through the NATO countries, Tony, and I didn't care for you as a representative of the U.S. so I vamped Edward." I looked up at Edward. "Now you know all. Feel free to disappear in a puff of smoke."

"No, no, I'll do my duty as an American. Onerous though I find it."

"Nonsense, Cole," Tony said. "Not with our Louise. Anyway you have any number of understudies right here at Winfield Abroad. It's true most of them are barely voting age, but perhaps that doesn't count."

"Okay," I said, suddenly tired of Tony. "Did you want something?"

"No, just wanted to make Mr. Cole welcome. Do you want a tour?"

"I'd like that," Edward said politely.

"We'll leave Louise to titivate, shall we?"

I put some more mascara and some lipstick on, and looked up "titivate" in the dictionary (basically it means "primp"), then went to find them. They were in Tony's office. Tony was leaning back in his chair giving a lecture on Poulenc, while Edward, with his hands clasped behind his back, stared quite openly at the mess in the glass-fronted cupboards.

"Okay, Mr. America," I said, taking him by the elbow. "I'm here to liberate you." I started walking toward the door.

"So rude, Louise. Well, good night, Volker-I-mean-Edward," Tony said.

I turned around to face him. "I don't know why I even work for you, let alone do you favors and feed you."

"Because only I can make your kitchen drain work." His voice came floating after us.

"Aargh!" I said, practically stamping down the hall. "I love Tony dearly but he gets in these moods where he baits me and I know I'm being childish but I *cannot* control myself. Damn! It makes me so mad!"

Edward put a hand on my shoulder and pulled me toward him. After he kissed me he said, "Does that cool you off?"

I laughed a little shakily. "Hardly."

He touched my cheek. "Who's the Byron of the Black Forest?"

I turned away, and walked toward my office. "A man named Volker Freilich. We went out for about six months. Somehow Tony found out he used to read poetry to me. I will never hear the end of it." I went in and picked up my bag from my desk, and turned off the lights in my office. "Shall we go?"

Edward was quiet that night. I should say, quieter than usual. I didn't think too much about it at the time. We walked home through the place de la Concorde after dinner and got caught on a traffic island in the middle. Edward just put his arms around me and we stood there for a few minutes, my head against his heart. When we got to my building door, he said, "I don't think I'll come up tonight."

I was a little surprised, but I couldn't really remonstrate. And I decided there must be something on his mind to make him so subdued. Maybe he was regretting having said so much the night before. Maybe he wanted to slow the whole thing down. That was fine with me. So I just said, "Thanks for walking this far," and he smiled and kissed me good-bye. I noticed that the Mobylette wasn't parked in its usual place as I crossed to climb the stairs.

THE PHONE RANG the next day just as I was leaving work. I considered not answering it. I wanted to get home, and phone calls at the very end of the day are never things you can dispose of quickly. The Girl Scout in me prevailed.

"Louise?" Edward's voice. "Listen, I need to see you."

"Well, you're going to. Can't you wait a couple of hours?" I teased.

"No, as a matter of fact...." He sighed. "Oh, hell!" There was real anger in his voice, and I suddenly felt silly for having been coy.

"What is it? What's the matter?"

"I can't explain over the phone. Can you meet me at your apartment?"

"What, now?"

"Yes." Pause. "It's important."

I looked at my watch. "It really can't wait?"

"No."

"All right. I'll be there as soon as I can."

When I got there he was pacing back and forth on the roof. It was a gorgeous sunny evening but one look at his face made me decide against pointing this out. Still, he held out his arms when he saw me. But after he had kissed me he held me against his chest for a minute, with one hand stroking my hair. As if, somehow, he were sad. Then he lifted my bag from my shoulder and said, "Let's go in."

"You don't want to sit out here?" I asked, unlocking the door.

"No. I need the sofa. And a drink."

"Okay. Is wine all right?" I asked, going around the counter to get a glass.

"Do you have any scotch?" he answered, and went over to sit on the far sofa. As I got the bottle out and poured his drink I glanced over. He was just sitting with his hands clasped between his knees, frowning into space. And then I knew what it was. I could just see it coming. About the other night—he'd been carried away. Never meant things to get that far. Was very fond of me. Didn't mean to take back anything he'd said, but...et cetera.

Dumb. As I took the glass over to him, I felt dumb. I could have predicted the whole scenario. In fact I had. I had tried very hard not to take anything he said at face value. But I had let my guard down. What a sucker.

I put the glass down and sat at the opposite end of the sofa from him. Clearly this was no time for coziness.

He looked over at me and rubbed his face. "I don't even know where to start. Except..." He moved down the sofa so that he was sitting next to me. He put a finger under my chin. I didn't resist, but I didn't try to look cheerful either.

He sat back and took one of my hands. "Oh, listen, Louise. Everything I've said to you, I've meant. I can tell, looking at you, that you don't believe me. I know you're wary and I understand why. But I *do* feel something for you, something that is honestly special. I don't go around saying these things to every girl I meet. I'm sincere about this. And I wish…" He took a breath and started again. "I wish you could trust me," he said, looking into my eyes. "This would all be so much easier for both of us."

"Well, give it some time," I said. "I'm just cautious. I wouldn't lend you my life savings at this point either."

He let my hand go and shook his head. "No, that's not it. This is an official visit. I need to ask you some questions about your Mobylette." He moved back to the other end of the sofa.

Silence. "What?"

"Your Mobylette. You own a pale-blue Mobylette, license number"—he pulled a little notebook from inside his jacket and flipped the pages—"license number 750403. Yes?"

"Yes, but why do you need to know?"

"Did you take it out last night?"

"Edward! I was with you last night!"

"I know. But it was early when I dropped you off." He looked squarely at me, and for an instant I forgot my anger and confusion. Edward looked terribly sad. But then I remembered what he was saying.

"No, I didn't go out for a moonlight ride after I came home. I went right to bed. And why do you need to know? What is the problem?"

"Did you lend it to anybody?"

"Edward, why are you grilling me? Can you at least explain?"

And then two thoughts floated into my mind at the same time. He'd said "official visit." And Tony had borrowed my Mobylette.

"What do you mean about an 'official visit'?" I said slowly. And got up and walked over to the kitchen. Remembering my transparent face, and trying desperately to think. Tony had borrowed my Mobylette.

"Of course I don't think you went out for a moonlight ride last night," Edward said to my back. "But the fact is that your friend Sago was picked up in the Bois de Boulogne this morning with a concussion and a broken hip. Bruising indicated a hit-and-run. The police found a prostitute who'd seen him." Edward had his notebook in front of him but he didn't need to look at the notes. "She saw a pale-colored Mobylette and got the license number. It was around two A.M."

I got a glass from the cupboard without thinking. "And it was my Mobylette...." I stopped as something occurred to me. "Why are you asking me about this? Why you and not the police?"

"Because I put up a huge argument and made them let me bend the rules. It's part of my investigation."

I turned around and stared at him. "Edward, I think you'd better explain a little bit!"

He leaned forward and took a sip of his scotch. "God, I hate telling you this." He straightened up and took a deep breath. "My office is seeking evidence against a ring of anti-American terrorists. I won't go into all of it, but we are working on an information network based in Paris. We had evidence pointing to

Winfield College as part of the operation. I decided to get to know you as a way into the network."

Automatically I reached into the refrigerator for the bottle of wine and filled my glass, absently leaving the empty bottle on the counter. Then I walked slowly back across the room. I was stunned. I didn't care now about what he read on my face. I could feel it, all the muscles were frozen. I had to make a conscious effort to shut my mouth. And all I could think was—you felt dumb *before*.

I sank back down on the sofa as far from Edward as I could get. Put my glass very gently on the trunk. Looked at him. "I'm sorry," I said in my softest, most ladylike voice. "I'm not sure I understood that. You had information that Winfield was part of a terrorist information network and, as part of your investigation, you cultivated me? Did I get that right? I don't know much about the judicial system, but I didn't realize that was how district attorneys managed investigations. Isn't it supposed to be just a little bit more official? I mean—pillow talk? Is that what you had in mind?"

"I know. I know." He rubbed his eyes. "To begin with it seemed risky, but we couldn't just pull people in for questioning, it would have warned them and ruined everything. And Matt Steele really did suggest I call you. So there didn't seem any harm in it." He fell silent for a few moments. "And then..." I didn't help him out. "And then I...just...I let my emotions get the better of my professional judgment. Which I don't regret, to tell you the truth," he said, meeting my eyes. "Except that I've hurt you."

I glared at him. "And what makes you think I'm not part of the network? Maybe I'm the ringleader.

Aren't you being a little indiscreet? It's too bad you couldn't just keep your mouth shut until I really did trust you. Maybe you could have cracked the case. Maybe now I'll tell my terrorist friends about you and we'll all vanish into deepest Libya.''

"It isn't a joke. Why didn't you tell me about Volker Freilich?"

"Oh, you mean 'the Byron of the Black Forest'?" I said savagely. "I'm sorry, but I couldn't figure out how to work it in tactfully. Do you suppose we should have had a little confessional? 'By the way, the last person I slept with was Volker Freilich, a German creep'? Why didn't you tell me about *your* last girl-friend?"

He didn't flinch, but he took a big swallow of scotch. When he looked at me, his eyes were very sad.

"Louise, do you know about his politics?"

The question surprised me. "What, that anti-American stuff? Yes. He was always going to meet-ings and writing articles for their journals. Believe me, that's not why I went out with him."

"No, I know. It went farther than that, though. Oh, hell!" He stood up and started to pace. "I wish I could tell you. I wish I had told you at the start, but I couldn't, you can see that. And I can't now." He turned and looked out the windows, with his hands behind his back. "Are you in touch with Freilich?"

"No," I said. "I'm not. We parted on very bad terms."

"Has he tried to get in touch with you?"

I rolled my eyes. "After a fashion," I said.

Edward turned. "What does that mean?"

"It means," I said, looking straight at him, "that ever since we broke up a month ago he's been harassing me. Calling late at night and breathing. Knocking over flower pots. Trying to get in too. It isn't pleasant; are you sure you want to know about it?''

He came over and sat next to me. "Is that why you looked so alarmed when I mentioned the windows that night?" I just nodded. He reached over and took my hand, but I pulled it away.

"Right," he said softly. "Look. I have two professional responsibilities here. I had to ask about Freilich. And I have to ask about the Mobylette. Did you take it out yourself?"

I didn't answer for a minute. "No," I finally said.

"Did you lend it to anybody?"

I didn't say anything. But remembered Tony. And with a jolt, Tony's conversation with Mr. Sago.

Edward sighed. "Louise, we'll find out. It will take longer, and it will be embarrassing for you, since we'll have to question all your friends.''

"Maybe someone took it for a joy ride," I said.

"Maybe they did," he said. "Maybe the moon is made of green cheese.''

He stood up and looked down at me. "This isn't a threat. I'm just telling you. The police will have to follow up. You'll be hearing from them. I don't know if you're shielding somebody, or if you're so angry with me that you don't want to help. Maybe you'll help them. And help Sago, for what that's worth.'' He lifted his glass from the trunk and took it over to the sink.

He came back and stood in front of me. "There's one more thing. This isn't part of my job. I am worried about you. As I said that night, all those windows. This isn't a lark, Louise. This group that we think Freilich belongs to is *dangerous*. Do you remember the Baader-Meinhof gang?" I looked up at him, startled. "Yes, I'm serious." He sat down again, close to me.

"Please leave this apartment." I started to protest but he shook his head.

"Just to be on the safe side. I don't think there's any real danger, if there was we wouldn't let you stay here. But go somewhere else. You could stay with Gisele, couldn't you?"

"*We* wouldn't let you stay here" was all I said, mimicking him. "I'm staying."

He sat still for a moment, then got up. "Please. Don't ignore good advice just because you hate me." He waited a minute longer, but I didn't look at him.

"Listen, let me give you a phone number," he finally said. "An emergency number where they can always reach me. I'll wear a beeper."

I didn't answer. He sighed and reached in his pocket. "I'm going to write it down and leave it here. Please don't throw it away." He tore a page out of a little date book and wrote. "It's 4284.2053," he said, "in case you're too angry even to look at it." He looked across the room at me. Put the slip of paper on the counter. And left.

I stayed put. I dragged one of the paisley shawls off the back of the sofa and draped it around my shoulders. I was furious. Furious with Edward for his little ploy, furious with myself for having fallen for it. But more than that, I was scared and confused. I kept trying to go back to the facts. Tony had borrowed my Mobylette. He hadn't returned it by the time I got home. That was a fact. Also, Tony had had a fight with Mr. Sago. I had overheard it on the intercom.

Another fact. But they couldn't add up to Tony running down Mr. Sago in the Bois de Boulogne.

Back to their argument. What had Tony said? "We'll talk it over." That was all. It was true that he had sounded frightening. But "talking it over," even in a scary voice, wasn't the same thing as . . . I had an awful image in my mind. Odd little Mr. Sago, lying in some bushes with his legs all askew. It made no sense. I knew that Mr. Sago was irritated with something Tony had done. And that Tony was mad at him.

What was Mr. Sago doing in the Bois de Boulogne in the middle of the night anyway?

Anything. He could have been doing anything. There was no reason why he shouldn't have been there cruising for a hooker like everyone else, I told myself.

But what if he hadn't? What if he'd gone there to meet Tony? And they'd had an argument, and things got out of hand? Things got out of hand? What did that mean? It was all absurd. I couldn't imagine Tony, who was such a cold fish, ever letting anything get out of hand. And over what, anyway? Had they argued over opera tickets?

I would just ask him. I flung aside the shawl and stood up, leaving my glass on the trunk. I would just ask Tony. He could clear all of this up. It was silly for me to try to shield him when there was certainly a logical explanation. He was probably still at the office. I would go back there and get it all sorted out.

SEVEN

As LUCK would have it, I got a taxi right away and the driver sailed up to Passy so before I even had a chance to think over what I was going to say to Tony there I was, standing in our little courtyard with my keys in my hand. The building was dark, but that didn't mean anything. Tony was fanatical about saving electricity. He was probably sitting back in his den with a lonely forty-watt bulb.

And now what *was* I going to say to him? Behind me the traffic cruised smoothly by on the rue de Passy and I could hear plates clattering in the café across the street. "Tony, where did you take my Mobylette last night?" "Tony, how well do you know Mr. Sago?" My stomach twisted a little and I walked over to one of the benches. Tiptoeing on the gravel, as if Tony could hear me from inside. Over my head the wind rustled the leaves of the plane tree. "Tony, have you had a fight with Mr. Sago?" I felt sick. Not sick enough to throw up, just nervous-sick. "Tony, Edward says Mr. Sago was injured in a hit-and-run last night. By my Mobylette. Did you . . . ?"

In about two steps I was at the front door. Planning wasn't going to make this any easier. Or any more pleasant. I had my key out, but the door was unlocked, which was surprising. Tony always locked up behind the last person out, because he said he couldn't hear people coming in. Tonight I somehow had an image of him sitting in his office like a dragon resting on his pile of gold in the belly of a mountain.

Pretty fanciful. The house was dead quiet. From the front hall, I couldn't see Tony's door. I tiptoed past my office and down the corridor. Why did I feel I wanted to surprise him? Would he stammer out the truth when I suddenly appeared: "Tony, what have you done to Mr. Sago?" I could see the light seeping out under the door. This was going to be just awful. My hand was on the doorknob. There was no sound from inside the room. I admit I hesitated a moment longer. Wasn't there some diplomatic way to do this? "Oh, hi, Tony, I was just wondering about the phone call I overheard the other night . . ."

And then—CRASH! Actually it was a kind of slithery crash. Followed by some subsidiary slithering, and a voice that wasn't Tony's swearing. But by then I was inside the room and I saw who it was.

Gabriel, of all people, was standing with his back to me. And in front of him the doors of one of Tony's cupboards hung open. On the floor, the desk, the filing cabinets, covering the phone, the chair, and the rug were papers. Files, newspapers, examination books, computer printouts, pink message slips, and an unlikely roll of turquoise tissue paper that unfurled completely as I watched, festively draping Tony's typewriter.

"Gabriel, what the hell is this?" I said. It came out kind of shrewish. I don't think I realized how glad I was not to have to talk to Tony right away.

He jumped about a mile and spun around. I could tell from his expression that he was pretty relieved too. "Oh, it's you. I'm, umm . . . Nothing." And then he blushed. I'd forgotten that part of being a teenage boy.

It was sort of cute. But it still didn't explain the mayhem on the floor.

I walked the three steps that I could before stepping on the avalanche. "What do you mean, nothing? What happened, did you try to open one of the cupboards?"

"Yeah. I didn't realize I was disturbing a major ecosystem," he said. The blush had faded. Now he was just a little miffed.

"Well, of course you were. Didn't you even *look*? I think those things are full of every piece of mail Tony's gotten since 1979." I nudged a precariously balanced pile that shifted and scattered further, leaving me ankle deep in paper.

"No, I guess not. Is he going to be incredibly pissed off?"

"I imagine so. You know how much he hates to have people poking around in his office."

"Do you think we could get it all back into the cupboard?"

"We? What is this 'we' word, Gabriel? I have better things to do with my time than trying to restore Tony's artfully achieved havoc."

"Yeah, well, believe it or not, so do I. Maybe I'll just face the music."

"He'll go nuts, you know that." Once I had opened a personal letter of his by mistake and he threw such a tantrum that they could hear it in the café across the street. I know, because they asked me about it when I went in for lunch.

"I'm just going to have to deal with it," Gabriel said, surveying the mess. "I guess the least I could do is clear off his desk." He started shifting handfuls of paper and stuffing them back in the china cabinet. I watched him for a moment and put my purse down. Something had occurred to me.

"Gabriel, what were you doing in here anyway?"

"Oh, I was just looking for something." He didn't meet my eyes.

"What? I mean what were you looking for? In Tony's cupboards?"

"Oh, I, ah, wanted to find the records of a friend of mine who was at Winfield a few years ago. It's not really cool, I realize, looking at someone else's grades. So that's why I did it when nobody was here."

"Pretty weak, Gabriel. Pretty lame," I said, and walked around Tony's desk to face him. "Those records are in my office, not in this mess." I seized the handful of papers he was holding and tried to heave it into the cupboard. Wasted gesture; the cupboards were about six feet off the ground. I had to give the papers back to him. "Seriously. What were you doing here? It's after hours, you're not even supposed to have a key."

This time he looked me in the eye. There was a long pause. I could see him making up his mind to tell me.

"Okay," he said. "I might as well. Somebody needs to know about this besides me. Here." He finished clearing a place on Tony's desk. "Sit down. Let me just get this out of the way." He put the last load of papers in the cupboard and latched it. "Okay." He pulled up a chair cornerwise to Tony's desk and heaved his knapsack onto his lap. I hadn't even seen it before, buried under Tony's stupid papers. Without saying anything, Gabriel unlaced the flap and reached inside, groping for something that was deep in the bottom of the pack. Typically for Gabriel, it was an old-fashioned army surplus pack in olive drab. As he pulled out something wrapped in a bandanna, I wondered if the fact that I didn't like Gabriel's taste in backpacks meant that I was now getting old. Then I forgot about that, for Gabriel had unrolled the bandanna. And there, gleaming on Tony's desk, was an object shaped like a very fat little cigar, about four and a half inches long. It was oval, maybe an inch at the widest part. But that wasn't what mattered, because it was gold.

I recognized it right away, from going around museums with Daddy. "It's an etui," I said to Gabriel. "Louis Quinze, probably. God, look at it." The clasp to open it up was a ruby. The entire surface was decorated in a pattern of ribbons and flowers, with the elaborated scrollwork highlighted with diamonds. At each rounded end, a diamond sunburst surrounded a little enamel plaque. It was beautiful.

"Look," I said, and picked it up. I pressed the ruby, and the two sections of the case parted. I lifted off the top, to show Gabriel the cunning interior. "It's like a teeny little version of a purse," I said, carefully pulling out the minute vinaigrette, the scissors, the thimble, the perfume flask. "Sometimes these were made to be worn on a lady's dress, with another piece called a chatelaine. This one is very elaborate, very lavish." Even the perfume bottle had a diamond for the stopper. I picked up the lid and squinted at it. "I wonder if there's a coat of arms, or even the royal cipher...."

And then I suddenly realized. "Gabriel, where in the world did you get it! Oh, good heavens!" I quickly dropped it back on the desk. The lid rolled off and hit the floor. "It must be stolen. Right? I mean, it belongs in a museum! And here I am pawing it and the lid is probably dented. Where did you get it?"

Gabriel bent over to pick up the lid and put it back down, very gently. Then he looked at me bleakly. He looked a lot older in that minute, not a flippant happy-go-lucky kid but, well, a grown-up. He rubbed his eyes and ran his hands through all that hair.

"It's a long story." He hesitated for a minute, absentmindedly holding his hair in a ponytail and staring at the etui. "I'm just trying to decide where to start. I don't know what you're going to say. I mean, in a way, it affects you more than anyone."

I just sat there. He had to tell the story his way.

He took a deep breath. "Okay. You know how I'm interested in German theater. That's one of the basic reasons I came to Europe this year, and the only reason I'm not in Berlin is that my grandparents are still kind of cranky about World War II. So I've gone to Germany for performances. Not just the time you got so pissed off because I missed an exam, but a few other weekends. Usually I hitch."

I rolled my eyes. I should have known.

"Anyway," Gabriel went on, "last fall Tony and I were talking about a play I was going to in Berlin. I guess we got talking about opera and I couldn't help bringing up the work of this director Stuhlmann who does the Ring cycle fragmented, sort of like a cubistic view of Wagner, it's amazing. Of course Tony hates the idea of it, but I said I was going to a performance and offered to let him hear my tape. Which was going to be bootleg, but anyway, that's not the point. He was very interested. And then he asked if I'd mind taking something to a friend in Berlin for him. Something he didn't want to put in the mail. He said he'd have this friend meet me at the performance, it wouldn't be any trouble, so how could I say no? I didn't think too much about what it was, but hey, you know, maybe it was fragile, maybe he didn't want it going through customs, who was I to say."

"So you thought it was what, dope?" I said.

Gabriel shrugged. "Maybe. I didn't think Tony was much of a man for reefer, but I got the definite impression that it was a little hush-hush. And it was little. Packed in a box. I didn't try to get it open but I did shake it." He grinned a little. "You know, like trying to figure out what your Christmas presents are before you open them. Is it heavy for its size? Does it rattle or jingle? This thing was about palm size, light, no rattle. The guy was there like he was supposed to be. Tony didn't give any description of him, said he'd pick me out. Little guy, beard, glasses, dark overcoat. So that was that. The performance was great."

Gabriel leaned back and started to put a foot on Tony's desk, then thought better of it. "But on the way back, the French Customs officials gave me a lot of grief. I'm used to it, it's the hair and stuff. But this time they really took me apart. Took everything out of the knapsack, looked at every page in my notebook, the whole bit. And I was real glad that I didn't have Tony's mysterious parcel on me anymore.

"So when I got back here Tony asked how everything went and I said fine and we didn't talk about it anymore. Then a couple of weeks ago he asked if I had plans to go to Germany again soon. And in fact I was going to another performance piece in Berlin. So he asked me if I'd take something, and I said no. And explained about the customs officers, and pointed out that, really, I'm not the best choice for a mule."

"What's a mule?"

"Somebody who carries something illicit from one place to another. He was a little irritated, you know, he kind of snapped at me. But I figured he couldn't make me do anything I didn't want to do. I mean, I did get the impression the whole thing was a little under-cover. So I didn't think any more about it.

"That was last weekend. I couldn't get a seat on the train, so I was kind of camped out in the corridor with this pack. And I kept trying to shift it to get comfortable. Now, these army packs have all these compartments for God knows what, grenades and knives and ammunition or something. I don't usually use them." He lifted his pack into his lap and scooted the chair over to show me. There were three compartments on each side of the pack, and they looked empty.

"But on the train, there was this thing digging into my shoulder. Right about *here*." His fingers were on the bottom pouch on one side. "But I knew there was nothing in that pocket. And I dug around inside the knapsack and there was nothing harder than a pair of socks there. But somehow, there *was* something hard. And I figured out it had to be between the pocket and the knapsack. Look."

He put the pack in my lap, and I could see what he meant. The stitching had been cut, and there was a little opening about the width of three fingers. You could tuck something right in there between the pocket and the side of the knapsack, and it would be acces-sible only through that opening. And it would be se-cret unless somebody looked very carefully. I handed the pack to Gabriel. "Was it unstitched like this?"

"No. And it was pretty dark in the train corridor, so I couldn't see if it had been resewn. But I'll tell you, the stitches gave pretty easily when I tried them with my knife. And that army sewing is sturdy." Our eyes met. "Anyway, this was inside." He gestured to the etui, gleaming on Tony's wood-grain Formica desk. "I couldn't really see what it was but it felt—well, you know how it feels. Really *important*. I guess it feels like gold. So I took it into the bathroom to get a better look at it and I was completely blown away. First of all, what was it? And second of all, how had it gotten there?"

He put the pack down on the floor, and sat up straight. "Now I know what it is. And I guess I know how it got there."

I didn't even want to ask. I was starting to feel sick again. But I guess I croaked, "How?"

"The pack was here all day on Friday. I even asked Tony if I could leave it in his office. For safekeeping."

"Well, that's not really conclusive—" I started, but he interrupted me.

"Wait. I'm not done. I was mad. I knew right away it had to have been Tony who put it there. And this was what he wanted me to take to 'a friend' in Berlin. Now I don't know as much as you do about this stuff, and okay, maybe it was innocent, someone's grandmother's cigarette case or something. But I didn't think so. So I just put it in my pocket and took my big Swiss Army knife, the one with all the blades, and put it back in the same wrapping. It was some sacrifice, I want you to know," he said with a flash of levity. "I used that knife all the time. Anyway, I stuck it back in the same place and waited to see what would happen. I did just what I would have done, had breakfast in the train station, wandered around for a while, took a nap on a park bench only that didn't last long, they are really strict in those German cities. Anyway when I finally went to the performance, it was still there, I checked. And there was a part of the piece that involved the whole audience. Kind of a ceremonial thing. God, it was brilliant," he said, his eyes shining as he remembered. "We all lined up in a double line and at the head of the line they anointed us with oil put on with a feather, and danced us around the performance space, then sent us back to our seats. It was so powerful."

Then Gabriel remembered the rest of his story, and his face fell. "When I got back to my pack, the knife was gone." He looked up at me and didn't say anything more.

"Weren't you worried about customs coming home?" I said the first thing that came to me. I knew I was avoiding the real issue.

"That's why it took me so long to get back, I didn't get back until Wednesday. I didn't want to go on the train again so I got a ride with some people I met who had a car. But they weren't leaving until Tuesday night. We came through Belgium and they didn't even open the trunk of the car."

I hesitated. "And what are you doing here now? I mean, what were you going to do about this?"

Gabriel rubbed his face again, the way he had at the beginning of the story. "Nothing very rational. I guess I was just kind of nosing around, maybe hoping to fall across an explanation." Then he looked up at me. And paused. I remember thinking I wasn't going to like what was coming. Which was, "Louise, what about your father?"

EIGHT

I DIDN'T ANSWER. It was one of those incredibly long moments that seems to last a year. I could even hear the question echoing in my head over and over: "What about your father? What about your father?" until the words lost their meaning and were just sounds.

I looked down at the desk, at the beautiful object lying there. Very gently I picked up the lower half of it and peered inside. There was something small and round and flat like a coin, with a tiny flower engraved on it and one little diamond. It was stuck, as if somehow it hadn't been replaced in its accustomed spot. Without thinking I turned the etui upside down and gave it a little shake. Two things fell into my waiting palm: a tiny wand no thicker than a wedding band, with a diamond at each end. A needle case. And the spool of thread I'd noticed stuck in the bottom of the case. Everything for the handy housewife. Though I doubted that the possessor of this trifle ever needed to thread a needle if she didn't want to. Certainly not with this dark thread wound around the shank of the spool. I looked up at Gabriel, still toying with the spool.

"What about my father?"

"Well, Louise, think about it. You've never told me but I heard the story. And remember, I was here when he called you. He's stopped at customs carrying some fabulously valuable, *old*, *hot* object. I don't know what the cocaine was about, but I think the missal was the point."

"But how could..." My voice trailed off. I couldn't even say it. Tony? Even the thoughts that had boiled through my mind on the way up here, Edward's implied accusations, they were just implied. This was something definite. This wasn't something that could be explained away. Say it, Louise. Face facts. He's a crook. I swallowed. "How could Tony have switched briefcases with Daddy?" How could Tony be that kind of person? How could he build my kitchen counter and use my father to smuggle? How could he do a brilliant Hermione Gingold imitation and send Gabriel off as an unwitting courier? How could he have injured poor little harmless Mr. Sago?

How could he have done those things, and I never know it?

How could Tony Geist, my boss and, when the chips were down, best friend for five years, be lawless? And apparently violent?

How could I be so stupid?

God, what a day for being stupid. I reached out once more for the etui. Gabriel had been right, it had a special feel. Smooth, cool, rich. Solid. Trustworthy. Gold. It never tarnished. A completely pure element. Au, if I remembered rightly, on the Table of Elements. They fished it out of oceans and graves gleaming brightly. The spool was no bigger than my little fingernail. The black thread looked out of place. For some dainty, frivolous lady of the eighteenth century the color should be peach, or cerise, or aquamarine. One of those colors they gave names to like *feuille morte* or *soupir d'amour*. I held the spool closer, aware that I was avoiding thinking about what was important.

"Louise, snap out of it." Gabriel reached over and took the trifle away from me. "Wake up. I know he's a friend of yours. But we have to do something."

"I know," I said, looking at my hands in my lap. "I have to talk to him. That's actually why I was here tonight, I thought I'd find him."

"No, he's going to that Kathleen Battle recital. I came because I knew he wouldn't be here."

"Oh, hell," I said, looking at my watch. Suddenly, now that I thought I might not be able to talk to him, I felt I had to. "I wonder if I can catch him."

"Well, it could wait until after the concert, couldn't it?"

"I don't want to pace the streets for three hours thinking god-awful things about my best friend if I can help it," I said tartly. "I'll try to get to him before he goes. Here, let me put this back together. I'll take it with me." I started replacing the little pieces in the etui: the perfume bottle, the vinaigrette, the needle case. I had the top back on when Gabriel remembered he was still holding the spool, so I tore off a piece of turquoise tissue paper to wrap up the spool and slipped it in my raincoat pocket.

I got up and glanced around. "You should probably try to clean this place up a little more. I don't know what's going to happen—whether Tony will be in on Monday or not. And he'll probably have more important things to think about if he is. But still, there's no point in asking for trouble."

Gabriel stood up too and put a hand on my arm. "Are you sure you'll be all right? Do you want me to go with you?" It was sweet of him. He looked young

again. Maybe he was relieved that he'd gotten the
whole story off his chest.

"No, you clean up here. I'll be all right. Tony's a
friend, for God's sake." And I left him standing alone
in the one lighted room in the building.

TONY LIVED across the river in the fifteenth arrondissement. I'd never been there, but his address was in
my Rolodex and I'd leafed past it often enough to remember: 13, rue Letellier. Under a streetlight outside
I opened up my little red-bound *Plan de Paris*, the
map of Paris by arrondissement that I never went
anywhere without. Rue Letellier was right across the
pont de Bir-Hakeim and along the boulevard de Grenelle; probably not much more than a fifteen-minute
walk. Or, for that matter, three stops on the Métro. If
the recital began at eight I didn't have much time. A
taxi would have to negotiate one-way streets; I might
have to wait for the Métro. At least if I was walking I'd
feel like I was making progress, not waiting, frothing
at the mouth, on the subway platform. I set off down
the rue de Passy, in a hurry. And with my last words
to Gabriel echoing in my head: "Tony's a *friend*."

Was I being incredibly stupid? Compounding naïveté on top of naïveté? What did I expect to hear from
Tony? Was I hoping that he would somehow be able
to explain away the suspicion in my mind? What
would be the best possible outcome of this interview?

What would be the worst? I had to face it. Mr. Sago
was lying unconscious in a hospital bed. Would
Tony... My mind sheered off the prospect. I was glad
to concentrate instead on crossing the river. To my
right, the narrow sycamore-lined Allée des Cygnes
floated like a huge raft. Traffic zipped along both

quais lining the river, hundreds of little European cars driven by hundreds of macho French drivers, their honor on the line at each lane change.

Would Tony get mad? He had a terrible temper, but it was the yell-and-sulk kind. I would have said petulant rather than violent. Would he—and as I thought of this, I knew it was just what Tony would do. He was going to try to spin me some story. Truth was just an abstract concept to him. And a pretty worthless one, at that. He'd have a plausible answer for all my suspicions.

I realized, as I continued to walk as fast as I could along the wide busy boulevard de Grenelle, that I had relaxed. Physical danger was probably not an issue. But if Tony was going to make light of my suspicions, why go to him at all? Why not just take the damn etui to the police and let them handle it?

I gave that about three seconds' thought. I couldn't imagine walking into the nearest *gendarmerie* and plunking the etui down on someone's desk and telling the story Gabriel had just told me. A, they probably wouldn't believe it. B, it implicated Gabriel. C, I couldn't do it without talking to Tony first.

Even if he was going to lie himself blue in the face.

His building was hard to find but after zigzagging back and forth looking at street numbers I spotted it, just a couple of doors on a narrow passageway off the street. One door said *Serviere* on a name plate by the bell, so the other one had to be Tony's. I pressed the bell and tried the door at the same time, and to my surprise, the door opened.

But just as in Passy, it opened onto a dark hall. I called out, but there was no answer. Could I have missed him?

I closed the door behind me and groped on the wall around it, hoping to find a light switch. No luck. As my eyes grew used to the dark, I took a couple of steps into the room. Dimly I could make out some shapes: a sofa, a table. And now I could see the whole far wall of the room, which—well, it *glowed*. Not solidly, but in little windows here and there, four-inch oblongs of silver light, little red-and-green dots, some of which throbbed, small vertical strips and one fan-shaped patch of dim yellow. Slowly and carefully, with my hands out in front of me so I didn't trip, I walked toward it. Tony's sound system.

I knew he was a fanatic. But this was phenomenal. On one level I knew I was there for another reason, but nobody could have avoided being drawn to this— creation. It was like the computer in *2001*. With its pulsing little lights, and here and there a needle sweeping across the face of some indicator, it seemed to be intent on some task of its own. Running the world, or curing cancer. Reproducing Joan Sutherland's voice with terrifying fidelity.

"Louise?"

I jumped out of my skin and whirled around with my hands clutching my chest. It had just been a whisper, but I knew whose. "Tony, what are you doing sitting here in the dark?"

He hadn't actually been sitting. In the shadows I saw a figure emerge from a door, close it behind him, and move forward to flick on a lamp. It was a gooseneck desk lamp, so it shed a pool of light on the table, where a sheaf of papers lay with Tony's keys and wallet. A handful of CDs lay half-in, half-out of the light. "I guess I fell asleep," he finally answered. "What time is it?"

"What do you mean, you fell asleep? You were going to that Kathleen Battle recital," I said, indignant. I expected to get a runaround, but was it going to start already?

"Oh, she canceled," he said. "What are you doing here?" He was still standing over the lamp, but because of its shade his face was in deep shadow. And I couldn't tell anything from his voice. This was, after all, the best mimic I had ever heard.

"Tony, can we sit down?" I said. "And could you turn on another light?"

He hesitated. "Well, I don't have much time," he said after another pause. "I'm supposed to meet somebody for dinner."

"It won't take long." I moved a satchel full of crumpled clothes from one of the chairs at the table and sat down. He waited for a minute and sat opposite me. He didn't turn on another light, but now that he was sitting I could see his face. He looked wide awake, for what that was worth.

Now I had to say it. This was the moment I'd been dreading. Where should I start? With Gabriel and the etui? With Mr. Sago? With my father?

He didn't prompt me. He just sat there, not even looking at me. I had never, in all our time of being friends and working together, been to his apartment. Now I had come barging in, and Tony wasn't even reacting. He looked as if he were listening to something I couldn't hear. It made me a little mad, as if he were somehow robbing my accusations of their importance. Tony had something else on his mind? I'd provide him with something he really needed to think about. The spark of irritation put the words in my mouth.

"Edward came to my house tonight and told me that Mr. Sago was in the hospital," I said. "He was found in the Bois de Boulogne. He'd been hit by a Mobylette. They got the license number, Tony." I found myself leaning forward, trying to get his attention. He still wasn't looking at me. "It was *my* Mobylette."

He blinked. And I saw him pull himself together. "Oh, no. No, that's terrible." Genuine concern in the voice. At least, genuine-sounding. Worried look, now, behind those glasses. "But . . . well, I guess it is possible. I didn't want you to find out." Big sigh.

"What?"

"Well, I lent your Mobylette to a friend last night. He'd come over here for dinner and we got listening to some music and it was so late that I offered him your Mobylette to get home. He lives near you."

"I thought *you* were using it and *you* were going to be out late," I objected, remembering what he'd said when he first mentioned borrowing it.

"Plans changed."

"Anyway," I went on, barely listening to him, "you don't get to my house from here via the Bois de Boulogne."

Tony sighed again. "Well, he did say he might go . . ." Voice petered out.

"What, it's not for my delicate ears? Going to pick up a *fille de joie*? You are making this story up as you go along. Who is your friend?"

"I'm hardly going to tell you!" he said, with the first convincing tone of voice I'd heard.

"Well, you might think about the fact that I am now in trouble with the police, Tony. You might think about the fact that your assistant may not be at work on Monday because I'll have been hauled in for questioning. It's all very well to shield your friend, but I'd like to draw your attention to the fact that you're shielding him at *my* expense." I could hear my voice rising, but it was a relief to get this off my chest. The fear of the past few hours, the shock about Edward, my anger at myself: It was all turning into anger at Tony. "Out of some notion of loyalty, I didn't tell Edward I'd lent you the Mobylette. But when the police ask me, as they will, I'll just tell them. I'm going to let you and your 'friend,' if he even exists, which I doubt, fend for yourselves." I stood up and paced over to the stereo wall, where I stood with my back to the room.

"Wait a minute, calm down," Tony said, getting up and coming over to me. "It's all right, he'll face the music. I haven't heard from him but if he, God, if he did hit Sago then he'll have to take the responsibility for it."

So plausible. Calm down, Louise, be rational. You're flying off the handle. Tony of the superior intelligence will make it all okay. "That's not all," I spat out. "I just saw Gabriel up at Passy. He told me about the etui. About how you wanted him to take it to Germany. And you snuck it into his pack when he said he wouldn't. What is going on? Did you switch briefcases with my father? What else have I missed? Have you planted stuff on *me*? You're a fence, right?"

There it was. What I had wanted not to say. Not to think. Not to know. Tony Geist, head of Winfield College Abroad and international fence. No wonder he could afford this wall of equipment blinking in front of me. And tickets to Glyndebourne and La Scala, and CDs and whatever else.

But he wasn't going to let me brood about it. He ignored the last half of what I said. "The etui? You mean *he* has it?" And he grabbed me by the arm. We were still standing in the shadows, feet away from the only lamp. But there was no missing his eagerness. For the first time tonight, Tony was all there. He was paying attention. I could see reflections from the sound system glinting on his glasses: There were half circles with needles flickering where his eyes should have been. But I could sense the urgency.

"No. He wanted to get rid of it."

"So where is it? Louise, I have to get my hands on it. I'll explain everything. But this is crucial, it's— everything. It's worth my life. Honestly." His hand was tight around my arm, and I could feel, across the space between us, the pounding of his heart. Now that I had gotten through to him, Tony was afraid.

And without an instant's hesitation, I said, "It's in your top desk drawer at work. Neither of us wanted to take charge of it."

He let go of my arm and was across the room before I knew what he was doing. "Thank God. I'll just go get it. Listen, I'll explain everything to you. I know how it looks. I understand you're suspicious. And angry." He kept on talking while he opened a door and took a jacket. He snatched his keys and wallet from the table, and extracted his passport from the papers piled under the lamp. "But I just have to go now. Come on, I can't leave you here."

He came back over to me, now wearing the dark jacket. He took me by the arm again and deftly flipped a few switches and twiddled a few dials on the system. "All right, now let's go," he said, and started to hustle me toward the door.

"But wait a minute, Tony, where are you going? Don't you think you owe me an explanation?" Suddenly the balance of the confrontation had shifted again, Tony was slipping away. I was irrelevant. All he cared about was that etui.

"Yes, of course I do. But listen." He turned me around to face him. "I'm serious. This is—" And he paused. Then in a flat tone he said, "It is a matter of life and death. Mine. Go to your apartment. I'll call or come by when I can. I'll explain." And then he nudged me out the door.

I wasn't sure why I had lied to him about the etui. I could at least have saved him the trip to Passy, not to mention saving myself the explosion of anger when he came back to my apartment and told me the etui wasn't in his desk. And if it *was* a matter of life and death, as he claimed, didn't I at least owe him the chance to find the etui and save his life?

The problem was that I didn't believe him. I didn't believe more than half a dozen words that Tony had just said to me. Starting when he'd walked out of his closet, pretending he'd been asleep.

NINE

AND YET HE WAS afraid. That was the only thing that had rung true. He was afraid, and his fear had something to do with the etui. He had called it "a matter of life and death." Tony hated clichés. Ordinarily he would have laughed at such a melodramatic phrase. But as I stood there in the little cul-de-sac outside his door, I had an uneasy feeling. He had locked his door and sprinted off without another look at me. As if—well, as if his life depended on his speed.

Maybe I'd done the wrong thing. Maybe I should just have given him the etui. I shivered. But what if Tony was lying and just wanted to get it back because it was worth so much? Would I dash across town like a possessed person for a million-odd dollars worth of beautifully crafted gold?

Sure. Especially if it wasn't mine to lose.

I shivered again and pulled my raincoat close around my body. Now that I thought of it that way, I could feel the etui practically burning a hole in my bag. I had to do something with it, hide it or stash it someplace safe. It was starting to give me the creeps. The word "dangerous" flickered into my mind, but I squelched it. That wasn't what I meant. I just didn't want to lose it. That was all.

But even though I wanted to get rid of the etui, I didn't want just to hand it over to Tony. It was partly, I had to admit, that I was so furious. And hurt too. As I started to retrace my steps to the boulevard de Gre-

nelle, I took stock of just what had happened to my
cozy little world. Devastation was the word that came
to mind. It wasn't just the practical aspects that upset
me; what would happen to Winfield College if Tony
was a fence? Would I have a job? What would I say to
the kids? I couldn't even begin to imagine what the
repercussions were going to be. All our students being interviewed by the police? Gabriel, certainly, having to give evidence against Tony? If it came to that,
was I going to turn Tony in?

I couldn't even think about that. Time enough to
consider it when I got home to lick my wounds. The
principal of which was a sense of loss. I'd just lost my
best friend. As surely as if he'd been hit by a car, Tony
was out of my life. And so was Edward.

At that thought, tears came welling to my eyes and
I tried to tell myself that I was overwrought. Tired,
under a strain. Why should I be more upset about
Edward than I was about Tony, when they had both
made a fool of me? Edward, after all, was no more
than—what?—a potential boyfriend. Tony's place in
my life was much bigger.

But I had never entirely trusted Tony. Not emotionally, certainly. I was shocked, I felt stupid and naïve. (But who would suspect her boss of smuggling? a
little voice kept asking.) It was Edward, though, who
had begged me to trust him, while he used me.

I had reached the boulevard de Grenelle and had to
decide which way to go. For a moment, I had to be
realistic and ignore my misery. I didn't want to keep
the etui in my bag. I didn't want Tony to get it. I
wasn't just being vindictive; I had a sense that once
Tony had this thing in his hands, my chances of getting him to listen to me and answer my questions were

nil. I wanted to be able to tell him *honestly* that it was
safe, and that neither he nor I could get at it. I could
leave the etui in a locker at a station, but I'd still have
the key and Tony could go fetch it. I could give it to
somebody else, like Gisele. But Tony could just go
over there.... I considered hiding it in my apartment,
but I knew that wouldn't work. I'd probably keep
looking at the place where it was hidden.

I stopped to wait for a light to turn and noticed a
tabac across the street. The door was open and I could
see the display of chocolate bars lined up by the cash
register. I wasn't hungry, but the thought of a chocolate bar struck a chord. Sweets in time of stress. By the
time I got across the street, a middle-aged woman was
already at the counter, buying stamps. She wanted
something complicated, not the usual 2.20 francs for
a letter, but the right amount to send a little package.
She claimed to know exactly how much it would cost,
but the clerk kept telling her she should take it to the
post office to be weighed. The discussion was getting
pretty heated, and I reached in my bag to get out my
wallet. I might have the exact change for a Mars bar.
As I heard the man say "Madame, if you are not in a
hurry you could take this package of yours to the post
office in the rue du Louvre. It is open all night and
they will..."

I lost track of what he was saying then, because my
hand had closed on the etui just as he said "rue du
Louvre."

The perfect hiding place for the etui; the French
mail. I'd wrap it up safely and mail it to myself. It was
Friday; it would be stuck in the postal system at least
until Monday. Probably Tuesday. Long enough, any-

way, to get some kind of truth out of Tony. And long enough for me to decide what to do about him.

I left the *tabac* with the pair still quarreling. Sweets could wait.

I must have caught some of Tony's anxiety, because now that I had decided what to do with the etui, I wanted to get it done right away. The only place I could think of to buy packing materials was Joseph Gibert, the big stationery store on the boulevard St. Michel. I would go there first, then cross the river to the post office. I looked at my watch as I headed toward the nearby metro station. Eight-fifteen. I sighed. It was going to take at least an hour to accomplish this. And then by the time I got home, Tony would probably be there in a lather. One step at a time, I thought bleakly, and sent a mental nod of thanks to the RATP when a train whirred into the station just as I reached the platform.

But that was the last good luck I had. Joseph Gibert was still open when I got there, but oddly enough they didn't have just the right-sized mailing envelope for a Louis XV etui. I had expected to get a too-large envelope and pad it. But in a store devoted to the needs of college students, padding material was hard to find. I wasn't completely cavalier about the etui; It was priceless, I knew that. I didn't want it to get dented or scratched, so I knew I'd have to cushion it in something. Finally I left the store with an envelope, a pad of tracing paper, and a roll of tape. I was not going to be turned away at the post office counter because this package was inadequately wrapped.

But when I got back in the Métro there was a long wait before the next train came. I paced up and down on the platform, wondering if I should just go back upstairs and walk across to the Right Bank. By the time the train finally came, I figured I could have walked to the post office and home again. I tried to tell myself to calm down. After all, what did it matter what time I got there? Nobody was chasing me.

All the same, my heart sank when I walked into the high-ceilinged, slightly dingy main room of the post office and saw a long line. I managed to wrap up the etui (shielded from prying eyes by Gabriel's bandanna) and reinforce the envelope with tape, then scrawl my address across the concave surface of the package. For safety's sake, I wanted to put on a return address. I gave it a moment's thought: Gisele? But after hesitating, I wrote down Edward's name and address. He wasn't a potential boyfriend anymore. But he was still The Law. I found that just faintly comforting.

All this time, standing at the chest-height table constructing my package, I had been eyeing the line, which didn't seem to be moving at all. Of course, it was one of those practically surrealistic urban scenes. Who goes to the post office at nine o'clock on a Friday night? The desperate.

There were several groups of swarthy foreigners, who were, I knew, going to stand for long moments at their respective windows, gesturing wildly as the one with the most French tried to understand which forms had to be filled out to send their parcel the size of a small refrigerator to Teheran. Of course, they all smoked incessantly. There were a number of thin, intense, anonymous-looking men, staring into space and jiggling their legs as they waited. Around the middle of the line a pair of women nudged each other and grumbled stagily about the service and people who tried to cut in lines. Near me a pair of American girls in Chanel T-shirts talked a little louder than necessary about the French boys they met at Sciences Po, the political science faculty favored by the upper middle class. Gonzague this, Jean-Luc that, house in the Sologne, Ecole National d'Administration, *Madame la Comtesse*, Fiat, cute. They smoked too.

The minutes dragged by. I know, because I kept track of each one of them. The big clock on the wall was two and a half minutes faster than my watch. I spent twenty-three minutes shifting from foot to foot, inching along toward the front of the line. And getting more and more anxious.

Was I doing the right thing? Shouldn't I just turn the etui over to the police? But I couldn't face the ordeal that would involve. Hours of skeptical questions, at best. Anyway, I could still turn it over in a few days, when it arrived in my mailbox. But what about Tony? What if... I tried to avoid the thought, but it insisted. What if he hadn't been lying? What if he really was in danger?

I wasn't equipped to think about it. My mind kept running up against the problem like a mouse trying to scale a wall. I couldn't get a grip on it. If Tony was a fence... I tried to reason it out logically. If Tony was a fence, he was dealing with criminals. Who might be violent. And he had been afraid when I mentioned the etui. That much, I was sure of.

But he had lied to me before. Often, it seemed. I must have been incredibly naïve. Because now that I looked back, there had been signs. George, caught with 600,000 francs in his car at the Swiss border. Tony hushed it up at the time—had he been using George to send currency into Switzerland? Obviously. I shook my head, thinking about other clues I'd missed. Of course his pay from Winfield wouldn't stretch to cover all of his opera tickets and CDs and travel for performances.

And this was the man I trusted with my Mobylette, my keys, everything in my apartment, not that there was anything in... My keys. It all fell into place. Tony had a set of my keys. That night before Daddy left, he could have seen us go off to dinner, then let himself in and switched briefcases. A cinch.

The line inched forward about half a step. I looked at the package in my hands, squashy and irregular, with my address staring up at me in my own handwriting. It didn't look like a million bucks. But somebody must be pretty mad that it had gone missing.

So was I, if it came to that. Why couldn't Tony just have taken it to Germany himself? Why couldn't I still be blissfully ignorant? Now I wanted to get rid of the etui more than ever. Get rid of it and turn the clock back to before Edward's phone call. I sighed, thinking about how cheerfully I had answered him.

The Chanel twins were nattering on and on and behind me a large silent Frenchman kept nudging a little closer than I wanted him. Finally it was my turn. How did I want to send the package? First class, third class, parcel rate? It needed more tape. Did I want to insure it? That was a laugh. Insure it for what, a million dollars? If it got lost in the mail I'd be glad.

Finally, wearily, I headed home. It wasn't even ten o'clock, but I dragged myself through the streets as if I'd been out all night. I trudged unseeing down the rue du Louvre, past the round Bourse, the discreet stockbroker's restaurants doing a quiet dinner business, the tourist cafés near the Louvre. I turned right on the quai du Louvre and followed the grimy wall of the museum as the traffic sped by on my left. I'd be home soon. Tony would be there. I would have to explain why I'd lied about the etui. And ask him about smuggling. I didn't want to. I wanted to go hide somewhere.

I wouldn't, though. I'd face the music. Daddy's legacy—never shirking the unpleasant task. At a break in the traffic I crossed the quai and turned onto the pont du Carrousel. I could see it perfectly clearly. Tony was going to yell. I was probably going to yell too. Yes, I probably would. Fencing under my nose; I would yell. And he would try to justify himself. And I would pretend to listen . . .

Finally I'd reached my building. It was all I could do to drag myself up the stairs, and I was praying with each step that I would see only darkened windows when I got to the roof.

Prayers unanswered. The windows blazed. I shut my eyes. Was there any way to avoid this? I could just turn around and go back downstairs. . . . My feet kept walking toward the door, though. My hand turned the doorknob and my feet walked me inside. My eyes fell on the man getting up from the couch and my brain, very slow to catch up, registered that it was not Tony. Nor—why had I hoped so, even for an instant?—was it Edward.

No, it was Volker walking toward me across the room. Volker holding my shoulder to kiss me on both cheeks. Volker saying he had just dropped by to see how I was. Volker not explaining how he'd gotten in. Volker who belonged, Edward had told me, to a terrorist group. A violent terrorist group.

"How did you get in?" I asked. Maybe that didn't sound too polite. Oh, God, don't let him be offended. I tried to smile.

"Oh, Madame Cabrol, you know she still likes me. You look tired."

"Yes, well, it was a long day."

"And how is everything at Winfield? How is Tony?"

"Fine the last time I saw him," I answered. "He was going to a Kathleen Battle recital tonight." Why did I add that? As a dodge, I thought. If I can make Volker believe everything is normal, maybe he'll get bored and just leave. But if I try to kick him out he'll want to stay and discuss it. And he must not find out that I know *anything* about him.

"And your students?"

"Oh, the usual. It's pretty quiet now. Serena has a new boyfriend as of three days ago. Gabriel's landlady thinks he has bedbugs."

Volker didn't even laugh. "Does he? You know they are very hard to stop."

"So I've been told," I answered, wondering if Volker had really come over to talk about bedbugs. And if not...I set down my shoulder bag on the counter and shrugged my raincoat off. "And what have you been up to?"

"Oh, the same. The usual. Have you seen this new film by Wim Wenders?"

"No," I said brightly. "Is it good?"

"*Ja*. It is brilliant. Brilliant metaphor for life in Germany today."

Nothing could have sounded less interesting. "Oh, well I'll have to see it."

"*Ja*, and Klaus Maria Brandauer, I remember you like him, he is in it. And Hanna Schygulla. Very good."

I nodded. "Well, good." Pause. Had Volker come over to talk about *movies*?

"Your father was here to visit?"

"Yes, he was here for a week or so."

"And he is well?"

"Oh, fine. He and Tony went to see *Wozzeck* one night. He hated it. But otherwise he had fun." What if Tony came while Volker was still here?

Volker strolled across the room and plumped himself down on the sofa facing me. "You are going to travel this summer?"

Clearly he was planning on settling in for a while. "I'm just going to take my shoes off," I said. "I'll be right back." As I reached the bedroom door, the phone started to ring.

"Hello?" Why did I hope it was Edward? But there didn't seem to be anyone there. "Hello?"

There was a funny scratchy sound on the other end. Not breathing, it was too loud and ragged. Then, faintly, I heard my name. "Louise? Don't hang up. It's me." I stood stock-still. Suddenly I wasn't tired. "It's Tony."

I gasped. "What?..." I started, but he broke in. Still weakly. The scratchy sound went on. It was his breathing.

"Don't say anything," he whispered. "I know Volker..." pause. "There."

"How?" I whispered back, but I got no answer. He was trying to say something else, there was a kind of hissing sound. "Hhhhhee." Another pause. "Dangerous." Silence. Then a strange, terrible sound.

Something between a moan and a sob and a hiccup. Without thinking, I started to say "What happened to you?" But with what must have been a surge of energy, Tony gasped. "Don't. Don't ask. He beat me. Wants...etui. Get away." And then there was a clatter. As if he had simply dropped the receiver.

"Are you all right?" Volker's voice came from right behind me. I knew I couldn't erase the shock from my face as I hung up the phone and turned to him.

"Yes," I said, and allowed myself to shiver. "It was an obscene call." I sank down on the bed. Volker sat down next to me, very close. I kept shivering. He put an arm around me. The shivering got worse. I tensed all my muscles to try to get it to stop. The man sitting next to me had just beaten Tony. I took a deep breath. I had no idea what he wanted from me.

"Volker, have you been calling here late at night?" I blurted out, then flinched. Why did I say that?

"What, on the telephone?" he answered. He looked puzzled. For what that was worth.

"Or come here while I was gone?"

"No! Why would I do this? If I want to see you, I come when you are here." He shrugged. Seemed simple enough.

I got up, away from that arm. Went to the closet. Took off my high heels. Put on a low pair. Tony said get away. Would low-heeled loafers be good escape shoes?

"Well, come out and have a glass of wine," I said brightly. I had an instant's wild vision of getting Volker paralytically drunk. But of course Volker drank only white wine. Had to keep his mind sharp for his eternal struggle against American imperialism. I told myself I wasn't really funny.

"Is someone calling you up late at night?" he was saying behind me. "Like this call now?"

"Yes," I said, unthinking, "and somehow I thought it was you."

Suddenly he had me by the shoulders. He turned me around firmly. "Listen. I do not do these things. I know we are not lovers now, but why would I frighten you like this?" His blue eyes looked down into mine. He had on a beautiful sweater, cable knit in a speckled blue. Impeccably clean white shirt. Was this the wardrobe of a terrorist? One of his hands came up and brushed the hair away from my face. "No. That is not what I want," he said. And leaned down and kissed me.

I managed not to cringe. In a way I was relieved. I didn't know why he was there. I didn't have any idea why he would beat Tony up. But this, Volker being amorous, I thought I could deal with. For a while anyway. For as long as it took me to figure out how to get out of the house without alarming him.

Which actually turned out to be no time at all. For as Volker sat down on the sofa again, I went behind the counter to get out the wine. There was a short glass in the sink: Edward's scotch glass from earlier in the evening. Ouch. And an empty wine bottle on the counter. I had finished the wine myself.

"Oh, look," I said, holding up the empty bottle. "I finished the wine and forgot to get more. I'll just run down to get some." There was a good wine store two doors away. Of course I had no intention of going there.

"All right," he said. A little eagerly, I thought, for someone who was supposed to be romancing me.

Shouldn't he, as a gentleman, have offered to go himself?

I slipped my raincoat back on and put a hand toward my shoulder bag to get out my wallet, but Volker leaped up. "No, no, I will give you money," he said with his hand in his pocket. My mind whirled. I didn't want to go out into Paris without my wallet: passport, credit cards, money. But I wanted to get away. And I didn't want Volker to suspect anything.

"Oh, it's all right," I said, groping around in the bag.

"No, no. I insist," Volker said, coming over to me. He pulled my hand from the bag and put a fifty-franc bill in it.

"Well, that's very nice," I said, and smiled up at him. "I'll be right back." And I walked out.

I could barely keep myself from breaking into a run the moment the door was shut behind me. I took deep breaths and made myself pace slowly across the roof. It took about a century. But the minute I hit the stairs, I was scurrying like a rabbit.

I could hear Madame Cabrol's television as I got to the bottom, so I had to slow down again. She poked her head out as I walked by her window. "*Bonsoir*, mademoiselle, you are going out when you have guests? It is a pleasure to see M. Freilich again!"

Willing myself not to rouse her suspicion, I stopped. "Yes, I'm just going to get some wine." And then in the midst of my anxiety, my eagerness to be gone, a little thought emerged clearly. "Madame, M. Freilich has not been here at all for a month or so?"

"No, no." She shook her head. "You would know."

"No, while I was out. To leave a message or anything."

"No. Not for a month or more. *Bonsoir*, M. Joubert," she called out to the occupant of the third floor. "I have a package for you..." I slipped away then. Out into the street, and away.

TEN

THE QUESTION WAS, where to? I stood on the pavement outside the great doorway of my building for a moment. It was a normal Friday night on the boulevard St. Germain. Warm enough for the café tables to be full. The sidewalk was littered here and there with fallen chestnut blossoms, bruised and flattened under scores of feet. If I walked into the wine shop, the café next door, the *tabac* around the corner, I would get a smile and a pleasant *"Bonsoir, mademoiselle."* I could cash a check in the *épicierie* around the corner. Of course it was closed at ten o'clock.

I had a doctor and an accountant and a dentist. I knew a good mechanic to fix my Mobylette, and a great travel agent. The woman who ran the nearby *patisserie* would save me her last *gâteau Pithiviers* if I asked her to.

A *Pithiviers* was not going to do me any good at the moment. And neither were all those cordial professional relationships that made my life so pleasant. At lunchtime, a week ago, I had strolled to the place du Trocadero, and looked out over the Seine and the Eiffel Tower, Les Invalides, and the champs de Mars with an idle feeling of relish. Possession, really. As if I owned the damned place.

And now here I was on my own doorstep, not daring to go back inside. And feeling, as I had never felt even in my first hours in Paris, like an alien. Frightened and alone.

But that, I told myself, with a bracing rush of practicality, was not entirely true. I had friends. Friends who would help me. Gisele would be a good start. Even if she couldn't put me up, she had a whole network of emergency lodgings through the Alliance Française. Or she could lend me money enough for a hotel room. But I'd better be on my way. My pretext of wine-buying wasn't going to give me a lot of time. Soon Volker would wonder why I hadn't come back.

I was halfway up the block when I followed that line of reasoning to its conclusion, and though I kept walking, my pace slowed. On some level, I was expecting Volker to come after me. Volker knew Gisele. If I went to her, I'd just be dragging her into this. Into—whatever it was. I didn't want to use the word "danger," even to myself.

Why should Volker come after me? Maybe he had just come to see how I was and try to get me into bed. I didn't really believe that: I was just testing the notion. Why tonight, of all nights? Why unannounced? Even when we were going out, Volker had never just dropped by. And if he wanted to see *me*, why let me run out to do this errand? He had always been punctilious in the past, formal and old-fashioned about little things like not letting me buy the wine. I was just trying to reason it out step by step, but I already knew the answer because Tony had told me. Volker wanted the etui, and he thought I had it. And my volunteering to go out for a moment gave him the chance to look through my bag. Where he was not going to find it.

I had reached the river, and I had to decide where to go. No, that wasn't really it. I had to admit to myself where I was going. I was planning to cross the pont de la Concorde, take the Métro to Etoile, get off and walk several blocks down the avenue de Friedland—to Edward.

Edward had been right—Volker was violent, Tony had injured Mr. Sago, and I should have been more careful. On an ordinary day, in the sunlight, well rested, after breakfast, feeling like myself, I would have hated to concede that. Nobody likes being wrong. As it was I was not thrilled about the way Edward had used me. I was certainly not going to his apartment to throw myself into his arms and tell him all was forgiven. But he was a representative of the United States Government. And—he was right after all.

Besides, Volker didn't know about him.

When I walked down into the Métro station I made an automatic gesture to reach for my *Carte Orange*, my monthly transit pass, before I remembered that it was still in my purse, sitting on the kitchen counter. Actually, probably spilled out on the dining-room table by now, with Volker pawing through it. I pulled his fifty-franc note from my jeans pocket and bought a single yellow cardboard ticket. The crumpled ten-franc notes and change the clerk handed back looked pathetic. If Edward wasn't at home, I wouldn't get very far on 45 francs 40 centimes. But he would be. Of course he would be.

When the train pulled into the station I sank gratefully into a seat, leaning my head back against the wall of the car. I shut my eyes and let my whole body sag. I heard the conductor announce each stop, the electronic tone that signaled the car doors' closing. Champs-Elysées. Franklin D. Roosevelt. George V. One more stop. A few blocks' walk. Then I would be able to tell Edward everything. About lending the

Mobylette to Tony. And Gabriel finding the etui, and Tony's reaction. I felt a rush of concern when I thought of Tony's voice on the phone. Well, Edward would send an ambulance for him. Maybe he would let me sleep on his sofa. It wasn't even that late, but I was almost numb with exhaustion.

Hope and eagerness propelled me up the stairs of the station at Etoile and down the few blocks to the building where Edward had told me he lived. I would tell him everything. He would decide what to do with the etui, and do something about Volker. Have him arrested? I didn't know. It wouldn't be my problem.

Edward's building was an apartment house not unlike mine: built a little later and several floors taller, with smaller windows and less ornament. I rang the bell. In a few moments I heard the *click* that released the massive lock, and the huge door was drawn open slightly. A sad-looking man in a cardigan and slippers stood there. I explained that I was looking for Edward. He looked sadder. Yes, M. Cole lived here. But he was not at home.

I wasn't very quick to catch on. How could he not be here? When would he be back? The man had no idea when he was expected. He kept very irregular hours, M. Cole. Would mademoiselle care to leave a message? *Un petit mot?*

Un petit mot. I realized I was clutching the door frame. A little note to say what? "Dear Edward, you were right about Tony and Volker and I am in deep trouble. Please help, Louise." No, silly. I was inside the door now and the man was shuffling off to get a pencil and paper. Think, Louise. How can you make this work?

Of course, he'd given me a phone number. For an occasion just like this. Oh, damn him for being right anyway! I'd crumpled up the paper scornfully (even without an audience). But he'd told me the number. I don't forget numbers. It was 4284.2053. "I'll wear a beeper," he'd said. "They can always reach me."

But just in case. In case he wasn't wearing the beeper, in case "they" couldn't reach him. I needed a plan.

Edward couldn't stay out all night. It was ten-thirty now. He would have to come back. I could try to meet him here—but no, that didn't make sense. I didn't know when he was coming back and I couldn't just wait around. Better to make a rendezvous. Set an hour that would give him plenty of time to get there if he got home late. But not too late so that it would be unsafe for me, alone. Find a place that would still be open and populated.

The man was shuffling back with paper in his hand. Eleven, twelve—Edward might still be out at midnight. Better to make it one o'clock, to be on the safe side. What would still be open at 1 A.M.? Le Drugstore, pretty near my apartment. Too close to Volker, I couldn't chance it. Any number of bars. But I only had forty-five francs. And I might—I tried to think of this calmly—have to try to find a bed for forty-five francs. Maybe one of the station hotels? That was it: I'd meet Edward at a station. I knew the boat train to England left the gare du Nord late at night. There would be enough people around for it to be safe.

But what if we missed each other? Somehow I would have to fend for myself but I could try for another rendezvous. Quickly I scribbled, "Edward: I need help. Meet me gare du Nord 1 A.M. Failing that..." I paused only for a moment. Anything obvious. "... in front of Notre Dame 7 A.M. Please." And then I couldn't help adding "Desperate." I just signed it "Louise."

I gave the note to the man and heard the door thud closed behind me. For an instant, I felt a bit forlorn. But I couldn't afford to. I couldn't let myself slide into self-pity. It was only a matter of two hours or so. I had almost fifty francs, I was well clear of Volker. I could try to call Edward. Even if I didn't get him I could find some café and simply *sit* until it was time to go meet him. Not such a hardship. But first I needed to try to get Tony some help. I was still furious with him. I knew I'd never forgive him. But he had called me to warn me about Volker. And he was badly injured. For the sake of five years of friendship, I had to try to do something for him.

It was such a staid neighborhood, not the kind of place where the cafés stayed open till all hours. Well, I'd just walk until I found one. I turned eastward, toward the neighborhood of the Grands Boulevards. A little bit more commercial, and I hoped more likely to be awake. But as I headed toward the Boulevard Haussmann I spotted an orange awning on a side street. The lights were still on, the chairs and tables still on the sidewalk. A couple of them were even occupied. As I drew near I got a whiff of the classic Paris café scent: coffee, Gauloises, a hint of strong soap, and an edge of vinegar. When I walked in the place was bright and cheerful. The barman was just pouring a couple of glasses of red wine. The waiter was polishing a table. The buxom brunette at the register was complaining to both of them about the laziness of a mutual acquaintance. When I asked for half a dozen jetons she didn't interrupt her narrative for a moment. Where was the phone? I asked. She pointed down a flight of stairs, where, indeed, a sign read TELEPHONE. W.C.

The phone was stuck in a dark little alcove right at the foot of the stairs. There was a phone book lying on the floor beneath it, and a couple of cigarette butts, as if someone had had a long, troubled conversation. I slipped the jeton into the slot and dialed. I could hear Edward's voice saying the number: 4284.2053. I shut my eyes as the phone rang, and wondered how they would answer the phone. In English? In French? "Edward Cole's office?" Would Edward himself answer?

"Chez Lucie," a voice said in my ear.

"What?" I said stupidly.

"Chez Lucie. Je peux vous aider?" Then, in unctuous English: "May I help you? Is it to make a reservation?"

Great. The Paris phone system strikes again. Well, maybe I'd just misdialed. I explained that I was *"mal branché"* and hung up. Put another jeton in the slot, and slowly, checking each number, dialed again: 4284.2053.

"Chez Lucie." This time I was aware of the din in the background: voices, clattering dishes, a wisp of music.

Oh, no. Please, no. Maybe I'd dialed wrong. "Is this 4284.2053?" I asked, and repeated the number in French.

"Oui, madame. Je peux vous aider?"

I hung up. No. He couldn't help me. And neither could Edward.

No, that wasn't right, I was being melodramatic. I stood up straight and took a deep breath. I had left a message for Edward. Talking to him would have been helpful. But the situation wasn't hopeless. It really wasn't. Sure, I was disappointed. But I wasn't crushed. Oh, no.

My eye fell on the phone book, open at my feet. I flipped it over: It was current. Worth a try, maybe.

Upstairs I could hear the waiter order two cups of coffee and a Benedictine. When I finished my telephoning I'd see if I could get something to eat, maybe a sandwich. This was as good a place as any to wait, since waiting was obviously going to be my course of action. I leafed through quickly to find the entries for "Etats-Unis." Just possibly there might be one for the attorney general's office. I ran my finger down the listing: consulate, embassy, visas, tourist office. Short and sweet. No attorney general. I thought of Tony, lying by a telephone with the receiver dangling. He needed help. But I dialed the information number at the consulate just in case. Got a long taped message, in both French and English, about the procedure for obtaining a visa. Waste of a jeton.

The only hospital I could think of trying for Tony was the American Hospital in Neuilly. I couldn't imagine that any Parisian dispatcher would send out an ambulance when I couldn't describe Tony's state. It was going to be hard enough to persuade someone in English that an American desperately needed medical help.

The man who answered the phone (in French) passed me on to an official-sounding woman. She, also in French, passed me on to another number. I prayed I wouldn't get disconnected. The phone rang and rang, eight times, ten times, then an American male voice answered: "Emergency."

"Thank God," I said. "I've been trying to get through. I need an ambulance. A friend of mine has been beaten..."

"What? This is the emergency room, I don't dispatch ambulances. Are you in Neuilly?"

"No, Paris."

"Call the Poste Centrale, they'll send someone."

"No, you don't understand, I don't know how badly he's injured. Look," I pleaded, talking fast, willing him to stay on the phone, using an argument I hated to resort to. "You know the French. If you don't have all the right papers they'll let you die in the gutter..."

"Hold on," the voice interrupted, and I could hear him shouting something about a saline drip. "Sorry. What's wrong with this guy?"

"I don't know," I said, relieved that he would at least listen. "He was beaten. He got to the phone and called me. He sounded"—his ragged breathing echoed in my head—"he sounded pretty bad."

"How do I know this isn't just a hoax?"

I shut my eyes. "Do grown women call ambulances on false alarms in the middle of the night in foreign cities? Do you know how hard it was for me to get to you?" An irritating beep sounded in my ear. "Hold on, I need another jeton, just wait." I pushed it into the slot.

"Oh, hell," he said, and sighed. I didn't break his silence. "Look, I'll see what I can do. What's your name?"

"Louise Gerard."

"Give me a phone number where I can reach you."

I hesitated for a moment. No point in going into my whole story. I gave him my home phone number.

"Now you say this friend of yours just called you, you haven't seen him?"

"No."

"Okay. Lucky for you it's a quiet night. I can't promise anything, you know. Where is he?"

I gave the Passy address. "It's set back in the courtyard, and the door should be unlocked. If it isn't, break a window."

"Yeah. We would anyway. Now listen. You go over there right now. You may get there before we do. *Don't move him.* Try to keep him warm. Got that? Don't move him."

"Okay," I said. It didn't matter. I couldn't go to Tony. Volker would find me.

"And call the municipal ambulances. I may not be able to talk my supervisor into letting me send this one out. Call the police too. They'll help. Let me have the phone number at that address. In case I can't help you."

"Okay," I said again, and gave him the number.

"Good luck," the voice said. "I'll do what I can." He hung up.

I stood with the receiver buzzing in my ear. I still had one jeton. The phone book was open on the floor. I would call the police. Not for my sake. For Tony's. Even if they didn't want to believe me, they would have to send somebody just in case. And they would find Tony and get him medical help. Awkward questions were beside the point now.

I was squatting on the floor beside the book, flipping to "Police," when I heard something from upstairs that made me freeze.

A voice was asking if a redheaded woman had been in. Not very tall, wearing a raincoat over a black sweater and jeans. Volker's voice.

I didn't wait to hear the answer. I flew, in the only direction I could, toward the W.C.'s. There was a grimy door with a padlock in between them. The padlock hung open. I took an instant to close the padlock carefully, leaving the hasp of the lock free. The door would look securely locked, I hoped. Then I slipped behind the door, pulling it to behind me.

It was evidently a storeroom. I felt carefully in front of me with my feet, in case the floor was uneven. I couldn't afford to make any noise by falling. At my right hand, I felt a big drum. There was a little space behind it, and the floor was dry. Quickly and quietly I squeezed myself behind it and hugged my knees. My heart was pounding so hard I thought it would jump out of my chest. I put my hands over my eyes and pressed against them. Maybe I thought if I couldn't see him, he wouldn't be able to see me.

The door had been heavy, but it didn't fit very well. As my eyes adjusted to the dark I could see a thin wedge of light on the floor. And now I could hear feet coming down the stairs. "Louise?"

The footsteps stopped. The telephone receiver rattled slightly. It would still be warm from my holding it. I knew my ears were sharper than usual. I could hear the tiny sounds, creaking of shoe leather, coins rubbing together in a pocket, that meant Volker was bending down. Looking at the phone book. Which was open to "Police."

The coins jingled again. Volker was standing up. Two steps. A creak; he was opening one of the rest-room doors. It swung shut. Silence, followed by the

low roar that meant French plumbing had been acti-
vated. Volker was, after all, only human.

Then the creak again. Footsteps, now right outside
my door. I tried to squash myself down even farther.
Another different squeaking hinge. Then a different
set of feet coming down the stairs: *clip, clip, clip.* High
heels: and the patroness saying "No, no, monsieur,
you cannot go in there."

"But I am looking for—"

She cut him off. "And I have told you she left. I saw
her go. Philippe was in the kitchen, Marc washing the
glasses. They did not see her. I am at the cash register,
I see who comes in and who goes out. Your redheaded *demoiselle,* she came in, bought jetons, came
down to use the phone, came back upstairs, thanked
me nicely and went out."

Silence. Volker wasn't budging.

"All right. You want to look in the ladies' room? I
will go in with you. *Voilà.*" The door creaked. The
heels clicked. Terrified as I was, a tiny corner of me
enjoyed the notion of Volker being bullied by this
woman. Two slow steps. She kept the door open. It
whined slightly as she leaned against it. "There, you
see. She is not in here. Look all over. It is very possible that I am lying. Please, you must assure yourself
that I am not. She is small, I think you said. Perhaps
she is in the garbage? Or beneath this pail?" She was
tapping a foot now.

More slow steps. "Very well, madame. I am sorry
for troubling you," Volker said. He didn't sound angry, but there was a puzzled note in his voice. Good.
Let him wonder. Two sets of footsteps went up the
stairs.

Then: *"Bonsoir, monsieur."*

I sank back in the darkness. My mind was blank, and stayed that way for several long moments. My whole body was shaking, and I let it. I put my head down on my knees and tried to breathe deeply. Gradually the tremors went away. It was nice there in the dark. I didn't want to leave.

How had he known where I was?

Could he have followed me? No. He would have stayed in my apartment for a while. Until he began to think I wasn't coming back. How long would that take? Ten minutes? Fifteen? Say fifteen.

And yet here he was, right on my heels. He had known exactly where I would go. Maybe finding this café had been a coincidence. But he had come directly, like a homing pigeon, to this little corner of the avenue de Friedland. To Edward's apartment.

Which meant he knew about Edward. He knew where Edward lived and that I would go directly there.

And he also knew, if he'd questioned the concierge, that I was somewhere nearby.

He might even have read the note I left. He might even be at the gare du Nord at 1 A.M.

How had he known about Edward? Oh, God, of course. If he was spying on me he would know. I remembered the night when the phone had started to ring right after Edward left. Volker must have seen that. Could he have taken an apartment across the street? Was that how he kept track of me?

Something scuttled in the corner. Great, rats. That was all I needed. I stood up slowly, stretching my legs. But I wasn't ready to go outside. Rats or not. I tried to shift the drum I'd been hiding behind. It seemed steady, so I perched on top, pulling my feet up. I just needed to think a little bit longer.

And there was an awful lot to think about. The whole picture was suddenly much bleaker.

Volker knew I was nearby.

He knew about Edward.

He might even know about our rendezvous. Bleak was the word.

The scuffling suddenly got quite a bit louder, and I heard a new appalling noise: squeals. I banged my heels against the drums and the noises stopped. Small comfort. I couldn't stay there forever. Either the rats would run me out or someone would hear me banging and come to investigate. I had to think of a plan.

I couldn't do much about the fact that Volker knew roughly where I was. Be careful, that was all. Walk around like someone in a spy movie, peering around corners. And the fact that he knew about Edward— well, the harm was done. If I'd known ahead of time, I wouldn't have come to this neighborhood. And in a way, since Edward had given me the wrong phone number, it was a good thing I had. I would have had no other way of reaching him.

Unless Volker had read the note. I cast my thoughts back to the concierge, trying to guess how their conversation might have gone. Is M. Cole here? No. Do you know when he will be back? No. Has anyone come asking for him? Yes. Red hair, et cetera. She left a note for him. Now this was the tricky part. If Volker said, "Could I see it?" would the concierge have let him? I really didn't think so. Most Paris concierges, like most Parisians, were fierce about doing things the right way. Being helpful and open was almost never the right way. In fact, I thought with a little trickle of relief, the harder Volker pressed, the more likely the sad concierge was to resist. I would need to be careful. But my rendezvous with Edward was probably still safe.

I sat on the drum for a little while longer, thinking about nothing much. It was warm, a little too warm. My sweater began to prickle around my neck. The scuffling started again. My thighs hurt anyway where the lip of the drum cut into them. I slid carefully down to the floor. I was going to look a sight when I emerged. Of course that was the least of my problems.

Slowly, stretching my arms and legs, I felt my way to the door. The bright light made me blink. I turned into the ladies' room to see if I was filthy. The face staring back from the mirror was pale, decorated with a black streak on the chin. My hair, which I had wrapped up loosely in a scarf, looked like a pile of unraveled knitting. I spent a few moments washing, trying to comb my hair with my fingers, trying to rub away the dark marks under my eyes. They were built in. Finally I climbed the stairs again.

Madame was at the register. *"Bonsoir,"* I said. And hesitated. Had she known?

She nodded, with a sly smile. "The door to that storeroom is never locked. *Bonsoir, mademoiselle. Et bonne chance."*

I walked out into the street. That was the second time in half an hour someone had wished me good luck. And I realized now, I needed it.

I looked at my watch. Eleven o'clock. I had done what I could for Tony. Now all I had to do was make it to my rendezvous. And keep out of Volker's way.

I was tired. I was hungry. I wanted to sit still somewhere and think. I had a lot to think about. It was getting late. A café on the touristy Champs-Elysées would be expensive, but what I wanted now more than anything was to sit down. So I walked the few blocks to the bustling boulevard, scanning the streets for any sign of Volker. He might, if I was lucky, have already given up on the area. Maybe I should go somewhere else as well. But there was something deeply reassuring about the idea of a well-lighted and touristy joint where nobody would notice me. It was, after all, getting late. There just weren't that many parts of Paris (or any city for that matter) that were safe for a woman alone near midnight. I thought briefly about trying to find a cheap restaurant in the Latin Quarter. But I didn't have that much money. And I was tired. And besides, right in front of me was a garish "Restaurant-Self-Service Café," with amateurish pictures of hot dogs and ice cream cones painted on the windows. The menu posted by the door was an immense laminated affair in four languages. Just the ticket.

When I sat down, near a side door at the back, I didn't dare order more than a cup of coffee. It was going to be expensive, and just in case Edward wasn't at the station...

When the coffee arrived I unwrapped both of the cubes of sugar in the saucer and dropped them in. I stirred the coffee carefully, watching the froth of the milk glide around in the spoon's wake. The first sip tasted like heaven. I made myself put my spoon down and wait a moment before the second sip. In front of me, by the window, a group of six large blond tourists were digging into elaborate constructions in ice cream. An American family was trying to get a small boy to eat a hot dog, but he just clamped his mouth shut and shook his head. I wondered idly why he was up so late and then realized that it must be dinnertime in America.

Friday night in Boston. Daddy would probably still be at work. I thought, for a single minute, of calling him. But what good would it do? He couldn't help me, not at that distance. It was just a matter of sticking out the next few hours.

Now that I was sitting down in a cheerfully ordinary place, I could afford to think about the phone number. If only it had worked! I spent just a few seconds imagining what it would be like to have talked to someone who knew where Edward was, someone who might have a soothing voice—just so that I felt less alone.

But I couldn't dwell on it. Stiff upper lip, Louise. Face the music. Edward gave you a wrong number, and that's that. Stupid man. Couldn't he even remember an eight-digit phone number?

That was better. Annoyance was surely a healthier frame of mind than regret. I would manage.

If Volker didn't get me first. I took another swallow of coffee, and faced it. Volker knew about Edward. And he had beaten up Tony and come after me.

Slowly, Louise, step by step. It doesn't make any sense now. But start with everything you know about Volker. He is a member of a terrorist gang. Edward said that. It still seems hard to believe. Volker, the Goethe fan, the dandy, who does a brilliant tango. But somebody did some considerable harm to Tony. And Tony himself said it was Volker. So you have to accept it.

Tony was a fence, smuggling stolen objects out of France. He didn't admit it, but it fits. He was using

Gabriel to send that etui out of the country. To Germany. It didn't get there.

I thought back to our exchange. Lighted in that weird way, by the desk lamp and the flickering sound system. Had Tony been surprised to find that the etui didn't get to its destination? No. He'd known. He'd talked about it the way you'd talk about something that you were worried about and glad to find. What's more, his apartment had been dark, and he'd been in his closet. Tony had been hiding. That was clear. But his passport was right there on the table, along with... I tried to remember what the rest of the papers had been. There had been CDs, I remembered that, bathed in light. And the passport, with something bright sticking out of it. I hadn't made the connection at the time. But now I realized: What bright rectangular papers did people stick into their passports? Plane tickets.

Of course that could mean anything. It could have been an old ticket, left from a recent flight. But I could see it in my mind's eye, with crisp corners, not dogeared or folded. And Tony had been careful to tuck it into his jacket pocket.

So just before I got to his place, Tony had been on the verge of going somewhere. Then when I came unannounced, he hid. Not very effectively, because the door had been unlocked. His slipping into the closet was more like a child hiding under a bed, hoping not to be seen. And when he saw who I was, he came out. It wasn't me he was hiding from.

Then I told him where the etui was, and he ran off to get it. An hour later he'd been badly beaten. Had he been fleeing because the etui hadn't gotten where it was supposed to go? Fleeing because he knew somebody would be after him? Somehow smuggling art seemed as if it shouldn't be so violent. That was stupid. My ideas about art thieves must have come from Cary Grant movies.

I took another sip of coffee. The large blonds (Swedes? Danes?) were plowing stolidly through their ice cream. The American family was giving up and leaving. Tony had called to warn me about Volker. He knew *I* was planning to go home, but how did he know that Volker was going there? He must have told Volker where I was and that I had the etui. That was simple enough.

But why did Volker want it so badly? Why did he beat Tony? Was Volker involved in the fencing too? He could have been, I conceded. Even high-minded terrorists might need a little illicit income.

Still, how would Tony have the contacts for fencing, or smuggling, or whatever you wanted to call it? Volker *might* have helped there. I didn't suppose it took any great knowledge of the art world to smuggle, but Tony was so indifferent to anything but opera that it seemed like an unlikely sideline for him. Bootleg tapes would have made much more sense. Then, as I lifted my cup to my lips, I remembered Mr. Sago.

Mr. Sago was currently lying in a hospital bed. And in a better situation than Tony, at that. Tony, who at my dinner party had pretended he barely knew Mr. Sago—but was calling him "Albert" on the telephone the next day. I cast my mind back to that dinner party. Tony had come unexpectedly. He hadn't known ahead of time who the guests were. He... I put my cup down. He had been unnerved by Edward. I nodded slightly, remembering. He had quizzed Edward about his job.

I could see it quite clearly: the two men sitting side
by side on the roof after dinner. Tony leaning forward, intent on his questions. Edward impassive, with
that calm that I found so alluring. The calm that had
fallen away at the end of the evening, when he kissed
me.

Oh, stop it. I wrenched my mind back to Tony and
Mr. Sago. There had been something at dinner: That
was it. I'd been talking about my father being caught
with the missal and Mr. Sago had squawked with surprise. And he hadn't been able to take his eyes off
Tony afterward. He'd followed Tony out. And the
next evening I had overheard that phone call.

I couldn't remember the exact words now. Damn!
All I could remember was being embarrassed and not
wanting to overhear much. Mr. Sago had been furious, telling Tony off. And Tony had said something
threatening about who approached whom... And that
he'd had another project in hand.

It wasn't at all clear. It was only a guess. But maybe
Mr. Sago had approached Tony as a courier. And was
angry that Tony had placed the missal on my father
instead of carrying it himself? He'd said something
about negligence, I thought.

But then shouldn't Tony have been afraid of *Mr.
Sago* tonight? If, say, Mr. Sago had hired Tony to
smuggle the etui out of the country, and Tony had
screwed up. Then Mr. Sago would be getting back at
him. No, that wasn't it. Mr. Sago was in the hospital.
But why had Tony injured him? To keep him from
finding out about the etui? Could he have known by
then that the etui didn't get to its destination? And
where did Volker fit in?

On the other hand, maybe I had interrupted Tony
on his way out of the country. Maybe that was what
the passport and plane ticket had meant. If that was
true, if his danger was so great that he had to disappear, then knocking Mr. Sago down and breaking his
hip might have seemed pretty minor.

I swallowed the last of my coffee and thought about
ordering another cup. I had time. I was safe. I looked
around for the waiter. I caught his eye and gestured to
my coffee cup, and then a movement out of the corner of my eye made me turn around. Volker was coming in the café's side door, not ten feet away.

ELEVEN

I BOLTED.

I had no idea until that moment what adrenaline can do. But the sight of that handsome man in his blue sweater drove me out of that café like a rabbit driven from cover. Somehow I dodged the tables and chairs, pulled open the door, and sped out onto the sidewalk in seconds. I knew Volker must be right behind me. I knew he was taller than I. We'd never run a race, but it seemed a good bet that he ran faster. On the other hand, I was afraid.

There were still people out, and I was vaguely aware that they looked after me as I pelted by. I bumped into a few. Didn't bother to apologize. As I flew past a car dealership, I noticed a green light and I crossed the street, glancing back to see if Volker was still with me. Just as the light changed against him, he charged out into the traffic. I heard honks and the squeal of brakes, but no impact of metal and no voice crying out. I turned right, toward the Etoile. The arc de Triomphe loomed ahead of me, bathed in a cool blue-white light. Around and around its base zipped hundreds of cars, weaving in and out, cutting across each other's path, not yielding a moment's speed. It had always amazed me that Parisians drove around the Etoile at forty miles an hour. Now I was heading toward it at a dead run, on foot, with a very angry man behind me.

Before me a pedestrian walkway pierced the pavement. The City of Paris's concession to pedestrians' safety at the place de l'Etoile was to put them underground. Not a bad idea—by day. I liked it less by night. All the same, I ducked down the stairs.

The passage I was running along was tiled. It was clean and well-enough lighted. Small comfort; I hate being underground. A tunnel branched off to the left: AVENUE MARCEAU said the sign. To the right, a wider passage. I took it. I didn't dare stop to listen for footsteps behind me.

I had no idea where I was headed. My sense of direction has never been good, and underground I was completely lost. The helpful tiled signs had disappeared. The concrete floor made a lot of noise as I pounded over it. Surely anyone listening for me could follow by sound alone.

The tunnel curved a bit. An advertising poster on my right hand had been defaced with black markings, and a door in the wall with a DEFENSE D'ENTRER sign on it was covered with graffiti. A narrow tunnel branched off to the left. The sign said ARC DE TRIOMPHE. Floating up the passage came the sound of a flute, playing "Sheep May Safely Graze." I took the turn.

The floor was sloping downward now. I slowed down a bit, straining to hear if there were footsteps following behind me. I even turned around, looking back. Which was why I didn't see what was in front of me.

My first thought was "Oh, please, not now." And my second was "between a rock and a hard place." For there were three boys leaning against the passage in front of me. Three big boys, young men really, and all of them scary-looking. Two had shaved heads. The other had more hair than I did, dyed a sooty black. All three of them had on pointy-toed boots, with shiny metal caps on the toes. All three wore black leather jackets and jeans. And all three had chains dangling from their hands.

There was a moment of silence as they looked me over. Behind them, the flutist was still playing. I just stood there gasping. I knew the words: "Sheep may safely graze and pasture in a watchful shepherd's sight." Useful. Without a word, without a glance at each other, the three boys pushed themselves off the wall with their shoulders and moved into a loose line, so they were blocking the tunnel.

I looked back over my shoulder.

"Bonsoir, mademoiselle," one of them said. He had pimples.

I didn't say anything.

"J'ai dit, bonsoir, mademoiselle." He also had a very strong, guttural Parisian accent.

Without making a conscious decision, I answered in English. "I don't speak French, I'm sorry."

They exchanged a glance. Then the one with the dark hair stepped forward. "Ee say, good even-ing, mees. You are Amairicain?"

I shook my head, I didn't know why. Maybe I just hoped to keep them talking.

"Eenglish?" Shook my head again.

"Canadienne?" offered one of the skinheads.

This was dumb. Now I'd have to invent some nationality. Quick, any English-speaking country; I knew they wouldn't realize my accent was wrong.

"South African," I said, and smiled to placate them. "Now could I go by?" I stepped forward.

Wrong move. They straightened up and closed ranks. Now the three of them were standing with arms folded and legs apart.

The dark-haired one was saying in French "Africa? But she isn't black," while the pimply one answered,

"They have whites there, idiot."

Black Hair said to me, "You are not black, mees." And he stepped forward and raised a hand to my hair. He tweaked a strand out of the scarf and pulled it gently. Keep it friendly, I thought. Don't make him mad. I tried to smile. I tried even harder not to pull away. He stepped a bit closer.

"Ecoutez," hissed a skinhead. Black Hair froze. So did I. I heard what they did: feet pounding along the passage.

Suddenly Black Hair grabbed me by the shoulders. *"Allez, mademoiselle, bonne soirée,"* he said, and pushed me off toward the flute. He slapped my rear, like a cowboy slapping a horse to make it run. I hardly needed it.

I kept running toward the flute sound, on the downward grade. Then suddenly I could hear a new sound, the honking and car engines from the Etoile. To my right, another narrow passage branched off. I ran toward it and saw stairs. At the top there was darkness, but it was the glowing darkness of the city. I flew up the steps.

And there I was, in the center of the place de l'Etoile. Far over my head loomed the coffered underside of the arc de Triomphe. A few steps away, framed in sober bronze, burned the perpetual flame at the Tomb of the Unknown Soldier. A slight breeze lifted the lock of hair pulled loose by Black Hair. It was eerie, being alone in that spot that was usually packed by tourists. In spite of the noise around me, the threat behind me, I had an instant's solitude and, in a funny way, an instant of peace. Ahead, in the long elegant vista laid out by Baron Haussmann, lay the Champs-Elysées. Wide and straight, brilliant with light, the avenue sliced through darkness to the place de la Concorde. It was only dimly visible from there as an extra spot of glowing light, and the obelisk a shadow in the midst of the glow.

I was all alone, and somewhere not far away was Volker. I doubted that the three punks had delayed him much. He might not have turned where I did and come up for air. But he would find me soon.

On the road right next to me a taxi honked as a pale-blue Citroën cut it off. Then the Citroën squealed to a halt, and with a somehow satisfying *crunch* the taxi hit it. It was one of the old Citroëns, a Deux-Chevaux, and it crumpled like a soda can where the solid bumper of the taxi (a big Mercedes, naturally) rammed it. In a second the two drivers were out on the sidewalk glaring at each other. All around them, the traffic slowed. I glanced over my shoulder. Another pedestrian walkway led up from underground on the other side of the Arc. Emerging from it, still facing away from me, was Volker.

Once again I ran. This time I knew it was foolhardy. I should have just backtracked, slipped down the stairs into the underground passageways. But how could I, knowing that those three punks were down there? If I met them again, it would look as if I wanted to. Too much like an invitation.

I vaulted the low fence between the pavement circling the Arc and the mayhem in the place de l'Etoile.

Around the Citroën and the Mercedes, locked together in a metallic embrace, the traffic was at a dead
halt. Drivers leaned out windows to comment and ad-
vise. Not wanting to attract Volker's eye by sudden
movement, I tried to walk steadily, passing in front of
a big black Citroën DS, squeezing between the bump-
ers of a Renault and a Ford. As I got farther out from
the center, the traffic started moving. Looking back,
I could see Volker silhouetted by the brilliant light on
the monument. He was staring out into the traffic,
shading his eyes. Instinctively I turned left, toward the
darker avenue Victor Hugo. If I could only get out of
the light...

A Volkswagen accelerating toward me honked. If
only I could get out of this unhurt. I'd hoped to get
across that little patch of pavement before he did. I
kept my eyes to the right, scanning the oncoming cars
for gaps. All I could see were headlights, double dots,
continuously aiming toward me. There, a single dot
meant a motorcycle: I took a couple of steps forward,
then had to jump forward yet again as the car with one
headlight nearly brushed me. *Screech!* A Fiat had to
swerve hard to miss me. They were on all sides now,
coming faster. I didn't dare look back to see if Volker
was on my heels. Saving my skin, getting across the
road was all I could think of. I saw a gap and skit-
tered across it. Someone leaned on his horn as he
zipped by. Yes, I know. I could imagine what I looked
like, appearing suddenly in the dark, a ghost in my
long, loose raincoat. Something else not to think
about. A string of cars followed close on each other. I
glanced back. I'd come almost halfway. A gap. I ran
across, waiting while a car passed, and ran farther.
Someone passing behind me yelled something rude.

Here on the outer edge of the Etoile, the gaps were bigger. I could make better progress. But the cars also moved much faster. I could get more hurt.

I scanned the pattern to my right. There, and there, staggered, two long dark spots where no cars were coming. Not yet, not after this car: after *this* one. I ran. The plane trees at the head of the avenue Victor Hugo were in sight now. Four or five more rows of cars to cross. Behind me, suddenly, I heard a long scream of brakes. Voices raised, shouting. I turned back, without wanting to. I got a fleeting image of lights clotted together. Then another gap opened up on my right, and I scurried.

This time I made it all the way across. A limousine barreling into the avenue Kléber nearly clipped me. But I stepped onto the curb with an incredible feeling of gratitude. The Pope kisses the ground when he gets off a plane, I thought. I'll come back and kiss this spot tomorrow.

Assuming I get to tomorrow. I still didn't have much of a lead on Volker.

Automatically I had turned left and started walking back eastward, toward the Champs-Elysées and, eventually, the gare du Nord. I crossed avenue Kléber and kept walking fast, looking back occasionally. There didn't seem to be anyone following. Of course now I was moving in and out of shadows, as I crossed these residential avenues lined with their hundred-year-old trees. I was glad to be walking instead of running. I could feel sweat trickling down my back and I was still breathing hard. But now what? The avenue d'Iéna would take me down toward the river. For a second I thought longingly of home. My big sofa, a kimono, a bowl of soup… Would Volker find me there?

Probably. It was too easy. I kept walking. Avenue Marceau; the next street was the Champs-Elysées. I looked back. Under a streetlight, I saw a flash of blue. Wearily, and at a shadow of my former speed, I took off again.

I couldn't go on much longer. I wasn't strong enough. If Volker just kept on coming after me, sooner or later he'd catch me.

I headed a little to the right, to run in the shadow of the buildings. Should I duck into a side street? Try to lose him? The problem was I didn't know the neighborhood that well. Rue Galilée: Where would that take me? Probably into a quiet residential section, where I'd be the only person out. I was gasping for breath now. When I first got to Paris I used to jog every morning in the Luxembourg Gardens. It hadn't taken me long to absorb the French indifference to fitness. Volker, on the other hand, lifted weights. I had a stitch in my side. I pressed against it with my hand and looked behind me. I didn't see him. That didn't prove anything. I didn't dare stop. Ahead of me I spotted the George V Métro stop. Without thinking, I accelerated toward those stairs. Just like a rabbit, I thought, I couldn't stay out in the open. When I got to the token booth I didn't wait to buy a ticket. For the first time in my life, I jumped the turnstile. Daddy would have been appalled. But as I glanced back at the gesticulating token clerk I reasoned that if the gendarmes came after me, at least I'd be safe from Volker. I ran down the escalator.

And fetched up on the platform, a clean, brightly lighted space. There were the usual immense advertising posters. There was a bench. There was, I realized, no possible place to hide. Only one Métro line went through George V. There were no tunnels for changing trains. If Volker followed me this far, he had me.

I stood at the end of the platform, panting, with my head down like a sprinter after a race. If Volker followed me this far, I didn't have the energy to go any farther anyway. I would have to depend on a train to put some distance between us.

A minute or two passed. My breathing slowed. I straightened up and walked over to the bench, but I couldn't relax enough to sit down. I looked up the escalator but didn't see any gendarmes coming to arrest me. There weren't many other people around. Instinctively I had chosen the inbound side, where the trains would take me eastward. On the opposite track a woman in a raincoat was reading a newspaper as she waited for the train to Neuilly. Should I go to Neuilly, to the American Hospital, and throw myself on the mercy of that nice doctor I'd talked to? Stupid idea. Anyway, I only had to hang on for another hour or so. Get to the station. Find Edward.

What would I do if Volker came? What if he came down the escalator right now? I turned to look. Riding serenely downward was a bland-looking man in a brown corduroy suit. No sign of Volker. A distant rumbling set the platform vibrating slightly. Too soon to tell which way the train was going. The lady with the raincoat, across the tracks, stepped forward to peer down the tunnel. On my side the man in the corduroy suit did the same. The train was coming from our left, heading east toward Vincennes. It pulled in smoothly. The doors opened. I stepped into a car. As we pulled out of the station I looked back to see if Volker was coming down the escalator. He wasn't.

But how had he found me in that restaurant on the Champs-Elysées? How had he known where I was? He must have waited around the café where I phoned, sure that I would come out. Or maybe it was just luck: good for him, bad for me. Maybe he'd just been walking by and spotted me.

The expression on his face as he walked through the door of that restaurant had not been friendly.

I looked at my watch. Eleven-thirty. An hour and a half. Not a very long time to keep going. But Volker's turning up like that had scared me. I'd been stupid to stay so near Edward's apartment. Maybe, deep down, I'd hoped to go back there. Maybe I'd thought I would catch him at home before one o'clock. I'd certainly ignored the probability that Volker was still somewhere around.

The train started to slow down and came to a halt. An indistinct announcement came over the loudspeaker. Something about "delay"—stating the obvious. I was thrilled. There were four passengers in my car: a couple of students whispering together, a spectacled man in a gray sweater, and me. Completely innocuous. I was grateful for that. Maybe we could be stuck here for a nice long time.

How much longer could I go on eluding Volker? Soberly now. He had gone right away to Edward's neighborhood and, I had to assume, to Edward's house. What made me think that he hadn't read my note? And wouldn't be at the gare du Nord at one?

But Edward would be there too, I argued with myself.

Or at least I hoped he would.

Well, why wouldn't he?

Why would he, though?

Oh, come on. Any human with an ounce of good-will would have to respond to that note. And Edward had demonstrated goodwill. He'd been helpful about Daddy, thoughtful when we were out together, solicitous this afternoon. Almost as if he'd known that trouble was brewing. Ugh, that was an awful thought.

The two students in the corner were necking now, with the usual Parisian oblivion to their audience. I had always been amazed by that indifference, until that night with Edward. We'd been as shameless as any sixteen-year-olds. Funny, in a man as restrained as Edward. It had seemed almost out of character at the time. I'd been flattered. I'd assumed that his attraction to me had swept away his inhibitions. Pretty heady.

Then it turned out that he was just trying to work his way into Winfield. Had he had to go so far? Couldn't he have just become a friend?

Yes. He could have. It would have been more professional. Less risky. Gotten him the same results: the information he wanted.

So then, why? Why go through this act of total abandon? At the very least, it was a loss of dignity. It must have been distasteful on some level.

Or had it been for real?

My instant assumption had been that it wasn't. He had to be putting it on. But rationally, objectively, did I think Edward was capable of dissembling like that? I rubbed my face with my hands. Heaven alone knew why I was worrying about this now. But I couldn't dismiss my thoughts. Honestly, Louise. Anger and hurt aside. Think back to that night, as you were walking along the quais with Edward. Was he faking it?

Who knows? Men always think they mean what they're saying.

But why say it?

Why say it? Why pretend anything? I hadn't exactly required any urging. And there had been that look on his face. This was not a mercurial man. Not, I would have said, a man easily swept by emotion. And no, not a man who could fake things easily. Laurence Olivier could have faked that look of—what?—need and vulnerability. But Edward was if anything a little bit stiff. Not demonstrative, not an actor.

So. Maybe he had meant it. Maybe he *had* been carried away. I shrugged. I told myself it didn't make any difference. I was still sitting on a stalled train yards and yards underground, trying to get away from Volker. It didn't make any difference, because I was counting on Edward anyway. I had never really doubted that he would help me. On that level, I'd trusted him all along.

But it gave me a little hope. There was just a tiny shred of brightness now in my thoughts. When I got to Edward... Getting to Edward might mean more than just safety. I would still be cautious with him. I still wouldn't trust him completely. But having even the possibility restored... even thinking that there might be something beyond tonight made me feel stronger.

Now the question was how best to get to the gare du Nord. I could go straight there. I tried to visualize the familiar subway map. I could stay on this train to the Châtelet stop and go north on the Orléans-Clignancourt line. I'd get there too early, though. And I couldn't take the chance that Volker might be there.

It was hard to believe that in this whole city I couldn't find a way to get away from that man. Surely he wasn't omniscient? There must be a way, somehow to evade him.

Drive around in a taxi, barricade yourself into a hotel room, lose yourself in a nightclub or at the movies. None of them possible with only forty francs and one jeton in your pocket. I smiled inwardly, thinking that at least I'd saved money by jumping the Métro turnstile and running away from the bill for my coffee.

With a jerk, the train started moving. The loud-speaker started rumbling again. Something about train out of service. I rolled my eyes. What a night for mis-fortunes! But at least this made up my mind for me. I'd walk to the station from the next stop.

TWELVE

MEEKLY WE ALL shuffled out of the train at the Champs-Elysées station. The young lovers in my car broke their clinch only to resume it on the platform. They were probably the only ones who wouldn't mind waiting for the next train to take them to points east.

When I got aboveground, I realized I didn't know exactly what route to take to the gare de Nord. I should have looked at the map in the Métro station. Of course it hardly mattered; I had time to take a less-than-direct route. The station was northeast to me, so I headed north on the avenue Marigny. Then I would turn east on the rue du Faubourg St.-Honoré, and north again on the rue Royale, past the Madeleine. Clean, brightly lighted streets in the heart of elegant Paris. Bound to be safe. Even, I thought with a shot of courage, entertaining. I always loved looking in the windows of this quarter's boutiques.

I was walking along the gardens behind the Elysée Palace. Of course the president's private garden was shielded from view by metal panels lining the tall iron fence. But branches from the president's trees hung over the street, rustling in the breeze, dappling the light from the impeccable streetlamps.

Cars passed me in convoys, regulated by traffic signals a block or two away. Between them, quiet reigned. I started to relax. I could hear occasional sleepy twittering from fortunate Elysée birds. Clean

Elysée leaves made a pleasant rushing sound. My footsteps sounded clearly, clip, clip, clip.

And slightly delayed, so did another set of footsteps. Clop, clop, clop. Somebody walking behind me.

My heart started racing instantly, but I wasn't going to panic. It could be anybody. It wasn't that late. Maybe it was the president of the Republic out for an after-dinner stroll. (Ha.)

If it had been Volker, he would have caught me by now.

I sped up a little. I was walking alongside the Elysée building now. This had to be one of the most secure spots in Paris. Armed guards on every corner, cameras monitoring every passerby. I turned right. Sentries stood like dummies in boxes on either side of the Elysée gates. A car whooshed by. A set of footsteps turned the corner.

Without waiting to get to a crosswalk, I veered across the street. Paused, oblivious to what I was seeing, at the window of Louis Féraud. Nothing behind me. I moved on again. Art gallery, men's suits, Italian sheets. *Clop, clop, clop.*

It could be anybody. Anybody in the world could just happen to be on the same route as I. Darting glances in both directions, I crossed back to the south side of the street again, a few yards in front of a car, and tucked myself into a doorway. Whomever was behind me would have to wait until the cars passed, and I'd be able to get a glimpse of him without his seeing me.

I waited. More cars passed, as did a pair of businessmen in dark suits, coming from the direction of the British Embassy. I peered out. The sidewalks were empty.

I felt silly. Obviously the man behind me had gone into one of the buildings I passed. There were probably still some apartments above the stores, and he must live in one of them. I was getting paranoid.

Still I waited in my doorway, five minutes by my watch. I saw a very merry dinner party getting into several taxis, a street cleaner with his twig branch, and lots of cars. The street cleaner didn't go *clop clop*.

I set off again, reassured. I was being a fool. The sooner this all ended, the better for me. There was a gorgeous apricot-colored suit in the window of Yves St. Laurent Rive Gauche. As I stopped to get a better look, I heard the footsteps again.

I whirled around but couldn't see anyone. For an instant I considered running toward the footsteps, chasing them for a change. Maybe I would catch whoever it was.

Maybe that wouldn't be too smart.

Automatically I left the window and kept walking, trying desperately to think. What did this mean? Could it be Volker, just trailing along behind me? Waiting to see where I went, perhaps. Hoping that I would lead him to the etui? But it hadn't *sounded* like Volker. I couldn't have said exactly why. Maybe this man was shorter, his steps closer together.

But if it wasn't Volker, who was it?

There couldn't be two people chasing me.

Calm down, Louise. This guy isn't chasing you, he's just following you. I glanced back. Of course he was out of sight. I couldn't hear him either, but we were nearing the rue Royale.

On impulse I turned right, down the rue Boissy d'Anglas. I was thinking I'd give him one more chance *not* to be trailing me. It was just possible that someone had been taking the same route as I. Marginally possible that he had coincidentally paused when I did. But walking around the block behind me seemed conclusive.

Boissy d'Anglas was busy, since it formed the westernmost edge of the place de la Concorde. I wouldn't hear him until I turned right again, onto the avenue Gabriel.

If it wasn't Volker, who was it? Who else could it be? A colleague of Volker's. That was the obvious answer. But I had a panicky minute thinking about the other possibilities. And I remembered something odd. I had asked Volker if he had ever called me up late at night, and he'd denied it. I thought I believed that denial. So who was *that*? Could there possibly be two sets of people that were interested in my activities? Interested enough for undercover surveillance?

But it wasn't all that undercover. After all, the phone had rung when I was there. They—he, surely?—had left signs, like the overturned geraniums, of the visits. Even the man behind me wasn't exactly keeping his presence a secret. Wouldn't any smart tail be wearing soft-soled shoes? Maybe not sneakers, but crepe soles anyway. Of course any self-respecting Frenchman might object to the very idea of crepe soles. But Germans had terrible taste in shoes. Witness the national uniform of sandals worn with socks. What's more, a German tail would, with Teutonic thoroughness, dress for the job in sneakers. So the man behind me was obviously a Frenchman. Q.E.D.

I told myself this was no time for frivolity, but my reasoning was only half frivolous. I'd reached avenue Gabriel, and turned right. It was a good deal quieter. On the left, rows of trees and a bit of Parisian park separated us from the Champs-Elysées. In a block or so we'd come up to the back of the Elysée Palace; square one. I concentrated hard, trying to hear footsteps.

I was walking slower now. Ahead I could see the red-and-yellow disc that signaled a bus stop, attached to a stanchion. There wasn't really room to hide behind it. What about ducking across the street into the park and trying to slip away through the trees? I looked back. I couldn't see anyone. But behind a car, trundling deliberately along the avenue, was a bus. The number 52 bus. I knew it well. I sometimes took it home from work, as far as the Opéra. This was probably the last bus to run. I jogged the few yards to the bus stop and read the route indicator. The final destination was St. Cloud, at the southwestern edge of the sixteenth arrondissement. A nice long way away. If my tail wanted to stay incognito, he could hardly hop on the bus with me. I flagged down the bus and got on.

Quite a night for public transportation, I thought as I paid my fare. I walked toward the back of the bus and looked out the window as we pulled away. There was a man standing still in a shadowy spot. Though I couldn't see his features, he looked to me like a man who has just missed a bus. I couldn't say I was sorry.

I sat still for a while, trying not to think. The bus turned up onto the rue du Faubourg St.-Honoré, and I looked at the shop windows as we went by. This far west they became less screamingly chic, and the everyday crept in. A stunning display of ironing boards, for instance. We passed the church of St. Philippe du Roule. The *patisserie* across the street made the best coffee eclairs in the entire city.

It occurred to me that getting on this bus had not been completely clever. For one thing, it was going in the wrong direction. If I took it to the terminus, I'd be very far away from the gare du Nord. Possibly I could find a taxi—I didn't know St. Cloud at all and couldn't guess how busy it might be—and equally possibly I couldn't pay the fare to get back to the gare du Nord at one o'clock.

Not to mention the fact that, if my tail had any sense, he could figure out where this bus was going. And be at the destination when it got there.

Of course he could still be behind me in a taxi: "Follow that bus." Hell.

The bus had turned into the boulevard Haussmann and was trundling along toward avenue de Friedland. I had forgotten that: It would go right by Edward's apartment. I looked at my watch: just on midnight. I shut my eyes and wished hard. Please let him be there. Please, please, please.

I signaled for the next stop at the Balzac statue and scurried a little way into the square behind Rodin's massive portrait in bronze. Just to be on the safe side, I watched for a taxi stopping on either side of the street. None did. That didn't really mean much; only that the man following me, if he was still following me, had enough sense not to be completely obvious. In spite of his shoes.

Approaching Edward's building, I tried very hard not to hope. I tried to push out of my mind the insistent images of being told that he was there, going up to his door, falling into his arms. For one thing, they were a cliché. For another thing, if he wasn't there I would be devastated.

As I waited for the concierge after ringing the bell, I realized I was clenching my hands so tight that my nails were digging into my palms. As I heard the lock *click* and the door begin to swing, I shut my eyes and made one last inarticulate wish. *Please....*

"Ah, mademoiselle," the concierge said. "Here you are again. You are looking for M. Cole still?"

I nodded, trying not to be eager.

He nodded back. "He is not here." I tried to tell myself that I hadn't really expected him to be. "But he has been here. He left a note for you. Wait. I will get it."

He turned and shuffled away. I stepped inside and pulled the big door closed behind me. Just in case.

Edward had been here. He knew. He would be there. Less than an hour now. I could make it. It was going to be all right.

The concierge was coming back now, holding a piece of paper. "Mlle. Gerard? It is you?"

"Yes," I said, and held out my hand. He looked from the signature to my face and back, as if he were trying to match them up. I managed not to grab the note from him. He finally put it in my hand.

It was short. "Louise: I'll be there. Be careful." Signed simply "E." I wanted to clasp it to my heart.

"Did he say anything else?" I asked.

"No. Only to give you this note."

"What time was he here?"

"About an hour ago."

I wanted to know every detail. "Did he go up-stairs?"

"Yes." The concierge finally seemed to sense my eagerness for information. "He came in a car, and the driver stayed down here. He went up and stayed for, oh, fifteen minutes. He changed his clothes. Then he came back down and gave me this note. He told me if anyone else asked for him, he was out of town. Then he drove away."

"And has anyone else asked for him?" I said, curiously.

"Yes." The concierge shook his head and made a face. "It was very odd. A young man, I would say, with a limp. He tried to stay out of the light. But I could see, his left eye was all swollen. He asked for M. Cole and said it was urgent." The concierge shrugged. "I said I could not help him."

I would have caught on faster if what the man was saying had seemed possible. But...I glanced around taking note of the dimness near the door. He couldn't mean... "What color hair did he have?"

The concierge pursed his lips. "Dark. Curly."

"Did he have on glasses?"

"Yes." He nodded, clearly casting his mind back. "But they were broken."

It couldn't be. When Tony had called me, he sounded—I could hear the rattling breathing and the slurred speech—finished. He had just dropped the phone, leaving it dangling. Passed out, I thought. Lying on a floor, bleeding; I shut my mind to the images. He couldn't have recovered enough to make it here.

"I would say he had been in a fight," the concierge was going on. "He didn't smell of drink. Or anything else. But his clothes were torn. Blood all over his shirt." He gestured at the front of his brown cardigan. "From his nose, probably. I don't know why the police didn't pick him up. I told him he should see a doctor. But all he wanted was M. Cole.''

"And did he leave a name?" I asked.

The concierge nodded slowly. "Yes. He said he was M. Geist."

THIRTEEN

I GOT MYSELF OUT the door in a haze of confusion. How could Tony have been at death's door at ten o'clock and here at Edward's door an hour later? Maybe his injuries hadn't been that bad? But then why pretend? To scare me? Why? And why come to *Edward*? Tony had been breaking all kinds of laws. Why should he seek out a man who would probably turn him in? What was going on?

I stood outside the building looking vaguely up and down the street. Tony had been there just an hour earlier. He might still be nearby. I looked down at the pavement, thinking disjointedly about blood. Could I track him somehow? Did I even want to try to find him? Could I take the time?

Yes. I could. Edward had said he'd be at the station. I could take a taxi there. It would use all my money, but that didn't matter anymore. Soon enough I'd be safe, and I might be able to help Tony.

I had no idea how he'd gotten there. It had to have been a tremendous effort. He must have been exhausted. He couldn't have gone very far away. He might even have staggered off somewhere to rest. While my mind was reasoning this out slowly, my feet had already decided. I crossed the avenue de Friedland back toward the Balzac statue. There was a little park there, and where there was a park, there would be benches. Tony might have dragged himself there.

It was hardly even a park, just a little pocket of space carved out between the rue Balzac and a wedge of buildings. Memory told me the benches lined its northwestern perimeter. The streetlights diluted the darkness somewhat, but as I approached the benches I couldn't make out more than a bundle here or there. *Clochards*, the Parisian equivalent of the Bowery bum. The first bundle I came to had a patch of very sore-looking leg protruding from its ragged trousers. Even in the half light I could tell it was not a fresh bruise. Therefore, not Tony.

The next fellow was sleeping on his back. Bearded. A pair was curled together two benches down. My eyes were adjusting. I looked down to the end of the row and knew right away, by some extra sense, that the dim figure huddled on the end of the bench was Tony.

Still, I walked up to him slowly. I guess it was a combination of caution and tact. I didn't want to startle him into lashing out. I didn't want to frighten him. On some level, I didn't even want to catch him unaware. Unprepared for human contact, friendly or otherwise. So I coughed and rubbed the toe of my shoe on the sandy ground.

He was obviously awake; he stiffened and tried to roll over. I couldn't bear it. I rushed over and knelt on the far side of the bench, facing him through the slats. "It's okay, don't move," I said. Trying very hard not to flinch at the sight of his face.

I didn't know what I felt about Tony anymore. I still hadn't really taken in the fact of his smuggling, let alone his making a heroic effort to warn me about Volker. I couldn't make sense of what he'd done to Mr. Sago. But kneeling there on the gritty earth, with my face just inches from his, I did know that I felt pity. For the wounds, of course. But even in that gloom, I could see that he'd had what was for him a greater blow. His pride was in shreds. Tony had finally taken a fall.

"I was an idiot," he whispered.

I didn't answer. Didn't even move, though the pebbles under my knees were starting to dig into my flesh.

"I thought I was smarter than they were." Pause. "Volker and his minions." Another pause. "You'll appreciate this. I thought anybody that good-looking had to be stupid."

"Oh, Tony." I groaned.

"I know. What a mistake. Underestimating your opponent. Did he get it?"

Of course he was talking about the etui. "No. After I talked to you, I wasn't sure what to do with it. I mean, I didn't want it on me, but I wanted to think before turning it in. I didn't want to just go to the police with it."

"Is it someplace where you can get it now?" Tony broke in. "I'm not asking *where*. But Volker—he really wants it, Louise. He *must not* get it. I don't care what you do with it, throw it in the river or something."

"It's okay," I started to say, but he didn't seem to hear. He was still speaking urgently, with his eyes shut. It seemed as if all the energy in his body was going into making sure I got his message.

"It's crucial, I can't begin to tell you how important. I know before I said it was life and death but I mean it . . ."

"It's *okay*, Tony," I said, putting my hand as gently as I could over his mouth. It seemed the only way to stop this stream of panic. "Lower your voice, you're shouting. You're going to wear yourself out. The etui is somewhere I can't get it. So don't worry."

"Will Volker believe you? Do you have proof?" He opened his eyes and turned his head a few inches to look at me. "Because he..." Tony made a weak gesture toward his face. "Oh, Jesus, what a mess." His eyes shut again.

"Look, it doesn't matter. I don't know where Volker is and God willing he doesn't know where I am so he won't get a chance to ask." Something that had been bothering me suddenly reached my consciousness. "What's all the fuss, anyway? I mean, I know the thing is worth a mint. So why throw it in the river? It's not a bomb or anything?"

"No. It's not a bomb. And of course it's hot. You realized that."

"Yes, I did realize that," I said. "And I felt pretty stupid when I figured it out. It gave me a shock, Tony." I couldn't keep the reproach out of my voice. "To think you'd been smuggling all this time. And my *father*; using my father to get that missal to England! That was really low."

"Lower than you know," he said very quietly. I realized at the back of my mind that his voice was steady. "There was a lot you didn't notice, Louise. It wasn't just the smuggling. I was pretty careful about that. But—" He broke off and rolled away from me, so that he was lying on his back and facing the sky. His face was lighted more distinctly now. I had never seen a broken nose before, but his clearly was. The eye toward me was all right; it was the other one that was swollen.

"If I didn't feel like this was the end of the world, I wouldn't be telling you this," he said, staring upward. I slid my feet out from under me to sit on the ground. "Did you ever think... No." He stopped himself. "When you stopped seeing Volker. The phone calls? And the geraniums tipped over? That was me."

Since I was staring at him in surprise, I could see that he shut his eyes. As if he were waiting for, what, another blow?

"But I thought it was Volker," I said stupidly.

"No."

"But I kept seeing Volker, I was sure he was following me."

"I wouldn't know about that. But you run into people a lot, it was probably just coincidence."

"But," I kept protesting, "a couple of times there was someone *there*, I know. At my apartment."

"That was me. I was keeping an eye on you."

All I could say was "How?" Of course the real question was "Why?"

"I have your apartment bugged. That was how I knew Volker was there tonight. And how I knew you were alone, or had come in late: That was when I called."

"Bugged? How did you...? God, Tony, this is incredible."

"Yeah. All that equipment in my apartment; it's not just for playing CDs. I actually know quite a bit about tapping phones and surveillance."

"But why *me*?" I cried. Two benches down, a bundle stirred.

"Jealousy."

I waited for more. Finally I said flatly, "I don't get it."

He took a deep breath and flinched. I started to scramble to my feet but he put a hand out. "No, it's okay. I think I have a couple of broken ribs, that's all. Louise, I was in love with you."

I sat down again. Looked down at the ground, where of course I couldn't see anything in the shadows. I wasn't really taking it in. It was too much. Too many shocks tonight. Too many blindnesses on my part. Never in a million years would I have guessed. Tony! The cranky, sexless intellectual! Who was capable of great kindness and infuriating thoughtlessness, but who had never in all the time I'd know him made a single statement about his emotional life. I'd worked with Tony and been his friend on terms of some intimacy, but without exactly that: becoming intimate. He was private. I didn't push. It was true he could have been hiding anything for those years. And now he told me that he had been.

"I know," he was saying. "Big shock. Me. When there are big handsome guys like Volker and Edward Cole around. I knew I never had a chance. But it got to me. Knowing that I didn't. You were never going to think of me in those terms."

"But bugging my *apartment!*" I said, belatedly horrified at the realization. "You've got to realize that's ... it's an invasion of privacy, but it's also really twisted!"

"No," he said calmly. "I just wanted to be more involved in your life. I was discreet. I didn't listen all the time. The night Cole was there, I just kept checking to see when he was gone. In any case you were out of earshot on the terrace."

"The phone too?"

"Of course."

"You know it's illegal to tap somebody's phone," I said, grasping at another argument that I thought might puncture his weird logic.

"In France? I wouldn't bet on it. Anyway, illegal..." He tried to shrug, but winced again.

"But..." I said, still aghast. He interrupted me.

"Never mind. It's all over now. Where is Volker?"

"I don't know," I answered. He was right to recall me to the present. I turned my watch face up to the light and peered at it. It said twelve-thirty.

"What?" Tony asked. "Are you in a hurry?" There was a faint acid tone to his voice that I was familiar with. I realized that I'd always known instinctively what it signaled: hurt feelings.

"I'm supposed to meet Edward," I said. "Volker's been after me all night. He's uncanny, the way he's followed me around. I can't go home. I don't have any money to hide in a hotel. I can't just wait around here for Edward to come, because Volker knows about him. So I left him a note." And I explained about the two assignations.

"I suppose I know why Edward?" Tony said.

"Oh, come on, Tony. He's the cowboy in the white hat. Not to mention the fact that he is, as you just mentioned, big. And the last time I saw you, you were sweating with fear, and the last time I heard from you, you were at death's door. What else am I supposed to do?"

"I know, I know. Here. In case you miss him." He started to dig in his trousers pocket. It obviously hurt him, but before I could offer to help he pulled out a handful of bills and gave it to me. "Volker was kind enough to leave me this."

"Well, thank you," I said doubtfully, unfolding them. There were several five-hundred-franc notes, a two-hundred, three hundreds. Tony always had carried a lot of cash. Was that another clue I had missed? I thought as I peeled off the two hundred and two hundreds and gave the rest back. "I don't need all this and anyway, what are you going to do? Maybe you should come with me."

"No," he said.

"Why not? You came here to find Edward anyway. You wanted to see him, so—you'll see him."

"I wanted to tell him Volker was after you. He knows that now. Why should I turn myself in?"

"Then what will you do? You should go to a hospital. I had an ambulance from the American Hospital at Neuilly sent to find you at the office," I told him, remembering suddenly. "They will have broken the windows, I told them to. To get in. The place will be wide open."

"At this point I don't really give a damn about Winfield College Abroad," he said. More acid. "And I'm all right."

"No, you're *not*," I objected. "You should see your face. And the concierge across the street says you were limping, and you have a couple of broken ribs. You have to get some kind of help."

"Well, maybe," he said. Not giving in. "I'm not going to tell you anyway."

"Oh, please," I said, exasperated.

"No, listen." He turned his head toward me. "I don't want you to have to choose between telling Edward about me and protecting me. I know you're loyal; it's one of your virtues. But I don't want to test your loyalty. And I don't want to know which choice you'd make. What you don't know, you can't tell Edward."

"Okay," I said, suddenly moved. Tony always could surprise with these flashes of empathy. "Can I ask one question?"

"One. You have to go."

"What happened with Mr. Sago?"

Tony sighed slightly. "That was a mistake. I can't explain it all, it would take too long. *He* was the fence, really. I started just helping him to get things out of the country. He was furious about your father. I did botch that. Though I didn't think he was going to get caught. I didn't know they were going to search everyone."

"But why *him?* Why not just hop across the Channel yourself?"

"It amused me," Tony said.

"Oh, that's nice. Ruin a life for your own amusement." I started to get up.

"It didn't ruin his life. It gave him a great story to tell at Boston dinner parties."

"But it could have."

"Your father isn't the kind of man whose life is ruined by something like that. He's a lawyer and knows powerful people. Anyway he shouldn't have gotten caught."

"Anyway it shouldn't have happened. That's probably what Mr. Sago said."

"No," Tony answered. I was standing over him now. He hadn't turned his face upward to see mine, but kept staring sideways. "What happened with Sago was inexcusable. But the rest isn't as bad... Well, it is. But there are factors..." Now he did look directly up at me. "It's not quite as bad as you think. Go on, you'll be late."

I hesitated. I might never see him again. He had been my best friend for five years. He had bugged my apartment. He was in love with me. He had used my father to smuggle. He seemed sorry about Mr. Sago. But not about much else.

I didn't know how to say good-bye.

"Go," he said. I turned and took a couple of steps. Then I turned around and came back. Leaned down, kissed him on the forehead. I was still confused about him. But a final good-bye... His hand came up to my shoulder. He whispered, "Thank you." Then I turned around and walked away, leaving him there on his park bench, among the *clochards*.

FOURTEEN

TONY WAS RIGHT. I didn't have a lot of time left. But now at least I had enough money for a taxi. I walked out of the little park onto the avenue de Friedland. There should be taxis, I thought, coming down from the Etoile. Of course a cabby cruising for a fare wouldn't look here. I looked at my watch again. Twenty to one. Hell. I started to run. Rue Balzac cut into the Champs-Elysées. It seemed more likely that I'd get a taxi there.

But I was luckier than that. A few yards ahead of me a pale-yellow Mercedes stopped and let out a passenger, flicking on his *"Libre"* light before the doors were shut. I waved my arms and sprinted toward him. In minutes we were rolling along boulevard Haussmann.

He was one of the taciturn ones. I was grateful for that too. I couldn't have borne to chat with a stranger at that point. Instead I sat back, resting my head on the upholstery, and shut my eyes. I kept seeing the image of Tony's face, turned upward to the light, as he told me that he had been in love with me.

In spite of it all, I wished him well. In spite of the fact that he'd been bugging my apartment? Spying on me? Ugh. I shivered a little, thinking about Tony in that electronic lair of his, listening to my telephone conversations. It was very creepy. And then there was his criminal activity. At last I understood what had been going on—or at least I understood part of it. Mr.

Sago made a more probable receiver of stolen art objects than Tony did. He was well educated, had a good eye, traveled a lot, was respectable-looking. The only missing characteristic was a leaning toward crime. But maybe he justified it all to himself somehow. Redistributing the goods of the world. Getting them into the hands of more desirable owners. Somehow, even knowing Mr. Sago as little as I did, I felt sure that he had some elaborate rationale for what he did and never considered its illegality except as an inconvenience.

But that still left Volker. How did he fit in? And why did he want that etui so badly? How did he even know about it? Had Tony foolishly confided in Volker? Out of some yearning to establish himself as a macho man? Given my new knowledge of Tony I could imagine it—"You may think I'm a sexless wimp but actually I'm a fearless fence." Could be. And maybe Volker thought he was just going to intercept the etui. Hijack it and sell it. The person it was meant for could hardly complain that he hadn't gotten delivery of his stolen goods.

As the taxi pulled to a halt at a red light, I looked out at the slightly dingy street. Rue Maubeuge, a sign told me. The shuttered stores and apartment buildings, neon hotel signs that looked like they dated from the early sixties, all had a worn, depressing look. I rubbed my hands over my face and yawned.

Had Volker beaten Tony to try to get information from him? Probably. Or maybe he'd been enraged to find out that the etui was gone? It was possible. In spite of myself I could picture it: Volker going in a matter of seconds from easy confidence to shocking, appalling anger. All the more frightening because it

was still under control. Dangerous. That was what
Tony had said. So had Edward. And he had reminded me about the Baader-Meinhof gang.

But he had been talking about a terrorist connection, and an information network. He must have been
wrong, I thought, leaning forward in the taxi. I could
see the entrance to the station, brightly lighted, ahead
of us. I looked at my watch: five to one. Perfect.

Edward must have been wrong about his "information network." It was probably this fencing network that had confused him. Stolen goods instead of
classified information passing illicitly across international frontiers. Surely, to someone observing from
the outside, the signs would be the same.

I paid the taxi driver and walked into the station,
looking eagerly for Edward's tall figure. The long
concourse was nearly empty. All the little shopfronts
were sealed with steel shutters. A porter trundled his
baggage cart past me, and at the other end of the concourse, near the entrance to the tracks, I could see an
elderly couple walking slowly toward me. But no Edward. Still, I was a little early. And also, I realized, I
had stupidly not specified a spot within the station.

It wouldn't be hard to find him with so few people
about. I walked confidently down the concourse toward the tracks. Though I'd felt tired in the taxi,
somehow that fatigue had disappeared. Of course I
knew why. I kept looking around eagerly, searching
every corner and blind doorway. I'd already forgotten the past six hours. All I could think of was being
able to tell Edward that . . . I laughed to myself. That
I understood. Wasn't mad. That we could take up
where we'd left off.

I came out into the huge echoing space around the tracks. I'd always loved those old European train stations, with their glass roofs and little kiosks selling papers and candy, with the trains lined up side by side, and the whistles and shouts, slamming doors and hissing wheels as the trains pulled in and out. Even at 1 A.M., when the tracks gaped empty and the vast space took a dead-of-night chill, it seemed somehow hopeful and exciting. The notice boards at the head of each track were already set for the next departures of the morning: Calais, 6.20 A.M. Amsterdam, via Lille and Ghent, 7.10. I'd taken that train, I remembered, to go bicycling in Holland. Amiens, 10.45. On Track 6 the notice board still bore the time of the midnight boat train to London via Dieppe and Newhaven. As I walked past a workman finished tinkering with something on the track, leapt up onto the platform, and hailed another workman who was smoking a cigarette leaning against the Left Luggage counter.

I stood for a moment by Track 6, looking around. No Edward. I'd try the waiting room, and after that the ticket counters. Anyway, I was a little early.

The waiting room was dark, its swing doors locked. Down the hall, though, the lights were still on in the big room where travelers bought their tickets. I walked in. It was empty, all the ticket windows closed and dark. A door at the other side of the room opened out onto the entrance to the station. I walked over and peered out. No Edward. A group of short, dark men huddled over cigarettes a few feet away, speaking something guttural that I assumed was Arabic. One of them looked up and saw me. He must have said something to the group, because they all looked up. A couple of them smiled, showing yellowed teeth and the odd gold cap. I retreated into the ticket room.

I looked at my watch again. It was just a little after one. Now what? I couldn't stand at the entrance and wait for Edward unless the Arabs moved on. I walked slowly back down the hall into the main space. This was probably where Edward would come to look for me. I glanced around again. The two workmen I'd seen earlier were leaving, carrying grimy canvas bags with them. A janitor swept listlessly in a corner. For the first time I wondered: Did the station close down for the night?

Probably. But I'd be gone by then.

"Excuse me, mees, you have the time?"

I turned my head in disbelief. One of my friends from the entrance, grinning his flashy gold smile. I gave him a withering look and walked away. Of all the nerve. With clocks all over the station! How stupid did they think I was?

Of course he followed me. "Mees, you need taxi? Hotel? I know good hotel, I drive you." I didn't even bother with the withering this time, but I sped up a bit. Where was Edward?

I was walking down the concourse now, between the ranks of blank-faced stalls. My new friend was pattering along at my elbow, offering a limousine, nightclubs, the Ritz. I would have loved to just shake him off, like brushing away a fly. But he had those friends.

His friends were standing in an appreciative semicircle just inside the doors, watching our performance. I guess my failure to respond struck them as funny, because they were all laughing and calling out encouragement. I wheeled around, losing my escort.

But only for an instant. A fresh burst of laughter told me he'd done something side-splitting. He was probably walking behind me, imitating me. Fine. I was on my way to find the station master. Or a gendarme. Or someone large and official who could get rid of this man.

Except now they were two, I realized. That was what had been so amusing: reinforcements joining the fray. "Mees, you looking for someone? You need help with your luggage? You meess train?"

I was practically running now, trying to get away from the pair, but they kept pace with me. I went back into the big room with the tracks and looked around for anything wearing a uniform: a porter, a conductor. No good. It occurred to me that I might shout for help, but I vetoed that idea as soon as it surfaced. Too embarrassing. I hesitated for a moment, and my escort stopped too. Now they were suggesting they might take me home and feed me couscous. I kept thinking that the less reaction I showed, the sooner they would get bored. They couldn't keep this up. I spied a sign across the floor: W.C. DAMES. That was the answer. There would be an attendant on duty, and she might be able to shame this pair into leaving me alone. Anyway, they couldn't follow me in.

But when I got to where the sign pointed, there was a flight of stairs. Not too narrow, but they curved halfway down. Furthermore, there was no light. Of course it was closed at 1 A.M., and the attendant safely home in her bed by now. I took one look and wheeled around again. I wasn't going down a flight of stairs to an unknown destination with these two chattering Arabs at my elbows.

And the chatter was getting a little bit offensive. We had progressed from couscous to other offers and other suggestions. It seemed to me that the tone of voice was getting less jovial and more annoyed. What's more, it wasn't letting up. They were full of energy and kept coming up with new ideas. Now it was a ride to the seashore. How hilarious.

We went back out into the big space. At least it was open. And bright. These fellows could hardly whack me on the head and pick my pockets (or worse) here in plain sight. Without thinking, I looked at my watch. Quarter past one. Where was Edward?

"Mees, that is a nice watch. Mees, I buy it from you. What you want for it? Mees, you show me your watch again?" One of them reached for my wrist. I snatched it away and started to walk fast. Where was Edward? He could have been held up in traffic—no. Not at one in the morning. Couldn't get a taxi? Possible. Was I in the right place? Suddenly my heart sank. Had I written gare de l'Est? Think back.

No. I could remember my reasoning involving the boat train to London. I was in the right place. Was Edward in the wrong place? Or was he going to come at all? He must be. Oh, God. Was Edward standing in the gare de l'Est just a few blocks away, waiting for me? No. No, it couldn't be. I was walking down the concourse now, all but oblivious to the pair trailing along at my side. I couldn't face it. I had to find Edward.

I pushed open the doors of the station, ignoring the group of men calling out raucous advice. There were no cars in the sweep just in front of the station, no taxis pulling into the taxi rank. I stepped off the pavement into the cobbled roadway and peered out into the dark. I couldn't see anybody walking along the street. Just eerie, shadowy emptiness. It looked like a stage set. I covered my face with my hands. I would not cry. I would *not*. Something must have happened to Edward. To delay him, nothing more. It didn't matter. We had another rendezvous. And thanks to Tony, I had some money now. I would be all right.

The Arabs had all decided something. The pair had been reabsorbed into the group for a moment, as I stepped out to look at the streets. Now the entire group came closer. One man, a new one, stepped forward. "Mees, we have car..." he started. They inched closer. They were very close. One of them was right behind me. I could feel him, pressing against my back.

It was the last straw. I broke away in a run. I had no idea where I was going, but I had to get away from them. Would they follow? I thought not. Not the whole group, running after me like a pack of dogs.

I was crying. Running down a Paris street, with my raincoat billowing out behind me, crying. Wailing, actually. With tears pouring down my face. I looked behind me. They weren't following. The whole group was gathered again by the doors, gesturing and laughing. They weren't even watching me anymore.

As soon as I was out of their sight, I slowed to a walk, still sobbing. By now I couldn't have kept running if the devil himself were behind me. The burst of energy I'd felt at the station was gone completely. I was so *weary*. Tired of running, tired of thinking, tired of being afraid. Tired of trying to unravel all this mystification. All this confusion, plotting and scheming that had been going on behind what I thought was normal life.

The street was completely empty. I felt like the only person left awake in the city, and I was stumbling along in despair. Complete despair. I had been counting on Edward. All the time, running around the city. Running from Volker, through the cars, away from the footsteps. I'd just been thinking of Edward, not even really what I was going to do when I saw him: just the idea of him. Edward, standing there, waiting for me.

Of course, maybe... No. I wouldn't think it. But the thought came anyway. Maybe he was never going to come? No. No. Romance aside, he was reliable. Look at how he'd been about Daddy. Helpful, prompt, considerate.

But that was business, Louise. His business.

So is this, I argued back. The famous "information network." Besides, I couldn't be wrong about him.

And then I thought, You were sure as hell wrong about Tony.

No. I still couldn't see it. Edward was the kind of guy who helped old ladies across streets. I was sure of it. My note had made it clear that I needed his help. He would have been there if he could.

Maybe not. Maybe it's time for a different strategy. After all, the strikes against him are beginning to pile up. No-show at the rendezvous. The "emergency phone number" that was nothing more than the number of some bistro. And this is the guy who planned on cultivating me for the sake of trapping Volker. Hardly playing straight. And maybe he isn't playing straight tonight.

I drew a deep breath, to try to steady myself. Think practically, Louise. It's all you have left. Make a contingency plan. In case. Just in case Edward isn't there tomorrow morning.

Maybe wait for the consulate to open, go there first to get official help before approaching the police....

My nose was running. I stuck a hand in my raincoat pocket to see if, by any miracle, there was a handkerchief in it. My fingers met not linen but something smooth—thin paper? I pulled it out and heard something, a little metallic click. I looked down and saw, rolling away merrily under a streetlight, the spool from the etui.

And unraveling from it, what was obviously audio tape from a microcassette.

Automatically I was on my knees, capturing the spool before I could think how it came to be in my raincoat pocket. And then I remembered that I hadn't been able to fit it back in the etui with the rest of the tiny tools. I was still holding the piece of turquoise tissue paper I'd torn from that incongruous roll in Tony's office. I stuffed the paper back in my pocket and picked the spool up carefully, holding it high to lift the tape off the sidewalk. How could I not have recognized the tape earlier? I'd even looked at it, thinking it was an inappropriate color for the etui's owner. I was rewinding it now, slowly and carefully. I didn't want to touch the surface, damaging whatever was on it.

Whatever was on it. Even before I'd picked it up, as I saw the gleaming thread on the street, it clicked. This did not require reasoning out. Because this, obviously, was what Volker was after. Not the etui, valuable as it was. But the tape: the information. This was what he'd chased me around the city to get. And—I realized with a thud that made me hot all over—what he'd beaten Tony for. This was what Tony said must not fall into Volker's hands.

Not a soul had come into sight while I picked up the spool. I stood there, winding it up, wondering what to do with it. Put it back in my pocket? Take it to—whom? Edward, obviously. Equally obviously, I'd try that in the morning. Notre Dame, 7A.M. And if he wasn't there? Turn it over at the consulate, I supposed. Let them decide what to do with it. I wrapped the tissue paper back around it carefully, but put it in my jeans pocket instead of back in my raincoat. It just felt safer there, closer to my body. And now what?

My body told me. Sleep. Nothing else to do. Find a hotel. Thank God for Tony's money. Find a hotel, lock the door, wash my face. Take off my shoes. Lots of hotels nearby. Dingy, probably not very clean. But the kinds of hotels where people often arrived in the middle of the night without reservations.

Of course, I didn't have a passport. Slowly I started walking again. This was the rue d'Alsace, running the length of the tracks for the gare de l'Est. The hotels had names like Colmar and Le Rhin, to remind voyagers of home. The sign of one restaurant said "Spécialité Choucroute." Would the hotels also be Germanically clean? I doubted it. They all looked incredibly seedy.

Not very hopefully, I walked up the steps of the Colmar and peered in the glass door. I could see a bare staircase beside a concierge's desk, which was surrounded by a barrier of thick Plexiglas. Behind the Plexiglas a man shaped like Humpty Dumpty slept with his head leaning back against the wall and his mouth open. I tried the door, which was locked. I looked for a second at the doorbell surrounded by grimy fingerprints, then turned away. I couldn't bear to ring the bell, wake up Humpty Dumpty, and watch him snort himself back to life. More important, I didn't like what the grimy doorbell and the Plexiglas cage said about the guests of the Colmar. *Punaises*.

Exhausted as I was, I dragged myself farther down the street. There must be something better. There must be some nice solid place where German salesmen spent the night.

It was stupid, because the kind of nice solid place I had in mind would want identity papers. Which I didn't have. Whereas seedy places like the Colmar would probably accept a hundred-franc note instead of a passport. Still I kept going. I was too tired to be reasonable. I had an image of the kind of bed I wanted to sleep in, wide and firm, with no sag. And a reassuring lobby. With the kind of clerk, I reminded myself, who would be strict about identification and wonder where my luggage was....

I came out into the rue Strasbourg that ran along the front of the gare de l'Est. Across the street, facing the station, was a grand old nineteenth-century structure, all curlicues and bow windows. It announced that it was the Hôtel Strasbourg. It looked to me like an oasis, shimmering across a stretch of desert. I crossed the street.

Ten minutes later, I was back on the sidewalk.

I had gotten as far as being assigned a room. A quiet single, no bath, 300 francs. Then he asked for my passport. I acted surprised and said I didn't have it.

"Mademoiselle," the clerk said, "we cannot give you a room without a passport."

I pleaded. Told him it was nearly two in the morning and I had had my purse stolen. He asked me how

I was going to pay for the room. I showed him Tony's cash. Then, close to tears again, I told him I'd give him all of it if he would just let me have a room. The next thing I knew, he'd come around the counter and was escorting me to the door.

It occurred to me as I walked bleakly down the steps that he probably thought I was on drugs. Disheveled, incoherent, irrational. It was going to have to be the Colmar.

I crossed the rue Strasbourg again and looked up the rue d'Alsace at the Colmar's sign. It was one of those vertical arrangements of white blocks lighted from inside, with blue letters painted on them. The whole thing flickered a little, as if the bulbs inside were cheap fluorescent. It looked grim. I shut my eyes for a moment and told myself I wouldn't see the sign from inside. Or see the depressing concierge's cage once I was in my room. I wouldn't see any of it once I was asleep.

So once more I started walking. The last few yards, I told myself. Then up a few stairs. Then a bed. I didn't think I'd even undress. Just fall down on the mattress and pull the covers over me. I tripped and nearly sprawled flat on the sidewalk. No wonder the clerk at the Strasbourg thought I was on drugs.

There was a figure walking down the rue d'Alsace carrying a small suitcase. I made an effort to stand up and walk straight. One foot in front of another. Don't bump into this German computer consultant catching a late train back to Stuttgart. He probably already thinks Paris is a shambles.

It was only a few more yards. The man with the suitcase was walking briskly. He was younger than I'd thought. I concentrated on him, striding purposefully toward me. I took a step, he took two steps. Keep walking, you're almost there. He shifted the suitcase to his outside hand. Probably afraid I was going to take a grab at it, I thought. I was starting to feel light-headed. I might have to sit down for a minute on the Colmar's steps before I rang the bell. Oops; I car-omed off a building.

I couldn't see the man that well anymore, even though he was getting closer. I had the impression that he was walking even faster. Everything was getting a little foggy. I glanced up at the Colmar's sign: the glowing white blocks were dancing in an uneven conga line, though they didn't have much rhythm. It was more of a jiggly, uneven shaking.

The man with the suitcase was right under the sign. It looked as if it were going to fall down on him. I tried to call out. Then I realized who it was. And I really didn't care if Volker got buried by a mountain of dancing letters.

FIFTEEN

I DIDN'T actually faint. Somehow I managed to avoid that cliché. Heaven knows why I cared. I did crumple up and things went upside down for a moment, but I didn't black out.

I didn't actually hit the pavement either. Volker caught me.

I wasn't thinking clearly at all. In fact, I probably wasn't making much sense. But I did think about how I'd imagined that Edward was going to rescue me. And here was Volker, dropping his suitcase and rushing forward just in the nick of time. Now, if life was really the fairy tale that I apparently hoped it was, he would tell me that Edward was a member of a terrorist gang, and that he, Volker, was going to save the free world.... But he didn't. He put his hands under my armpits, dragged me to the steps of the Colmar, and told me to put my head between my knees.

I did, of course. He went back to pick up his suitcase. Then he came and stood over me. I could see his feet. Clad in polished loafers. They hadn't made a *clop-clop* noise on the rue d'Alsace, I thought idly. So he hadn't been the man behind me....

Cautiously I raised my head. I didn't feel dizzy anymore. Now I was looking at his knees. I tilted my head back to see his face. He was lighted from above, by the sign: There was a harsh glare on the top of his head and his forehead, but his eyes were in dark shadow. I shrugged to myself and leaned my head

against the Colmar's doorway. That was the moment
when I gave up.

I was aware, somehow, that Volker seemed to be
weighing a decision. He looked at his watch and at me,
apparently estimating something. "How do you
feel?" he asked. In a tone that sounded more like irritation than like concern.

No need to be polite, anyway. "Awful."

"Can you walk?"

I shuffled my feet a little bit, practicing. "I guess.
Not far."

"What's wrong with you?"

Surprise pierced the haze of my exhaustion. "Well,
I'm a little tired from running all over the city," I said.

"Whose fault is that?" We glared at each other, for
all the world like children squabbling. "Have you had
anything to eat all day?"

I thought back. "No," I said, surprised.

"You probably fainted from hunger," Volker re-
plied briskly. Clearly he'd made up his mind. He held
out a hand. "Up."

I looked at that hand for a moment. Clean, well
manicured. An attractive hand. I didn't much want to
take it. Volker snapped his fingers twice, the way you
would to a lazy old dog. "Come on."

And just about as gracefully as a lazy old dog, I got
up.

He didn't seem to know, at first, whether or not he
had to hold on to me. As we walked down the rue
d'Alsace, he kept a grip on my wrist, which I guess got
uncomfortable because he dropped it. But then he
must have gotten nervous that I was going to bolt
again, because he latched onto my elbow. I could have
saved him the trouble and reassured him that I wasn't

going to escape, but I didn't see why I should. Besides, I doubted he'd believe me.

As I'd expected, we went into the gare de l'Est. It was empty, echoing, just as the gare du Nord had been. Volker nudged me along past the same shuttered shops, the same blank ticket counters. He seemed to know where he was going. Soon enough I figured it out: a row of old-fashioned phone booths, the kind with seats. He sat me down in one.

"I am right next door. You are too tired to get away from me, and if you try it . . ." He squeezed my wrist very hard.

I didn't even bother to say anything. I just shook my head and shut my eyes.

He closed the door of my booth. He must have closed his too, because I couldn't hear any of what he was saying. Just his voice, rumbling indistinctly through the wall. I stretched my legs and the door opened a little. I still couldn't hear clearly. The intonations sounded German, but I couldn't have sworn to it.

There was a notice board not far away, listing the schedules of the trains. These were all going to the east, naturally. I saw Munich and Nancy listed as destinations, and Vienna. Probably the Orient Express stopped here. The last train to leave had been a train to Berlin. It left terribly late, I thought. Who would want to take a train to Berlin at nearly 2 A.M.?

Then I realized: Volker, for one. Walking with his suitcase down the rue d'Alsace. It hadn't even occurred to me to wonder why he was there. His appearing like that, the lone figure walking toward me, had seemed inevitable. Of course it was Volker, I'd thought as I fell. At that point he'd looked like Fate personified.

Instead of which, if my timing had been just a little bit different—if, for instance, I'd rung the bell of the Colmar the first time I passed it—Volker would be on his way to Berlin right now. And I would be safely asleep. *Punaises* or no.

I shut my eyes in a wave of dumb misery. I could hear the clatter of the phone hanging up and the door creaking as Volker came out. Some decision, clearly, had been reached. I wasn't even sure I cared what it was.

"All right," he said. "You need to eat something." And he held out a hand again to pull me up. The idea of getting up on my own in a dignified manner flitted across my mind. I didn't bother to try. I had no pride left. I let him heave me to my feet.

I didn't pay much attention to where we were going. In a demoralizing way, I was relieved not to have to think about it myself. He kept an arm through mine, holding me fairly close with a grip that was stronger than it needed to be. I couldn't really keep up with his pace, so I kept stumbling; once I tripped over a curb. He never swore or jerked me, but his endless, impassive patience was almost worse than an outburst.

He seemed to know the area well, because without hesitation he threaded his way through the empty streets. Left, right, cross here, left again, between parked cars and down narrow sidewalks. Cars passed, and I noticed a few windows and doorways were lighted in spite of the hour. Then we turned another corner into a wider street and I realized where he was taking me.

Paris, like every big city, has its zone of prostitution. The girls who worked the Bois de Boulogne were several ranks below the women in the bars at hotels like the Prince de Galles; and the girls on the rue St. Denis were still farther down the scale. I got a very good chance to see why that night.

It was warm still, so they were outside. They clustered in doorways and alleys, two and three together, moving in and out of the patches of light from the streetlamps and the windows. A blond-maned woman with a voluptuous chest paired with a skinny dark-haired pixie in black leather; a black girl in a blond wig with a pale thin woman in a lace bodystocking. The smell of marijuana drifted here and there, and a few of the women swigged from bottles. I was constantly conscious of movement in the shadows, a few steps into an alley or behind an open door. Cars cruised past slowly on the street, and the women would call out, mostly words I didn't know. Twice I saw cars stop, and women cluster around from the sidewalk, leaning over the windshield and calling out what I guessed were specialties and prices. Once two women got into a car; the other time the driver drove away and they all gestured vulgarly after him.

Volker didn't say a word as he walked along. He didn't even make much of an effort to be careful about where he was going. The first woman I bumped into had on a spandex halter and a red leather miniskirt that barely covered her buttocks. I couldn't help jostling her, with Volker walking on my other side. She teetered on her high heels, and though I didn't look back I could hear her furious swearing for a whole block. By then, of course, everyone was looking at us. There were propositions: Apparently we looked as if we were in the market for a threesome. A pimp, curly-haired and baby-faced, called down from a window to find out if Volker was trying to get rid of me.

Business was slow, I supposed, which gave them plenty of time to watch us. Groups would see us coming and press into a line that I had to brush past, a line of curious, taunting women. I tried not to look at them, so as not to anger them or invite animosity.

I know it wasn't actually far. We walked only a few blocks on that street before turning into a wider boulevard. But dazed as I was already, stumbling with fatigue and fear, it seemed to take a lifetime. Details magnified themselves crazily: a woman against a building with one leg tucked up behind her and her pelvis thrust out; a scrawny arm clattering with bracelets; a pair of blue eyes ringed with smeary black kohl; a dirty silk flower drooping from a topknot; chalky skin, a missing tooth. And always the glaring orangey streetlights and the raucous voices calling out in street accents, shadows flitting into corners and cars gliding slowly by and having to walk, walk, walk, with Volker's hand steely on my arm.

The thing was, we didn't *have* to walk down that street. Any one of a dozen others would have brought us out onto the boulevard where Volker turned. But he walked me down the rue St. Denis, I guessed, to make a point. A point about control.

By the time he steered me to a restaurant a few hundred yards along, I was shaking. He settled me into the corner of the banquette and I huddled against it, clutching my coat to me, trying to draw some warmth from the red vinyl of the seat.

I sat there, still shivering, staring into space. I think Volker spoke to me, and maybe the waiter looked at me with concern. But I wasn't really aware of them. I was back on that street, completely helpless. It was like one of those dreams that only end when you wake up crying. The voices kept calling out, the sharp little kicks bruised my shins, the eyes followed us angrily.

I tried covering my face with my hands, but that made it worse. The eyes came closer. I needed to shut out what was in my head, not what was around me. I needed to pull myself together. I needed to be able to think. Volker was sitting across from me and I had to be ready to deal with him.

I shook my head, trying to clear out the images. Opened my eyes wide, looked around. We were in a classic working-man's restaurant. Paper on the tables, a little bit of sawdust on the old tile floor, high ceilings and thirties-style lamps that would be worth a fortune cleaned up but here were just a nuisance because the bulbs were so hard to change. In spite of the hour, we weren't the only people there. Six men were drinking coffee and brandy and smoking cigarettes in a table in the corner, picking their teeth and muttering. The rest of the customers were scattered alone at tables, staring into space. I did notice a few covert glances our way.

The waiter brought a half-liter carafe of red wine and Volker poured a glass for me. "Here. Start with this." Obediently I did. It was very rough, and watery at the same time. It actually tasted wonderful. I drank half of it before I put the glass down.

"So?" I said wearily.

"So. Your soup is coming. While we wait for it, maybe you will tell me why you disappeared this evening?"

I shrugged and drank more wine. "Who knows?" I said "Whim."

"A whim to go out and have a cup of coffee in a tourist café on the Champs-Elysées."

"Yes."

"And a whim to go exploring a strange neighborhood in the middle of the night?"

The waiter came back and put a basket of bread on the table. I took a piece and ate half of it before I answered Volker. "Right."

"And this whim to stay out is so urgent that you end up practically fainting in the street."

"I guess so," I answered, subsiding against the banquette. Could I possibly have the strength for this?

Volker refilled my wineglass and took a sip from his own. "Why the Champs-Elysées?"

I looked away from him, toward the table of six men. "You know, Paris at night, the City of Lights." I barely knew what I was saying, but instinctively I wanted to put off saying anything substantial.

"Why this neighborhood?"

"Bad luck, I guess," I said carelessly, and looked up at him.

I guess it was the first time I'd really looked at his face since he scooped me up off the street. Looked and paid attention. He was a little flushed, and there was a glitter in his eyes. That was all. Nobody who didn't know him very well would even register these signals. But I knew him. And I knew that Volker was in a towering bad temper.

Suddenly I was alert again. It might have been the soup that the waiter put down in front of me just then. More likely it was adrenaline. All night long people had been telling me, I had been telling myself, that

Volker was dangerous. I had fled from him instinctively, based on that conviction. And there he was, across the table from me, glowering.

I couldn't think why he was so mad. He'd caught me, hadn't he?

I picked up my spoon and started to rake the gummy blanket of cheese from the top of the soup. The cheese was still bubbling on its crouton, and the soup scalded my tongue when I tried to taste it. There was this to be grateful for: During the battle of wits that was about to take place, I would at least have the strategic diversion of onion soup gratinée. Tell a lie, poke the soup. Pull a string of cheese to play for time. Heaven knew, as the world's worst liar, I was going to need tactical advantages.

Not that I had any idea what was at stake. What did Volker know? Would my playing dumb help? Could I possibly keep him from getting the tiny spool in the pocket of my blue jeans?

"Why did you leave your apartment?" he asked suddenly. His voice was very well controlled. It sounded almost exactly like a casual question.

Fortunately my mouth was full so I had time to consider. Whatever the exact connection between Tony and Volker had been, Tony was out of Volker's reach now. Nothing I said could harm him. I formulated a little rule for this inquisition: Lie only when necessary.

I swallowed and said, "Tony called me."

Did a shadow of surprise pass over those blue eyes? "And what did he say?"

"That you were in a rage. And you were coming over to my apartment. And I should be careful."

"Did he say why?"

"No. He didn't sound like he was in the mood to chat," I said sarcastically, then instantly regretted it. Somehow my impulse was to play as ignorant as possible, and I'd just let Volker know that I knew he'd beaten Tony.

"Oh? How did he sound?" He kept pressing the questions.

"I don't know, Volker, he sounded a little curt," I said, and buried my face in my wineglass.

"So you go running out just because Tony calls you with this...warning."

"Once I was out, I didn't want to go back. I know your temper. I didn't want to walk back into a fight." This time I looked up at him, trying to seem guileless and sincere.

"And why did you go to Edward Cole's apartment?"

It wasn't the question I'd been expecting. Should I show surprise that he knew? I tried to look puzzled. "Did you follow me there?"

His expression didn't change. "Why did you go there?" he repeated.

I shrugged, probably too emphatically, and turned back to the soup. "I couldn't go home, and I didn't want you following me in a rage to Gisele's place. I didn't think you knew about Edward. I hoped he would put me up for the night." The waiter reappeared with a plump omelette sizzling on its steel plate. Hoping to distract him, I said, "You should have some of that, I sort of have my hands full."

"*Ja*, you know, I think you do," Volker said flatly. He drew the plate toward him and, very deliberately, glancing up at me to make sure I was watching, cut into the middle of the omelette. The soft center, flecked green with parsley, oozed toward him. Then he lifted the knife, a sharp little serrated blade on a wooden handle. "Playing dumb is not so smart as you think," he said, glaring at me. And pointing the knife, still dripping, at my face.

It was melodramatic. Part of me knew that, and dismissed the gesture as just Volker overplaying a part. But there were those eyes, still glittering. And that voice. He sounded cold and impersonal, cold as a machine. But no machine could ever sound that frightening.

He held the pose for a few seconds, then put the knife down and folded his hands. "You know what else is not so smart? You think Edward Cole is going to rescue you." Volker shook his head. "Fairy tales. You go rushing to his apartment, but I tell you something. What do you know about Edward Cole?"

With my mouth full of soup, I didn't answer right away.

"What do you know?" he repeated. "Hmm?"

I shrugged. "He's an American lawyer, he knows a friend of mine, he seems trustworthy." Whatever my actual doubts about Edward might be, I was hardly going to share them with Volker.

"*Ja*, and why is this American lawyer here?"

I looked at Volker. "I don't know, you tell me," I said, and attacked a piece of cheese-crusted bread in my bowl.

"Well, I think he tells you he is with the government somehow. But the government is not the only people who need lawyers. Sometimes also the other side needs legal advice."

"The other side? What is this 'other side'?" I asked. "What are you trying to say?" But his shot had gone home. I could feel the stiffness on my face, and I knew he could see it. I had been worried about the "other side" before Volker brought it up.

"I only wonder. You have proof that he is what he says? Or maybe he is working—with me, for example." With a little smile he took a piece of bread and ate it, watching me.

I couldn't meet his eyes anymore. I just stared into my bowl, concentrated on my spoon. He always had been a malicious bastard.

I didn't really believe him. Really. It just didn't make sense. Anyway, he hadn't said anything specific. He hadn't come out and said Edward was a crook. He was just saying it to torture me.

And it worked. If Edward was on Volker's side, then . . . I put my spoon down and shut my eyes.

"You are all right?" Volker's voice came. Mock-concerned.

"Fine, thank you," I answered, and resumed eating. "And I don't believe what you're saying about Edward."

"You forget how well I know you," he answered. "I know you are not as stupid as you are seeming. I also know you are obstinate. You get an idea and you keep it." My face must have showed some surprise because he said, "Oh, *ja*, you were telling me I never pay attention to who you really *are*. I know who you really are. You are a silly stubborn American girl who is running away from her home and wasting time. You have only the father at home and he is too busy so you think 'aha! I show him I don't need him' and come to Paris. This is like a child! You are educated, you can do something for your country. But all Americans are like this. Children," he said with disgust.

I just stared at him, spooning in soup.

"You are playing," he said, returning his attention to me. "And you are playing very stupidly. You pretend you know nothing, I tell you what you know and you don't pretend anymore.

"First," he started, picking up the knife again, "there is Tony. Tony is..." Volker spat on the floor. My eyes widened at the display of scorn. "He is brilliant, he is worse than you. Wastes his life. He has stupid job running school for spoiled students, goes to opera, smuggles. He tells me he smuggles for the thrill. Thrill! So he need thrill, I tell him about the way to get thrill. He likes it. Thinks he is very clever. 'Killing two birds with one stone,' he calls it. He smuggles his little paintings and books and sometimes there is something extra in the package. He is already doing this: a little drugs here, a little currency there. He takes money from anyone, you know. Sago who he is working for doesn't know this.

"You know that is why Tony hurt Sago. He tells me this later. Sago is getting furious, hopping up and down and screaming, because Tony puts drugs in with old book and gives it to your father instead of taking it to England himself. Sago is making noise in Bois and Tony wants to shut him up so he tries to scare him. He says he doesn't mean to hurt him. This is probably true. Americans always stop short of necessary unpleasant actions." He glanced at the knife again and back at me before he put it on the plate. I just stared back. I was sitting stock-still now, with my spoon still in my hand. I had never guessed at this side of Volker. Never realized how much he noticed—and how much contempt he had for what he saw.

"Sago doesn't like when his shipments are mixed up with other—what is it Tony calls it? 'consignments.' I do not care so much. I think it makes him more careful. Only I tell Tony no drugs, no currency. Too dangerous. For me he is sending information." Of course: Edward's "information network." The tape wound on a tiny gold spool in my pocket. "Things we cannot send on the phones or in the mail. It is all for our cause," he said, suddenly fixing me with that blue glare. "We are going to have a united Germany and there will not be an American *bullet* in it! Not an American penny or an American can of soup! A united Germany has no need of America!"

That was the part I had heard before, though not with such passion.

"We are making plans," he went on, his voice lower but even more intense. "We are going to start with the military bases. Soon now we will be making our presence known." He leaned toward me and whispered, "We will start by destroying the bases, one by one."

He leaned back and took a swallow of wine, and gestured toward my soup, still with the knife in his hand. "Eat it. You must not faint again." It was a command, and I obeyed, though the soup was getting cold and the cheese congealing in a clump.

"Tony knew about this," Volker told me, resuming his lecture. "He knew about the bases and he was glad. Do you know about his family?"

"No," I answered, startled. The friendship between Tony and Volker must have been closer than I realized if Tony had told Volker about his background.

"They are good people," Volker pronounced. "They work hard in a small town called Michigan.

The father is in the post office. The mother teaches school. There is a brother in the army. He is football hero at school. Tony is the what, the misfit. He is bitter about this. He tells me he works hard in school, the parents tell him to get a job. He had scholarships and they want him to leave the university to go into the army like his brother. He complains that they don't understand him, he works and works at university and they don't love him, they only love the brother. Then he cheats on a paper. Copies somebody else. Very stupid.''

"You mean Tony plagiarized," I broke in. It did make sense. No wonder he was so quiet about his past.

"*Ja*, that is the word he uses, plagiarize. His parents are shocked, they kick him out of the house. They do not want to see this dishonest son again. So when I tell him about the plan for the army base, Tony is very interested. His brother is stationed in Germany. He doesn't know where but if it is maybe the same place, he thinks this is 'poetic justice.' He says this with hate. So he is helpful about passing plans. And maybe he is killing his brother," he finished. Even though it aided his fanatical cause, Volker obviously found this family betrayal shocking.

And so did I. I went on eating, but I couldn't help thinking: poor Tony. I could imagine the kind of "good people" his parents were: sober and hardworking and incapable of understanding the brilliant son they'd produced. How sad! It explained a lot about him, such as his arrogance and his emotional inconsistency. It didn't justify the hate, of course.

But what I knew, and Volker didn't, was that Tony didn't want the etui to fall into Volker's hands. Somehow he had had a change of heart.

"So now," Volker said quietly, "you know about Tony." The feverish look had gone from his eyes, as if he had vented his fury in his dramatic little speech. "Now you tell me where is this etui."

I scraped the last gobbet of cheese from the crock and swallowed it, watching Volker. He was right. Now I knew about Tony and what had been going on at Winfield. I also knew why the tape that was nestled in my blue jean pocket must not fall into Volker's hands. You could say that at last, I knew what was at stake.

It was a matter of human lives. Just as Tony had said. I didn't feel terribly heroic, but I thought I could probably get rid of the tape somehow, ensuring that Volker never got it and the army base didn't get blown up.

That wasn't the problem. The problem was that, in knowing what was at stake, I probably knew too much.

SIXTEEN

I KNEW WHAT Volker's group had been doing. I knew what their plans were. I knew how Tony was involved. What was to prevent me from turning Volker in and ruining the whole plan?

There were two possibilities. One was that Volker was going back to Germany, his work here finished. I had, after all, run into him near the train station. Maybe he was going to disappear, leaving no trace. If the group was set up on a cell system, his cell could just shut down without affecting the whole. I hoped that was what was planned, but I doubted it.

The other possibility... The other possibility I had to face. It was that somehow I was going to be prevented from telling anyone what I knew about Volker's plans.

I was still staring at him, thinking it all out. He met my gaze soberly and nodded. "*Ja*, you tell." He looked down again at the knife.

I remembered that he and his family used to hunt a lot in the woods near where he grew up. He had told me they lived all winter on game they'd killed: venison, boar, rabbits. This was a man who knew what a knife was for.

I leaned back against the banquette, still looking at him. The adrenaline high that had carried me though the last half hour was beginning to fade. "Take me home and I'll tell you," I said on impulse.

"No. You tell me here," he answered.

I just looked at him and shook my head. Now that
I'd said it, I knew that I wanted to go home more than
anything in the world. I needed to sleep, but more than
that, I craved—normalcy. Just a few hours in a normal setting, with familiar things around me, somehow seemed like the most desirable thing in the world.
Volker had called me stubborn. Stubborn I would be.
After all, I told myself, he could hardly start carving
me up in the middle of the restaurant.

He looked at me and sighed. I enjoyed that. It was
a very small victory but it made me feel better. "I will
not argue with a spoiled child," he said loftily. "You
will tell me at your apartment, but I warn you that I
have already been looking there." Of course he had.

He paid the check and started to put out a hand to
pull me up from the banquette, but this time I got up
myself. Naturally his hand latched around my upper
arm the minute I was standing. As we walked out of
the restaurant, our waiter said, "I am glad mademoiselle feels better," with a friendly smile. That helped
too.

As we waited on the street for a taxi, I tried to think.
I would tell Volker where the etui was. That presented
no problem. But how would I get rid of the tape in my
pocket? Could I possibly keep it hidden somewhere so
that it could be used as evidence against this gang? If,
for instance, I went into the bathroom: Could I hide
it in my laundry basket? Bury it in a box of face powder? Or stick it under the mattress? In a pillow? How
closely would Volker be watching me?

And what would happen after that? I felt safe
enough as we got into the cab that finally appeared.
He couldn't do anything to me until he had the infor-

mation he wanted. And then? Would he take me at my word?

Wouldn't he have to? Or would he try to get a different answer out of me? Because one thing was certain: He wasn't going to like what I had to tell him.

It was after three when we pulled over in front of my building. Volker had sat with his eyes shut for the entire trip and I'd wondered if he was dozing, but the minute the taxi stopped he paid the fare with the exactly appropriate tip. He had always been good at lightning calculation, I remembered. And he needed only four hours of sleep a night.

The big front door was closed, naturally. I punched four numbers on the electronic lock: 8420. It didn't release the catch. I tried again and swore.

"What?" said Volker roughly, and snatched at my arm. But he was too late, for I'd already rung a long peal on the bell.

"They've changed the combination," I said. "They just did it this week and I don't remember the new number."

"And you rang the bell! That nosy concierge will see us!"

"What does it matter? She already saw you once this evening." I tried to soothe him. But he was right. That was the whole point. I knew the new combination perfectly well; it had been functioning ever since I'd paid to have the lock changed after breaking up with Volker. But I *wanted* to wake Madame Cabrol. Maybe somehow I could get a message through to her that not all was well. She must know there was something wrong about my having to ring to get in....

It was a desperate silly move, but it was all I had. I didn't know what I hoped would happen; that she would rush Volker, overwhelm him, and tie him up with laundry rope?

I should have known better. I could hear her even before the door opened, well launched on a tirade. "Mademoiselle, may I remind you that there are decent citizens who need their sleep, and how long ago was it that this lock was changed..." Then suddenly she dropped the volume, as if she remembered that there were decent citizens on the second and third floors with windows on the courtyard. "...you of all people, to forget the number, it is a scandal, I hope this will never happen again, Mademoiselle Gerard, I do not expect such thoughtlessness from you."

Meekly we squeezed past her and started up the stairs as she pushed the big door closed, and went back into her ground-floor apartment, still clucking and complaining and shaking her head. I'd be hearing about that for weeks, I thought reflexively.

Then I realized, I'd be hearing about that for weeks—if I was lucky.

Volker must have left the apartment in a hurry, because the lights were all still on and it looked cozy and welcoming as I crossed the roof. I had a moment's panic as I opened the door: Would he have turned everything topsy-turvy, looking for the etui? Was I going to see sofa cushions cut apart, dresser drawers dumped upside down, plants upside down in their dirt on the floor?

A swift glance reassured me as I shrugged off my raincoat. The cushions nestled intact in their corners. Edward's pitcher of lily of the valley perfumed the whole room. The mismatched lamps with their Provençal print shades, the bowl of potpourri on the trunk, the shawls draped on the sofas, the faience on the dresser, Lily and Elsie calmly grinning at me, everything was as it should be. Warm and glowing and welcoming.

The only sign of trouble was the contents of my straw bag, dumped out on one of the sofas. That, naturally, Volker had searched. I saw down next to it and started reassembling its contents: address book, hair brush, six pens, red-bound *Plan de Paris*, wallet. The cosmetic case was unzipped, and I could see a lipstick on the floor by my foot, so I bent down to get it. I wasn't watching Volker.

Which was silly, because his foot came down on my hand. Hard. Hard enough and suddenly enough so that I cried out, and tears started in my eyes. I slipped down off the sofa, to try to take the pressure off my arm, which was twisted at an angle. But Volker just increased the pressure on my hand. I could feel all the little bones, separately it seemed, grinding and burning. The knuckles were like points of light, radiating pain and I cried out, "Stop it!"

"Tell me where is the etui," he said.

"In the mail." I gasped.

"What?" he cried, and stamped.

I could feel them popping. Little bones breaking like potato chips. I bowed my head into the carpet, curving the other arm over it. The pain—it was as if my whole hand were on fire, a ball of pulsing fire. I was cringing at Volker's feet. "In the *mail*!" I sobbed.

He stepped back and I guess I should have looked up to see what was going to happen next but I was prostrate, all I could think about was lifting my poor broken hand off the carpet into my lap and curling up around it, cradling the pain.

Then—crash! Or rather, a shivering tinkle, followed by a crash. I jerked up my head, alarmed. I could feel a current of fresh air drifting over me. Volker had broken a window. Clumsily I got to my knees, my hand drooping on my lap. And saw Volker, waiting for me to look at him, holding a faience pitcher over his head. When he was sure he had my attention, he hurled it through another window. I heard the same sequence of sounds: the shattering glass, then the pitcher smashing on the roof outside. Volker looked around again. Calm, methodical as ever. Picked up the pitcher of lily of the valley. I could see him looking at the window, thinking; but instead he brought the pitcher up high and hurled it down on the table, jumping out of the way as the water spattered around him, mixed with shards of glass. He looked at me again.

"Where is it?"

I shut my eyes and tried to swallow down a wave of panic and pain and nausea, pressing just under my chin. I couldn't lose control. Not yet. Not until he understood that I was in earnest.

"It's in the mail. I didn't want to have it near me. So I mailed it to myself."

He stared at me, incredulous. He was flushed with anger and breathing hard. He started to swear. I had no idea what he was saying: He could have been reciting nursery rhymes for all I could understand. But the venom and hatred didn't need translating. There were almost sparks coming from his eyes; you could have lit a match from him. In the middle of his curses he looked around again, deliberately, eyes seeking something to destroy. But not just anything. Something that would be satisfying: something that would break, and maybe break my spirit with it.

His eye fell on the Staffordshire pugs. I wondered to myself, Do I have to watch this? But of course I did. Because he picked them up very gently from the dresser. Brought them to where I was leaning against the trunk. I didn't look up. Didn't see him hold them over his head and hurl them to the ground one by one. I even had my head turned away, my eyes shut. But I could hear them, hear the china shatter as it hit the thinly carpeted floor. One of them, the second one, broke against the bottom of the trunk, as Volker improved his aim with practice. And I felt the little shards of china flying all over my legs.

I wanted very badly not to cry. I bit my lip and started to clasp my hands, but of course that was a mistake. Pain pulsed up my arm. And when I opened my eyes the first thing I saw was a largish shard of china on my knee. It was the muzzle of one of the dogs, its foolish grin intact, but severed from its beady eyes and its smooth china coat. There it was, disembodied, lying on my knee and smiling at me. My face crumpled and the tears came.

Volker flung himself down onto the opposite sofa. "*Ja*. This is one stupid story. Tell me better story."

"There is no better story. Do you know how I got it?"

For a moment he looked startled, then puzzled. "No. Tony only tells me you have it."

"What made you think *he* had it?" I asked cautiously.

"It has not arrived where it should. Several days ago. Finally I get message saying this. I go to Tony to find out what is up. He tells me shipment went wrong and you have it. Shipment went wrong! I tell him this is something he must take *himself!* I cannot have this information going in his system with little crooks! *Ja*, sure, it is my fault," he said, not with regret but with more anger. "I am *idiot* to trust this *American!*" he finished, glaring at me.

I sat still. Not the moment to talk about honor among thieves. He didn't seem to know about Gabriel. And if I was careful, maybe I could keep it that way.

"Well, I found it in his office," I said. Which was partly true. "And I went to see him in his apartment. I didn't know what was going on, but with my father, and then I had heard about Mr. Sago..."

"You heard how?"

"Edward." I looked sharply at him. "There, that's proof! He'd just come from the police. How else would he know about Mr. Sago being hurt?"

A look of mischief lit Volker's eyes for a second. "*Ja*, unless he was there himself."

"Oh, come on." I said, annoyed at myself for even having brought it up.

"*Ja*, well, you were wrong about him, of course you are angry. Why is he telling you about this accident of Sago?"

"I had lent Tony my Mobylette that night," I answered. Speaking of people I was wrong about.

"Oh, *ja*, naturally," he said, nodding.

"So I went to find Tony, to ask him about it. And instead I found this etui, and I knew it was worth..." I paused. "I don't know. Millions."

"So much?" Volker said, surprised. "And he is leaving it in his desk drawer?"

"I don't know exactly," I said hastily. "Maybe a million dollars. Have you seen it?"

"No," he shook his head. "Tony only tells me he is sending information with this etui. I ask him what is it, he tells me little gold case like cigar."

"Well, it's got a lot of diamonds on it, and it's beautifully made and it's Louis Quinze. So I knew it had to be hot, stolen. So I took it to Tony's apartment to ask him what he was doing with it. And he didn't tell me, he just wanted it back. But I was so mad at him that I didn't give it to him."

"He should have *taken* it, he is worthless!" interjected Volker.

"Well, he didn't. And I didn't know what to do. I didn't want to go to the police right away, I didn't want the thing around, so I mailed it."

"But the *mail!*" exclaimed Volker. "How can you be so careless? It gets lost in the mail, somebody maybe unwraps it and sees gold, it is gone forever!"

"At that point, I couldn't have cared less," I said flatly. "It was already stolen. Why should I care if it never gets to the right illegal owner?"

"My God, so you mail it," Volker said, drawing a hand over his eyes.

I just bowed my head. With one finger I touched the muzzle of the dog, still sitting on my knee.

"You mailed it how?" he demanded, after a moment's pause. "First class?"

"Yes."

"So it gets here what?" Volker was calculating to himself. "Monday, Tuesday at the latest. My God, you wrapped it well?"

"Yes," I said, thinking about those layers of tracing paper.

He sighed, obviously thinking. I picked the dog's muzzle up off my leg and put it on the trunk. Then I started moving the other pieces from my lap one by one onto the trunk.

"*Ja*, we wait then. I make phone calls to fix this. We wait."

"There's one more thing," I said very timidly.

"What?" he asked, already on his way to the bedroom for the phone.

I shut my eyes. There was no knowing how he was going to react to this. I no longer knew how to feel about it myself. "I left a message with Edward Cole. To meet me at Notre Dame at seven tomorrow morning. If I'm not there, he'll start looking for me."

The explosion wasn't instantaneous. It took Volker a few seconds to think through the complications. Then he put a hand behind the dresser, and, with one violent heave, turned the whole thing over in a cascading clattering crash. This time I was ready for the destruction. And as I shut my eyes to the racket, I thought, Surely they'll hear this downstairs. Then I remembered—the apartment was empty. The same thought must have occurred to Volker, because the flood of cursing abated. He walked back toward me, between the sofa and the table, obviously looking for something to destroy. I inched toward the center of the sofa, with my knees raised and my arms between them and my chest. Bits of china pug crunched beneath Volker's shoes as he crossed to the other sofa and plucked the shawl off it. He started to tear it, and it gave a bit in a weak spot. But the fabric was tightly woven and didn't rip. He clenched his teeth, took larger handfuls of fabric, shut his eyes as he tugged. It wasn't going to tear and I watched aghast as he kept pulling. His face turned purple as he strained. He looked ready to burst. Then he swore mightily and threw it toward me. I flinched as the shawl landed over me in a stifling bundle and clawed hurriedly to get it off. Was Volker going to come after me next? Was this how he'd beaten Tony? In an uncontrolled fury?

No. Because it wasn't completely uncontrolled. That was why it was frightening. Volker was deliberately using this destruction to let off steam. Nothing too loud, nothing to dangerous; just frightening and distressing. He was tearing apart my home. Except for the mistake of the dresser, he hadn't let this temper carry him into error. And now, to vent his rage, he started on the books. I suppose he thought they wouldn't make much noise. He started pulling them out of the shelves under the windows and tearing out the pages in handfuls. Ragged crumpled paper fluttered to the floor, to mix with the shards of Lily and Elsie.

I leaned back against the sofa, with the shawl still draped against my chest. He hadn't started on me. Thank God. Thank God for the impulse that had taken me to the rue du Louvre. Volker was going to have to keep me alive to get what he wanted.

There. I'd said it. Alive. All the fears of the last few hours, the fears that I'd kept at bay, receded. He had to keep me alive.

And then I thought: But what if Edward isn't there? He wasn't at the gare du Nord. What if he really *was* working with Volker? All too clearly, I could imagine the scene. Edward turning up at the cathedral with a cordial greeting in German for Volker and a cursory glance at me. The two of them easily holding me hostage until Monday's mail came. Unwrapping the etui.

Then what: me sheepishly producing the tape? Them bashing my brains out and pitching me in the river?

The tearing was slowing down. A book hit the back of the sofa with a muffled thud. Then one hit my shoulder. Without opening my eyes, I ducked my head forward and curved my right arm over it. Something smacked against my head with a flutter; a paperback, just tossed at me. He wasn't even trying to injure me. Just have his little game. Talk about children.

I just sat there as the missiles bounded off me. Most of them didn't hurt; once the corners of a small hard-cover met my scalp. Finally the shelves were empty and Volker said something scornful. I heard his steps go into the bedroom. He closed the door behind him.

I thought about bolting again. I could sneak out very quietly. He might not hear me go. But once I was outside, what? How could I hide from him until seven? Physically and emotionally I was too worn out for any more time in the street. I didn't even lift my head to see what time it was. It wasn't worth it.

Or was it? Could I get free? Could I take the chance? Could I face the consequences? If Volker caught me he would explode again. There was already my hand, throbbing now in my lap. What if he came out of the bedroom just as I was slipping out the door?

He needed me to take to Edward in the morning, but he didn't need me in very good shape.

How long would he be on the phone?

How far could I go, tired and hurt as I was?

Could I get Madame Cabrol to call the police? Maybe. What if I slipped down the stairs and woke her up and explained? Volker wouldn't stop to look for me in her apartment; he couldn't afford to make trouble like that. I could slip into the loge, her little booth opening onto the courtyard, and tell her not to turn a light on. We could whisper. We could even watch for him to go past, screened by Madame's lace curtains. And once he'd gone, we could call the gendarmes. Oh, yes, it would work!

I raised my head for the first time since Volker had started throwing books. The destruction was pitiful. All over the trunk and the sofas, torn pages like snow. Color pictures here and there, pages of different sizes, whole chunks where the binding had given way. Under the fall of paper, pieces of china pug.

With my right hand, I pulled the shawl from my shoulders. Pages fluttered to the ground. Carefully, trying to move as smoothly as possible, I got my legs underneath me. Every inch of motion jarred my hand and sent flashes of pain shooting up my left arm. How far could I get, feeling like this?

Not far. But I didn't have to go far. I braced myself for a pang and scrambled up onto the sofa, where I immediately collapsed facedown on a picture book of the Alps. I lay there, dizzy and gasping, clutching my left elbow, below which was a radiant pulsing mass of pain. Gradually my breathing slowed. It couldn't actually have taken very long. As I cautiously raised myself to a sitting position, a photo of a snowy Alp stuck to my cheek, and I brushed it away.

Now all I had to do was get myself out the door, down the stairs, and hidden under Madame Cabrol's bed before Volker got off the phone. I stood up. Not too bad. I took a step, trying not to grind Lily and Elsie into the carpet any further. The crunch sounded incredibly loud. Worse, the room started to sway again. Worse yet, I was going to be sick.

I couldn't swallow it back this time. I knew I wouldn't be able to. But some instinct made me run for the door, crookedly trying to shield my hand from being jarred.

"Halt! Stop!" came from the bedroom just as I wrenched the door open. I ignored Volker and ran. He came after me, of course, and grabbed my arm to bring me back. But he realized, almost soon enough, what I was doing. His shoes suffered a bit.

The pain of moving made the nausea worse, I guess, because I heaved and heaved long after there was nothing to heave up. Volker stood aside, probably not wanting to let me out of his sight.

When it stopped I knelt there a moment longer, exhausted. I felt sweaty and shaky and very weak. So much for making a break for it. My mouth tasted bitter.

"Now you are finished?" Volker's voice came.

I just nodded.

"Then you come inside. You may sleep now."

I scrambled slowly to my feet. No helping hand this time, not now that I wasn't about to get away. But he walked behind me across the roof and closed the door behind both of us. He followed me to the bedroom door, and I wondered for a horror-struck moment if he was planning to watch me while I slept. Instead, he ostentatiously unplugged the telephone.

"We will go in the morning to see Cole. You will be staying with me until I get the etui. After that, it depends on Cole. I will wake you up in the morning." He turned to leave the room with the phone under his arm, then stuck his head back in. There was a mirthless smile on his face. "You remember that I am a light sleeper." Then he shut the door.

I tottered into the bathroom. I considered not turning on the light, just brushing my teeth in the dark. I didn't think I wanted to see my face. But I thought I should see my hand. Maybe there was something I could do to make it feel better: hot water, cold water? Aspirin? Anything I could do in the three minutes I felt I could keep on standing up.

The face in the mirror, when I flicked on the light, was pale green. There were scraps of paper in my hair, and even a few chips of china that had bounced off the trunk. My eyes looked sunken, and there was still sweat on my upper lip and in my hairline. I looked down at my hand, lying on the porcelain sink.

It didn't look as bad as I had feared. It was swollen, of course. Turning red. The fingers were already getting hot and starting to look like sausages. There were tiny lacerations here and there from the soles of Volker's shoes, just pinpricks of blood nothing serious. It was still recognizably a hand.

Delicately I tried to move some of the fingers. Thumb was fine. Pointer was not. I gave up there. Using my right hand, I turned it over to look at the palm. Red streaks coming down from the fingers. No bones poking through the skin. It wasn't totally mangled. It just hurt like hell.

I managed to splash some water on my face with my right hand. It didn't do anything for the greenness. Brushing my teeth was harder: I had to lay the toothbrush down on the sink and hold it flat with my left forearm while I squeezed toothpaste onto it. I almost gave up, but was glad I hadn't. There was nothing more exciting than some Tylenol in the little wooden cupboard hung over the toilet. If I were some other kind of person, I thought, I might have something really useful here, like some codeine or some Percodan. If I were some other kind of person, though, I wouldn't be in this situation and I wouldn't need them. I took three Tylenol, knowing they weren't going to dull the throbbing in my hand even halfway. I drank three glasses of foul-tasting Paris tap water. I managed to get my shoes off but didn't attempt to take off my socks. Socks take two good hands. Then I crawled miserably under my duvet and turned off the light.

I tried lying on my side first. Fetal position, all curled up. But if I lay on my right side, I had to drape my left arm cross my chest, and the blood flowed into my hand and throbbed worse. And if I lay on my left side—well, I never got all the way over. I could tell it wouldn't work the minute my weight got as far as my left shoulder. So I lay on my back. I pulled a pillow across my stomach to take the weight of the duvet and placed my hand right next to the pillow. I shut my eyes, and waited to sleep.

It was all I had wanted to do for hours. And as I lay there I could feel the relaxation seeping through my body. But my hand, now that I had nothing else to think about, felt like... It felt like a lot of things, I decided. A hot air balloon. A rubber glove that someone was melting with a blowtorch. A ball of fire. I tried not to think about it.

The alternative subjects were worse, though. What was going to happen in the morning? A few hours away, I corrected myself. I lay there with my eyes squeezed shut, feeling wretched. Volker had been furious about having to go meet Edward. Surely that meant that Edward was not working with him? But maybe it just meant that there was some kind of friction between them. Maybe—and I gasped at the thought—Edward was the leader. And Volker was angry because now his incompetence would be shown up. There was something he'd said: "after that it depends on Cole." It certainly sounded as if Edward were somehow in charge.

I thought back. Tried to remember what had passed between Edward and me. Was there anything to prove that Volker was right? The helpfulness about Daddy. So what? The curiosity about Tony: He could just have wanted to get a different view of one of his minions. That night after the concert. . . . But some things didn't bear thinking about. I just had to assume that Volker was right. I wasn't sure it would make much difference anyway. Even if Edward wasn't working for Volker, what would he be able to do? I might as well accept that he was.

That was the low point. Lying there in bed, with the darkness all around me, I wished it would just press in and smother me. There was no way out. No hope. Nothing. I started to feel my eyes well up and tried to stop myself from crying. There had to be *something*. Something I could do? A tear rolled down my temple into my hair. Think, Louise, and stop feeling sorry for yourself! Be reasonable! What will happen after Volker and Edward get the etui? Maybe the picture's not that bleak.

Obediently I thought. Possibility A, they get the etui, the tape isn't there, they calmly leave for Germany, leaving me unscathed. Unlikely.

Or, B, when they find the tape gone they hit the roof and started quizzing me about what was in the etui when I found it. I could lie, say I'd never opened it, or say I hadn't seen anything else in it besides the little tools you'd expect to find there. That seemed possible—except that Edward could read my face. Anyway, if I got away with the lie, what would happen next? Would they just give up? Somehow I didn't imagine Edward as the giving-up kind of guy. I couldn't help a fresh burst of tears from escaping then. Pay attention, Louise! Could they give up, since I knew what I did? All that rigmarole about destroying military bases? Could they afford to leave me unharmed and able to talk? I couldn't see how.

Possibility C was that they got the etui, saw the tape wasn't in it, and Volker beat me to a bloody pulp then and there. Would Edward try to control him? Get mad too? No. I squirmed miserably at the thought. Not that. I felt sick. Nausea at the back of my throat. And always, at the back of my mind, the persistent thought that had been running like a refrain for hours: "How could you have been so stupid? How could you have been so stupid?"

Stupid, naïve, gullible, careless, idiotic. What a fool.

Daddy used to have a catch-phrase, one of those silly things he learned at boarding school or from his grandmother and really believed: "Prepare for the worst and hope for the best."

I guessed that meant I should prepare to meet my Maker. Mercifully it was at this point that my thoughts began to get a little foggy. I remember going back to possibility B and trying to work it through to a hopeful conclusion. Volker and Edward find the tape gone, I persuade them I've never seen it, and they—what? Head out to find Tony? An image of Volker surprising Tony on the park bench off the avenue de Friedland stuck in my brain and I couldn't get rid of it, but soon it was mixed up with other images and they began to make no sense, which was how I knew I was falling asleep.

I kept waking up, of course. If I moved, I jarred my hand and the pain woke me. Sometimes I would drift off and then jerk awake, worried that I'd overslept. Then I would look at the clock by my bed and realize that I'd only been asleep for twenty minutes. And my dreams were awful. Running in mud that grabbed my feet, standing stock-still in front of a tidal wave, trying to warn Daddy about a sniper. I woke up from the last one sobbing, with my pillow drenched and the hair at my temples wet from the tears that had dripped down my face. I tried to dry my eyes with a corner of the sheet and looked at the clock again. Only five o'clock. I shut my eyes and tried to relax my body inch by inch. I wanted to sleep so badly. I didn't want to lie there for the next hour and a half worrying. Oblivion was all I asked.

Instead of which, I was lying there waiting. Lying in the dark, waiting for Volker to tell me it was time to go meet Edward. And after that, I supposed it would be at least two more days with Volker, and maybe Edward, waiting for the etui to arrive. After which...

After which I couldn't possibly imagine. I lay there on my bed with my eyes clamped shut and my body tense again, trying not to think about the one possibility I'd been avoiding. I took a deep breath. Face it, Louise. Possibility D: You're afraid they're going to kill you.

There. I'd said it. It sounded completely fantastic. They couldn't. Even Volker alone couldn't.

But he's willing to kill all those American servicemen.

Bombing a military installation is not the same thing as killing someone yourself, I argued.

Look at what he did to Tony. Anyway, you could have an "accident." Fall in front of a Métro train. Get knocked on the head and fall into the river. Fall off your roof, for that matter.

My eyes flew open. This was ridiculous. There was no point at all in lying in the dark imagining how Volker was going to kill me. In about three minutes I was going to be hysterical if I kept it up.

"Prepare for the worst," said my father's voice in my head. The problem was, there was nothing I could do to prepare. The problem was I was powerless, and there was nothing I could do at all.

SEVENTEEN

I DID FINALLY SLEEP, fitfully. Even so, when Volker woke me it took me several minutes to figure out what was going on. I was upright in bed, my hand throbbing, before I knew where I was or why Volker was there. But it all came back too clearly when I went into the bathroom and caught a glimpse of my face.

I looked truly awful. One of the books Volker was throwing must have hit me hard because there was a bruise coming up on my cheekbone. The greenish pallor of the night before was now decorated with dark circles under my eyes, all emphasized by my black turtleneck. My hair was a bird's nest.

I looked down at my hand, and shut my eyes quickly. It looked even worse. It was quite red now, with bluish streaks here and there. It was swollen so much that the skin felt stretched to the splitting point. The throbbing had stopped, which was a plus. Except when I moved it, it was more of a steady, dull, intense ache. I ran the little basin full of cold water and rested my hand in it while I tried to tame my hair. But I couldn't get a brush through the tangled curls, and I couldn't twist it out of the way using my right hand.

"What are you doing? We need to go," Volker said, walking into the bathroom without knocking. I looked at his face in the mirror. Had I already angered him? Was he going to knock me around some more? But he looked calm. He hadn't banged the bathroom door against the tub, which he used to do when he was mad.

"I'm sorry, I'll be ready in a second. I was just trying to do something about my hair."

"*Ja*, I see," he said critically. "Shall I brush it for you?"

I hesitated. It was true that when we were going out, Volker used to love brushing my hair. Sometimes he would braid it elaborately too, in patterns he said he learned from his sisters. But did I want him touching me now? It was creepy, at the very least. Maybe he just wanted to get his hands in my hair to start pulling.

But he didn't wait to be asked. He just picked up the brush and began untangling the snarls, as impersonally as if I'd been somebody's poodle. He didn't say anything. I was glad of that. It would have been hard to answer cordial inquiries about how I'd slept.

I didn't really know what to do while he worked on my hair. (I've never known what to do in a hair salon either, and this was much more awkward.) I kept my left hand in the sink, because the cool water felt good. My mascara was right in front of me, on the shelf above the sink. I picked it up, and wondered if I could get it open with my teeth. Silently Volker reached over my shoulder and twisted the top off for me.

It was peculiar. I have to say. I put the mascara on and handed him the Chanel rouge whose sleek black case I knew I couldn't manage. He opened it and placed it on the shelf, giving me the brush. Last night he had crippled me; this morning he was doing the very things I couldn't do because he had mashed my hand into the floor. Was this the famous intimacy between captive and captor? Or an intimacy left over from when we used to dress up together to go out, and he would suggest a little more of the copper eyeshadow? Or was he trying on some obscure level to make amends? It was peculiar, but it was also oddly comfortable, as if this was a little moment of truce between the violence of last night and the confrontation that was about to come.

The gentian-blue eyes met mine in the mirror. "You are ready?" I nodded. "Okay." He put the brush back on the shelf and then, as a second thought, quickly did my hair in a simple loose braid down my back. I lifted my hand from the sink and started to dry it but it hurt so much that I just wrapped it in a linen hand towel. Maybe I'd just keep it wrapped up like this. Or, better yet, maybe I could make some kind of sling.

As I followed Volker out of the bathroom, I tugged a challis shawl from a drawer of the bureau and laid it out on the bed. Made a triangle, I knew that; and if I could somehow fasten it, of course you can't tie a knot with one hand...

Volker was standing in the door of the bedroom. "We go now. *Now*."

I straightened up and left the shawl on the bed. The last thing I wanted was to try his temper, and I thought his helpfulness wouldn't extend to making a sling for the hand he'd mauled.

I couldn't help peeking at Madame Cabrol's loge as we went by, but the lace curtains didn't so much as flicker. Apparently her vigilance had been used up the night before.

When we got outside, Volker turned automatically left on the boulevard St. Germain. "We walk. We have time."

I looked at my watch, and he was right, it was only six-thirty. We could easily make it to Notre Dame by seven. And it was a gorgeous morning. It would be warm later, but the air was still a little bit cool. Pud-

dles lay in the shadows, where the street and sidewalks had already been cleaned, and they reflected a
cloudless sky that was still only pale blue. Sparrows
hopped around in the gutters while more dignified pigeons, with their gray-violet plumage gleaming,
strutted boldly in front of us. Most of the stores were
still shuttered, but a waiter was putting tables out at a
café near the church of St. Germain-des-Pres, and a
young boy wheeling a basket of bread from a bakery
on a side street nearly tripped Volker, who didn't even
notice.

I sneaked another look at him. The face was set, the
expression distant. I guess I was trying to figure out
what he was thinking. Of course he'd never been one
of those people who gave his thoughts away. Self-
contained, self-controlled. Didn't it make any difference to him? Here we were walking along in this
strange bubble of peace as if he'd never wrecked my
apartment or crushed my hand. And as if the meeting
ahead of us were nothing very important.

I tried to imagine what Edward's face was going to
look like. I couldn't. I couldn't decide if he would be
ashamed, or sad, or just brazen and casual. We had
reached the rue de Seine and the traffic light was
against us, but Volker, still on automatic pilot, looked
for cars and then crossed. I lagged behind a few steps,
and he grabbed me by the arm and pulled me forward. But he slowed his pace a bit, so that I could keep
up. We walked on in silence.

There must be something I could do. Somehow I'd
been hypnotized into this weird acceptance, but hell,
what did I have to lose? I started to look around, considering. As if he'd been able to read my mind, Volker
grabbed my arm. "We go this way," he said, and

nudged me left on the rue Grégoire-de-Tours. I turned
obediently and stayed with him as he zigzagged
through the Carrefour de Buci. The stalls for the daily
food market were already being loaded. Men the size
of mountains were placing oranges daintily in glowing pyramids. What would they say if I wrenched myself free of Volker and asked them to protect me?

They'd think it was all a great joke. It was silly even
to dream. But once we got to Notre Dame, there
would be two of them, Volker and Edward, two large
strong men. Beside me, only a foot away, women in
head scarves tidied their cheeses on beds of grape
leaves or gently sprinkled water over the boxes of sor-
rel and *mâche*. So close. So normal. It seemed incredible that they couldn't see what was happening: that
Volker was marching me off to some horrific denoue-
ment. At one stall I noticed a flat of pansies tucked in
with the romaine and ruby-leaf lettuce, incongru-
ously, and then remembered that it was now fashionable to eat flowers in your salad. If you were ever
going to eat salad again. An onion bounced across the
cobblestones toward me and I gave it a savage kick
toward the gutter.

Volker looked down at me and smirked. "*Ja*, you
are feeling the strain a little bit?" Then in an awful
parody of tenderness, he pulled my right hand through
his elbow and stroked it. Basically, improving his grip
on me.

We crossed the pont Neuf and approached Notre
Dame from the quai des Orfèvres. The sun was in our
eyes, covering the Seine with glittering scales, so bright
my eyes were watering. I was relieved when we turned
on the rue de la Cité, into the shadow of the massive
cathedral.

The square in front of Notre Dame, usually bustling with tourists and hemmed in with gleaming buses, was quiet. A few *clochards* slept on benches, and on a patch of ground near the cathedral steps an enterprising Senegalese peddler, having staked out the best spot, was laying out his fake-ivory elephant tusks and chess pieces with elaborate care.

"It is only five until seven," Volker said, looking at his watch. "Did you make a particular meeting point?"

"No. But I think he'll be able to pick us out," I said dryly, and Volker just nodded.

We stood where we were for a moment. Volker was looking around, as if he might catch Edward arriving from one of the side streets. Then he took my arm again, and we strolled toward the porch of the cathedral.

We could have looked like any tourists. Up early, let's not waste a minute, maybe Notre Dame will be open. Stand back to get a good view of the towers; then move in close to examine the carved figures over the doors. There is the Last Judgment; there is heaven, there is hell, those must be the apostles, don't you think, there are twelve of them.

I kept my eyes on the cathedral doors. On the left, one of them was open, and as I watched an old man with a cane came hobbling out. Early mass? Lighting a candle to a patron saint? As we walked past the benches, one of the *clochards* stirred, knocking a pair of brand-new crutches to the ground. His hand came down to clutch them, but he didn't stir further. For a moment I pitied him, thinking of a life in which all you had to hold onto was a pair of crutches.

Then I saw Edward. He came out from the street alongside the cathedral, and he was hurrying. Even at that distance he looked rumpled, in an old tweed jacket and faded khakis. He hadn't seen us yet, in fact he was looking beyond us toward the far end of the square, but then he turned his head and spotted us. Volker took my arm. Edward began running toward us awkwardly, as if he knew there was no need to hurry but couldn't help himself.

He was slightly out of breath when he arrived in front of us, and for a moment stood panting, looking from me to Volker.

I waited for it. I stood there with my face as stony as I could make it. Holding myself straight. Braced for the blow. Waiting to hear him say "Well done, Freilich." Or "You stupid fool!" Or even *Deutschland, deutschland über alles*."

What I heard was, tentatively, "Louise? Are you all right?" And he stepped closer with a funny unfinished gesture, as if he didn't know what to do with his hands. There was concern in his eyes, and puzzlement, and something warmer I couldn't think about just yet. But one thing seemed perfectly clear: He didn't know who Volker was.

It was as if the sun had come out, or I'd come shooting up from underwater. I couldn't help it, I started to grin, even though the bruises on my face hurt.

Edward smiled back at me a little doubtfully, just as Volker squeezed my arm and answered, "Burglars. When Louise got home last night, she surprised someone in her apartment. He got away, but she didn't want to spend the night there."

Edward's frown deepened, and he said directly to me, "What? Who...?"

Before he could finish, and before Volker could cut me off, I said, "Volker." And like that, the situation changed. Edward's face was suddenly tense. Volker dropped my arm. And suddenly, so quickly that I couldn't see how, he was holding a knife. At least I assumed it was a knife. There was something cold next to my neck, and there was alarm in Edward's eyes. And I didn't think that Volker would risk a gun in such a public place.

"So," he said in a conversational tone, "Louise will come with me. You will not have us followed. If you have men hiding somewhere around here, you will call them off. If they try to overpower me..." I squealed. He had nicked my neck.

"Why take a hostage?" Edward asked in the same measured tone of voice. "What is it you want? If you only want to leave the country, I'm sure it can be arranged."

"No. That is, yes. I want to leave the country. I want to go back to Germany. But I must take with me something that is mine."

"What is it? Look, Mr. Freilich. Let's stop acting. I know who you are and I think you know who I am."

"Oh, *ja*, Mr. Cole. Official of U.S. District Attorney, I know who you are."

"And you realize I have resources you don't. The complete cooperation of the Paris police, for instance."

"*Ja*, so the police lick your boots. What else?"

"It extends a little farther than that. Phones, railroads, airline cargo, mails. We can have customs search all bags leaving the country. You say you want something that is yours," Edward said with a new intensity. "*I can get it for you.*"

He had been so quick in taking up Volker's suggestion about "something that is mine" that I had trouble remembering he didn't even know what "it" was. He didn't know about the etui. Or Tony. Or the tape, or the plans to bomb military bases. He was trying, blindly, to strike a bargain. I wished there was some way I could help him.

The knife was no longer tickling my neck. I could feel the warmth where blood from the cut had soaked into my turtleneck, but Volker's hand had relaxed and the blade was now hovering closer to my earlobe. Volker was thinking hard.

"You can get me what is mine. And then what?"

"I can get you out of the country."

Another pause. Edward was avoiding looking directly at me. Volker shot him a suspicious glance. "And then what?"

Edward shrugged. "I don't know. You know where you want to go. I won't guarantee you immunity from extradition, if that's what you're asking."

"So," Volker said, trying it out. "You return to me what is mine. You get me out of France safely. Why? What does this do for Herr U.S. Attorney?"

Volker and I were both watching Edward's face. He was making what had to be an unprofessional offer. What justification could he produce? He was silent for a moment. Then he blushed. It wasn't a pretty girlish flush, he turned an unhappy crimson. Ears and all. And he said, "Louise."

"What?" Volker and I barked in unison.

"Louise. I find whatever it is, get you out of the country. You release Louise."

There was a tense moment. I shut my eyes. And they popped open in surprise when Volker started to laugh. The humorless Teuton threw back his head and roared. "Excuse me," he finally said when he stopped. "I find it so amusing. The famous American skill at negotiating for hostages. This is fine with me. Only Louise stays with me until I am safe. Then I send her back."

"No. She comes with me now," Edward said.

Volker just shook his head. "This I cannot have. But I tell you what. You come with me to leave country. I decide how I go, by plane or train, you come, I send her back with you."

"And if you so much as raise your voice to her, you'll be in jail before you know it," Edward said quietly. "I'll be watching. I'll know."

"Oh!" Volker raised his eyebrows. "It is not Herr Attorney I am dealing with. It is what, a hero of chivalry. Maybe you don't make concessions like this for every American citizen? What makes our Louise special?"

"Never mind, Freilich. What am I looking for, what am I getting back for you?"

But Volker was too relieved to let it go at that. I'd seen him sometimes in these jubilant moods, when what he loved to do most was tease. More than once he'd needled me into a rage while he chuckled.

"No, no, you tell me, would you do this for everyone?"

Edward just looked at him. Then he straightened up in some visible way, took on a sudden extra air of dignity. And he said, "No. Of course I wouldn't. I'm doing it because I love Louise." Startled I looked up and saw that he was watching me.

"Don't glare at me like that," he said softly. "Please." His eyes held mine. For a few seconds, everything else fell away. I was aware only of Edward. There were five feet of Parisian cobblestones between us, but somehow I felt his arms around me and I could hear his voice whispering inside my head "Trust me. It's all right. Trust me." His gaze didn't waver. Steady and warm. I drew a deep breath and felt the point of the knife scratch my ear.

Volker moved the knife back down to my neck. "*Ja*, all right. This is very convincing. All for the love of a good woman. I don't worry about how you explain it to your boss when I am not to be found anymore. I tell you what you must find for me. You are to intercept the mail. You said you can?"

Edward just nodded.

"It is for a package mailed first class from—" He looked at me, "Which post office?"

"Rue du Louvre. Posted last night." It felt like a week ago.

"Addressed to?"

"Me," I said.

"And what is in it?" Edward asked.

"A gold etui," Volker answered. "This is a case, to hold little tools in."

"What does it look like?" Edward asked.

"I don't know. Louise, you tell him."

"Um, it's about four and a half inches long," I said, reminding myself not to try to gesture with my left hand. "It's gold, sort of a flattened oval, Louis Quinze I would have said, though I'm no expert. Studded with diamonds, and as I recall there's an engraved monogram and coat of arms somewhere on the surface, and let me see, wasn't there some enamel too?'' I was babbling. I'd had an idea.

"That is enough, I think," Volker cut me off. "In any case it is not necessary to open the wrapping. In fact, the wrapping must come to me intact or..." The knife moved caressingly along my jaw. I just stood there numbly, thinking hard. Volker had moved around now. He was standing almost squarely behind me, so that my right hand was free. I flexed it. He didn't noticed.

"What is in the etui, Louise? Did you open it?" Edward was asking.

Why did he want to know? Should I tell him? Volker didn't object, so I said, "Yes, I did, just kind of automatically." I pictured the tiny tools spilled out across Tony's desk, gleaming in the light from his desk lamp. "There were scissors, a thimble, a little bottle probably for perfume, smelling salts, a needle case..." Volker was listening intently. Edward was watching me. This was the moment. "And a little spool of thread. Here." I plunged my hand in my jeans pocket and tossed the spool behind me.

Volker, as I had hoped he would, jumped. The knife fell away from my neck as he reached for the spool and the black tape that was unfurling behind it. I didn't wait to see what happened next. I ran.

It was a risk. Volker still had the knife. But maybe, if he was careless for just a few more seconds, Edward could overpower him. If not—well, at least I had a start. I shot off across the square. We had been standing several hundred feet from the church, and every now and then during that conversation I had glanced up at the façade. It soared above me, familiar, beautiful, welcoming. Sanctuary. I headed toward the steps and the open door.

I had a clear shot. The square was still almost empty, though the first tour bus had drawn up and was beginning to disgorge its load of sightseers. They scattered randomly to stand back and get a view of the cathedral. An energetic older couple in clashing madras struck out toward the back of the square, toting camera bags. I had to swerve to miss them. I looked back, to see what had happened between Edward and Volker. It took me a second to find them, because Edward was on the ground and Volker...

Volker was coming after me. I glanced ahead to see where I was going and reflexively put out my hands. Backing up toward me was a tall fat man with a telephoto lens trained on the roofline. I couldn't stop. I hit him squarely between the shoulders and stumbled back a step, reeling with the pain in my left hand.

"Oof," I heard, a sound like air blowing out of a balloon. Then, in a Southern accent: "Damn it, where the hell do you think you're going, young lady? You could have done some serious damage, this here camera is a Nikon..." I didn't stop.

I was cutting diagonally across the square, heading for the open door. I was nearly there. But Volker knew where I was going; he was running in a straight line, almost level with me. I hardly had to turn my head to see him. He was skimming along by the benches, watching me, with all things a smile on his face. Volker, the bastard, was having fun. He was winning the race. He had already, it seemed, won the game; he wouldn't have left Edward lying there without grabbing the spool. After all, Volker had been armed. I thought of where his knife might be right now and launched an intense, wordless prayer to the towers of Notre Dame.

And when I looked back at Volker, he wasn't there.

He wasn't sprinting like a track star alongside the benches, beating me to the open door of the sanctuary. He wasn't ahead of me grinning on the cathedral steps. He wasn't coming directly at me, hands reaching to grab me.

I slowed my steps and looked over my shoulder.

Volker was lying sprawled on the ground by a park bench. Underneath him was a brand-new crutch. On top of him, sitting unsteadily on his back, was the bum with the crutches: Tony. He had another crutch in his hand and was trying to hit Volker on the head with it. But at such close range, the crutch was unwieldy and Volker was wiggling and bucking. It wasn't going to take much to unseat Tony.

I stood still and looked around. The tourists were straggling toward the steps of the cathedral, where their guide was waving a neon-orange banner and struggling with a megaphone. At the back of the square, Edward was sitting up, clutching an arm, and someone was bending over him. The bums were still asleep. Three feet away, the Senegalese peddler adjusted the positions of the ivory elephants laid out on a crimson blanket. He had bangle bracelets and chess pieces and crudely carved mugs and bowls. And he had some tusks.

No sooner was the thought in my mind than I had a tusk in my hand. I hefted it as I sprinted over to where Volker was just rolling over. Tony managed to stay straddled on top of him, but Volker's hands were now free. As I ran the last few steps, he reached for Tony's neck.

The tusk was not as heavy as I'd hoped. But then, I only had one hand to swing with. I gripped the tusk with the point in my right hand. Two yards away from the pair on the ground, I shifted my stride. Would the damn thing be long enough? One step, two steps . . . With a skipping motion and a backswing as high as my waist, I brought the tusk down along the ground. The timing was perfect. Volker was just turning his head away so the tusk whacked him behind the ear with a tidy, satisfying *thunk*. Instantly he stopped moving.

Tony looked up. "Where'd you learn to do that?" he demanded, as calmly as if I'd just performed a card trick.

"Field hockey," I admitted, gasping. Someone was yelling nearby, but I couldn't make out why. "I hope I didn't kill him."

Tony put a hand on Volker's neck. "No, his pulse is still strong. But I think you have a new problem." He looked up to the source of the yelling, which was now standing six inches away from me: the Senegalese peddler.

"You pay for that, miss, you pay for it two hundred francs, I am an honest man, I try to make a living, this is not for games, this is genuine ivory elephant tusk, it is a bargain, it is only two hundred francs."

I sat down on the ground next to Volker's body. From there the peddler looked as high as the towers of Notre Dame. He kept glancing over his shoulder to make sure nobody was stealing his elephants and bangles, then turning back to us to yell. His French was pretty elementary, and he kept switching into an even worse version of English. I leaned my head against Tony's knee. All of a sudden I was completely drained.

"What did you do with my money?" Tony's voice came from over my head. "You don't look like you had a night at the Ritz."

"It's in my pocket."

"So could you pay the gentleman for his genuine elephant tusk?"

"I can't get the money out unless I lie down. And if I lie down I'll never get up."

"What do you mean you can't get the money out unless you lie down? Those jeans aren't that tight."

My left hand was in my lap, throbbing viciously. I straightened up so Tony could see it. "The money's in this pocket." I pointed to the left front pocket. "But I can't, for obvious reasons, get this hand into it. No, forget it, it's all right," I said, and started to get to my knees. "Maybe if I stand up..."

"Here, I'll get it out," Tony said, and reached toward the pocket.

"If you make any offensive remarks about this I'll hit you with that tusk," I said as he took the folded bills.

"No. Too tired for offensive remarks. What did he say, two hundred?"

"Right." He peeled off three fifty-franc bills. "What are you doing?"

"You always bargain with these guys, you know that, Louise," he said, holding out the money to the peddler.

I shut my eyes. Typical Tony. "Give him the extra fifty francs, for God's sake!" I tore another bill from his hands and waved it at the peddler, who backed away thanking us and blessing us and our firstborn children forevermore.

"Thanks. I've always wanted one of these," I said, after a pause. But I wasn't really thinking about the tusk. I was looking for Edward. I scanned the back of the square, but I couldn't see him. Tony touched me on the arm.

"There." He pointed to a handful of men off to the side of the square. In the center, shouting into a walkie-talkie, was Edward. We couldn't hear what he was saying, but the men around him were shuffling their feet and looking abashed. One, I noticed, was dressed as a street cleaner, in a blue smock and carrying a twig broom. One was a businessman, one a baker. Two were bums.

"The reinforcements didn't show up?" Tony suggested, and I turned to look back at him.

His eye was now black, and almost shut. His glasses, reinforced with fresh white adhesive tape, sat gingerly on his white-taped nose. His lip was swollen and shiny with ointment.

His curly hair was matted and he was wearing a filthy green jump suit with the name of a garage embroidered on the chest. It was no wonder I hadn't recognized him.

"Where'd you get the spiffy togs?" I asked.

"Don't ask," he said. "My skin is offended at wearing this thing." He looked at me steadily. "Anyway, you don't look so great yourself."

"Yeah." I shrugged. "Don't ask." We sat for a moment idly watching the peddler cluck, fussing over his ivory and occasionally darting glances at us. Nothing seemed to matter too much.

"So, Tony," I said finally.

"Yes, Louise?"

"What are you doing here?"

"She finally asks the question I am willing to answer," he said, with what would have been a wry smile if his face had been normal. I glanced back at Edward who was a little calmer now. He looked over at us and said something to the street cleaner and the baker. They started walking toward us.

"I think this is what you might call protective custody on its way," Tony said. And now there was no mistaking the brittle tone in his voice.

"Never mind, just tell me. What did you do after I left you?"

"You know, you're very bossy, Louise. It's a wonder I ever fell for you." I looked at him fiercely, and he said, "Okay. I went to the hospital. They cleaned me up, strapped my ribs and my ankle, asked a lot of questions and wanted me to spend the night, but I spun a story about a new baby at home and they let me go." He looked down at Volker, who was starting to stir, and hitched himself more firmly onto Volker's stomach. "Then I got to thinking." He sighed and looked down at his hands. "I don't know how much you know. The tape?"

"I know about the tape."

"Where is it now?"

"Edward has it. Or else Volker does. I threw it on the ground between them just before I broke away."

Tony looked puzzled but said, "I'll get to that part of the story later. You know what was supposed to be on the tape?"

"Volker told me. Plans to blow up a military base." I didn't want to see Tony's face. "He said you knew. And he told me about your brother. I know it's not really my business, Tony, but I swear, if you didn't keep things so bottled up you'd be—"

"All right, all right," he interrupted me, but his voice wasn't angry. Only tired. "I know. I *do* know. And it wasn't as bad—do you remember, last night, I was telling you it wasn't as bad as you thought?"

"I remember," I said, still looking down at my hands.

"Well, I knew what Volker was up to. And at first I thought it was just fine. I mean, it's not as if the United States doesn't have its own weird little undercover projects, I mean, you have only to look at the CIA!" His voice rose a little, in a slightly defensive tone. I looked up at him.

"Right," he said, meeting my eyes, "get on with the story. It did start to bother me. I didn't really want to be involved anymore. But of course, once you're in, you can't get out. And then I realized what they were really planning. It was when you were going out with Volker, and I was listening in on your apartment. You know I speak German. Volker was pretty careless sometimes about the telephone conversations he had when he was there. But I guess he knew you didn't know enough to follow, and didn't worry about being overheard."

The baker and the street sweeper were standing over us now, but they made no gesture to reach down and handcuff Tony. He slid off Volker's body and started to stand up, still talking. "So I realized what they had planned. I don't know what Volker told you about my brother, and I'll admit I—" Tony paused with a hard look on his face. "I have to say, I hate him. I don't ever want to see him again. But I don't want him dead, or any other serviceman either. Let 'em die in wars if they want to, but being blown up by a sneaky bunch of ideological crackpots isn't what they signed up for."

Tony reached down for the crutch that wasn't beneath Volker and fitted it under his arm.

"So I thought, if Volker has me send plans about this project, I'll screw them up somehow. And that's what I did. Volker gave me the tape, and I spliced bits of it and dubbed over other bits so that it won't make any sense now. It would *sound* sensible, but when they actually tried to carry out the plan, it wouldn't work. And nobody would know, except Volker."

I remembered Tony's panic when I had gone to his apartment. "And that was why it was so important that he not get the tape back?"

"Right. I didn't think he would listen to it, but he might. And if he did, I'd be dead meat."

"Which you very nearly were anyway."

Tony shrugged. Edward was heading in our direction now. One arm of his jacket was torn open, and I could see that the fabric of his shirt had been slashed near the shoulder, and darkened with something. On the ground, Volker moaned, and the street cleaner knelt to his side. I clambered awkwardly to my feet.

"I would never have thought you'd fall for a man so much like your father," Tony muttered, then stepped away as Edward put an arm around me and pulled me close. I buried my head against his chest and wrapped my right arm around him. His jacket fell over my back and I stood there for a long moment, feeling his heart beat calmly, blocking out all thought. Then he moved, as if to dislodge me. I backed away, blinking. He kept his right arm around me, holding me in front of him. And then, as if he couldn't help himself, he bent down to kiss me just under the ear.

"Oh, Christ!" I heard him mutter, and he reached into his trousers pocket.

"What is it?" I turned up to him. He was spitting on his handkerchief, and started to rub my neck with it.

"You're bleeding, sweetheart. And I feel like a vampire."

I could hear sirens now, the *ah-oo-gah! ah-oo-gah!* converging on us from several directions. A police van screeched into the square and bounced over the cobblestones toward us. Then another, then an ambulance, then a sleek, official-looking Citroën DS with darkened glass windows. In an instant we were surrounded by a ring of vehicles. The tourists on the steps of the cathedral, about to be herded inside to look at the masterpiece in stone and glass, looked longingly in our direction.

"Who's the ambulance for?" Tony asked Edward, the first words he'd addressed to him.

"Whoever needs it most. I think we'll have to toss a coin."

I suddenly turned my head, horrified. "Edward, he got you, didn't he? I mean, he knifed you? I'm sorry, I shouldn't be leaning against you, are you all right?"

"Yes," he said, letting me go, "I'm really fine. But I need to say a word to..." He slipped through the growing ring of men surrounding us to lean in the back window of the DS.

"You know, we could sit," Tony said, pointing to the bench right in back of us. "I think we could be here for a while." He was right. There seemed to be some discussion developing as to which group was going to take custody of which one of us. I could see gestures toward Volker, toward Tony and me, thumbs jerked at Edward. I heaved a sigh. "Can I ask you one more thing?" I said to Tony as we settled ourselves gingerly onto the bench.

"*One* more."

"Why did you give the etui to Gabriel instead of taking it to Germany yourself? I mean, it seems so *dumb*. Especially after Daddy had been caught."

He turned to me, and there was a silly smile on his face. "Jessye Norman was singing that night. That's your last question."

So we sat there in silence, side by side like an elderly couple feeding the pigeons. Volker groaned as a pair of ambulance technicians fussed over him. A fresh supply of plainclothes detectives arrived, self-consciously eyeing the black Citroën. My head gradually fell toward my chest. I was just barely aware that I was falling asleep with my mouth open when I heard a voice coming from somewhere above me.

I looked up. It was the tall fat man I'd bumped into earlier. And he was saying "Excuse me, miss, are you all making a movie?"

EIGHTEEN

TEN HOURS LATER I was sitting on my roof. The sun was starting to skid downward, and my chair cast a long shadow. The traffic was obviously clotted to a dead halt on the street below; I could hear the usual symphony of horns and voices and engines, drifting up to me. There was a bottle of wine open on the table at my elbow and a bowl of cheese straws from Fauchon that I'd been saving for a special occasion. My left hand was wrapped in a light fiberglass cast, and I had just had a four-hour nap. I expected Edward any minute.

It had taken almost an hour to clear up the confusion in front of Notre Dame that morning. The ambulance driver wanted to take Edward away (as the candidate with the worst injuries) but had to be content with me. Tony, since he'd already had medical attention, got one of the police vans, and Volker, who came to with a furious rush of swearing, got the other. I saw Edward climbing into the Citroën as the ambulance doors closed on me.

Somehow he had managed to get hold of Gisele, because she met me at the hospital and brought me home. The orthopedist (or whatever they're called in French; that was one thing I didn't find out) stupidly put the cast on while I was still wearing my black turtleneck and then we couldn't get the arm of the sweater over the cast so we had to cut it off. Exit my favorite black turtleneck sweater. Though I probably would never have worn it again anyway, after that night. Then Gisele cooked me an omelette and let me tell her the whole story, and tucked me in bed when the pain-killer suddenly overwhelmed me and I almost fell asleep with my face in my plate.

While I was sleeping, she cleaned up the living room. She must have enlisted Madame Cabrol's help, because there was not so much as a shred of paper or a chip of china on the floor. She'd left a green salad and a roasted chicken on the counter, a vase full of peonies on the dining-room table, and a pair of chocolate eclairs in the refrigerator. And she opened the bottle of wine, and left a note saying that Edward would be by some time after six.

The doctor, being French, hadn't said anything about mixing wine with painkillers. Being American, I knew very well that I shouldn't. Having lived in France for five years, I went ahead, and was feeling pleasantly muzzy when Edward walked across the roof.

He had cleaned up too. His arm was in a neat dark-green sling, and he had shaved and changed into a rather dashing dark-blue shirt. He had a big paper-wrapped sheaf from the florist's in his right hand, but he just dropped it on the ground as he reached my chair and leaned down and kissed me.

Very gently, very sweetly. Then he sat down on the roof and rested his head on my knees, and sighed.

We sat there for quite a while without talking. There wasn't a thought in my head except contentment. The beautiful evening, a comfortable chair, my hand on Edward's shoulder, his hand on mine.

Finally he kissed my palm and said, "Your phone's ringing."

I hadn't even heard it, but as I listened I could hear the answering machine click to life. Gisele must have connected it to the kitchen phone so I could sleep. It was my father's voice saying "Louise, I've been hearing the most god-awful things from Nick Turner's friend the consul general. I gather you're still in one piece but please call when you get back to reassure your old father. Don't worry about waking me up." I didn't move a muscle. I knew he'd hang up before I could get to the phone. He never could remember that he paid for three minutes whether he used them or not.

"Waking him up? We're five hours ahead of him." Edward said, reaching for the empty wineglass.

I picked up the bottle. "I guess he thinks I'm going to be sent home from the police station at 3 A.M. or something," I said, as I filled his glass. "Speaking of which..."

"No," he said. "Not right now." And he stood up, a little awkwardly. I just lay back in my chair looking at him as he loomed over me.

"In the best of all possible worlds, I would scoop you like a he-man," he said. "But maybe just for tonight we could take that part as read." And he held out a hand.

I looked at it. And back at him. His ears were on the large side. There was gray mixed in with the brown hair, and crow's feet around his eyes. He was more than a foot taller than I was. And I knew that when I touched his hand a little river of heat was going to run right through me.

It did. Right through him too, I guess, because he pulled me upright with a single motion and his mouth met mine. Not particularly gently. I forgot about the wineglasses on the ground, and the flowers, and our slings and casts and even the fact that we were standing on the roof in full view of the apartment building across the street. Until the phone rang again.

We broke apart, breathless. Edward looked down at me and pulled my kimono back onto my shoulder. "Shocking," he said. The machine clicked on.

"Louise," a male voice said, "you don't know me but I'm a friend of your friend Joan Tanner, and I'm going to be in Paris for ten days..."

In two long steps, Edward was at the door. The voice cut off suddenly. Edward reappeared at the door, dangling the unplugged phone in his hand. "I told Madame Cabrol we weren't at home to visitors, so we should get some peace now."

"Better make sure the bedroom phone is unplugged too," I said, without thinking. And then I could feel the heat rushing to my face. What if Edward didn't... If that wasn't... He probably just wanted to talk things over, I hadn't meant to sound like that...

In an instant he was at my side. "I thought of that too," he said softly. And nudged me toward the door.

I leaned back against him, feeling his heat through the thin silk of the kimono. His good arm came around my waist, and he nuzzled the back of my neck. "You know," he whispered, "I've been thinking about this ever since you opened the door with that knife in your hand." His fingers found the knot in the sash. As we stepped through the door I turned around.

My hand was on the button of his shirt when he put his own hand over it. Guiding me gently backward through the room in short shuffling steps, he said, "Can I tell you now, Louise? Will you let me tell you now that I love you?" I looked into his gray eyes. Saw nothing there but sincerity. And, as he watched my face, a dawning smile. He kissed me gently on the nose as we walked through the bedroom door. "You don't have to say anything," he said, carefully closing the door behind us. "I know good news when I see it."

DINNER, when we got it, was a little more difficult. Since neither of us had two operative hands we were reduced to tearing the chicken apart like something out of *Tom Jones*. It was a good thing Gisele had opened the wine, because neither of us could have managed it. Fortunately Edward's flowers were more peonies so we just jammed them in with Gisele's. Neither of us was up to trimming stems or arranging things. And since there was a lot of explaining to get through, the whole thing took awhile.

Edward, of course, knew the end of the story. It turned out that he had been waiting at Notre Dame surrounded by plainclothesmen in clever disguises. He was wearing a microphone tuned into a walkie-talkie and the reinforcements were supposed to rush Volker at the signal. But they were all tuned in to the wrong frequency.

"So Tony really saved our bacon," I said, chasing a piece of lettuce around the plate with my fork.

"He did," Edward answered, watching me. "You know, it wouldn't shock me if you just picked that up with your fingers."

"Got to preserve the proprieties," I muttered, spearing it at last. "What's left of them, anyway."

"Precious little," he said, with a contented smile. "I like that phrase. Precious little."

He seemed to have strayed from the subject, so I tried to bring him back. "Where is Tony now?"

"Oh, he's in custody. We've made a deal with him on the conspiracy charges. It was a little inglorious, but Volker was the one we were really after. And of course he's not talking, so all the information I've gotten has been from Tony. And Sago, who's getting better."

He looked up from his plate, suddenly alert and businesslike. It was sort of sweet. "I think we have the picture pretty close to complete. Tony was the link, and we were all confused by the fact that he was smuggling for both Freilich and Sago."

"What about the fencing? Will they go to jail?"

"Sago may not. He's pretty frail, and he has some information about a ring of thieves that he might be able to use to plea-bargain. I'm still not too sure how that works in France."

"And Tony?"

"Yes. He'll have to do some time." Edward shook his head. "He seems pretty unrepentant. The one thing he was worried about was you. He felt responsible for getting you into trouble, and when he heard about what you went through, that chase through the place de la Concorde and all that, he was... Well, I think he was really sorry."

"As well he might be," I began, and then thought of something. "But wait, did I tell you about that?"

"No." Edward was smiling again, in amusement, I thought.

"Did I tell Tony? I didn't think I had."

"No. The one constructive thing I managed to do last night was put a tail on you. Not that he did much good. You lost him at the crucial moment."

"Wait, I know. The guy outside the Elysée Palace?"

"Right. He was watching your apartment, followed you to my place, and managed to stay with you through the place de la Concorde." Edward was suddenly sober. "He said it was terrifying. Worse than the time a drug dealer fired on him."

"Well, I want you to know he was a lousy tail," I said. "I mean, the least he could have done was wear sneakers. I could hear him coming for blocks!"

"Not only that," Edward said, "but he let you see him."

"He did? When?"

"In the Métro. Little man in a corduroy suit. Do you remember him?" I did, vaguely. He had come down the escalator when I was fearing I'd see Volker. "The thing was, once you'd seen him, he couldn't get on the bus with you or you would have been suspicious. So he phoned and told me you were—"

"Wait! Edward!" I broke in. "I'm sorry, I didn't mean to interrupt. But that phone number you gave me, that emergency number. I tried it twice and it was the number of some restaurant!"

"It was? You mean you kept it after all? I was sure you were so mad you'd just throw it away."

"Well, of course I did but you read it out loud and I remembered it. I don't usually get numbers wrong."

"What did I tell you it was?"

"You said 4284.2053."

He shrugged and got up from the table. "I have it written down here." He reached into his trousers pocket.

"I think your wallet is on the bureau," I said.

"Ah. Right. Just a second."

He was gone for a minute, and I got up from the table to sit on one of the sofas. When he came back in he said a little sheepishly. "Under the bed." And he held out a card as he sat down next to me. It was a normal business card with his name and phone number on it and, in the corner, another number written in red ink: 4248.2053.

I just looked at him.

He made a little face. "You might as well know the worst now. I don't know how to cook, I'm tone deaf, I hate to shop, and I can't remember numbers."

"You mean that creep in the corduroy suit was calling you up and I couldn't? God, that makes me mad! Particularly when I think about how much he scared me."

"I know," Edward said soberly, and pulled me next to him with his good arm. "And the next part is even worst. When he called he told me you were heading to St. Cloud, so I drove out there while he tried to get a taxi to follow the bus, but he couldn't. And then when I got to St. Cloud, you weren't there. Where did you go?"

"Back to your apartment. I realized I didn't dare take the bus all the way. I couldn't go that far from the gare du Nord because I didn't have any money. That was why I did all that running around in the first place. I'd left the house with nothing but fifty francs, so I couldn't just go to a hotel and wait until morning.

"So that was when you saw Tony?"

"Right."

"But when did Volker finally catch you? He wouldn't say, and Tony couldn't figure it out."

"Well," I said, trying to keep my voice level. "I went to the gare du Nord. And waited for you. As long as I could."

His arm around me tightened. "While I was arguing with a policeman on the boulevard de Courcelles. I got a ticket for running a red light trying to get back to the station in time. By the time I got there it was twenty past one and you were gone. Fed up with waiting?"

"Fed up? It wasn't like being stood up for a date," I protested. "I was—" I shut my eyes for a moment—"exhausted and scared and the idea of finding you was keeping me going, though I was worried about that phone number and thought you might not be there. And then you weren't, and these Arabs kept pestering me . . ." I shuddered. "It was a low point," I said, trying to make my voice sound dry and detached.

"I am sorry." Edward's voice came from somewhere right behind my left ear. "I am so sorry."

"Well, I'm not trying to make you feel terrible," I said, pulling his hand onto my lap and placing it palm to palm with mine. "It just came over me. Anyway, after that I just ran into Volker in the street. Pure bad luck."

"And he brought you here."

"Yes. Eventually," I said. There were some things I was not ready to think about.

His fingers slipped between mine and clasped my hand. He reached around to kiss my temple.

"He told me you were working with him," I said to my lap.

I could feel the deep breath he drew. "That was why you looked so shocked this morning."

I nodded.

"Well, I wasn't."

I shook my head.

Edward sighed. "You know, sweetheart, it's going to take you a long time to believe this. But some things *are* exactly what they look like."

"I guess." I squirmed around so I could see his face. He was looking steadily at me. What did I really know about him? He was kind. He was brave. He had great taste in flowers. He said he loved me.

He smoothed my hair back from my face. "I do, you know," he said. "I know what you're thinking. I do love you. But you don't have to trust me all at once."

"Well," I said, "I do trust you, sort of. But I still wouldn't lend you my life savings."

"Give it time," he said, and kissed me.

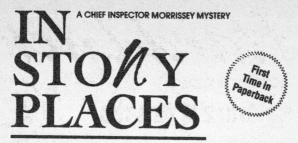

A CHIEF INSPECTOR MORRISSEY MYSTERY

IN STONY PLACES

KAY MITCHELL

First Time in Paperback

LOVELY ENOUGH FOR A KILLER

Murder stalks the quiet English village of Malminster. There's no connection between the victims, except that they're all young and pretty.

The murders seem random, and the killer is very careful. All Chief Inspector Morrissey's got is a fattening file of paperwork and nothing to go on but the latest victim's diary. Worse, he can't get a feel for the mind of the killer he's hunting.

But the killer is watching him—aware that Morrissey is getting close. Perhaps it's time he introduced himself to Morrissey's eighteen-year-old daughter....

"Unpretentious, brisk, an engaging example of the village procedural."
　　　　　　　　　　　　　　　　　　　　—*Kirkus Reviews*

Hard Luck

A Cat Marsala Mystery

Barbara D'Amato

First Time in Paperback

HIGH STAKES

Chicago journalist Cat Marsala has just begun her assignment on the state lottery when murder falls into the picture—literally—as a lottery official takes a leap in the middle of the multistate lottery conference.

Suicide...or murder? It's curious to Cat—and to the police—that the guy took his mighty plunge right before his meeting with her. Especially curious since he'd hinted at some great exposé material, like "misappropriation" of lottery funds.

"Cat Marsala is one of the most appealing new sleuths to come along in years."
—Nancy Pickard

Available at your favorite retail outlet in July, or reserve your copy for June shipping by sending your name, address, zip or postal code, along with a check or money order for $3.99 (please do not send cash), plus 75¢ postage and handling ($1.00 in Canada) for each book ordered, payable to Worldwide Mystery, to:

In the U.S.

Worldwide Mystery
3010 Walden Avenue
P.O. Box 1325
Buffalo, NY 14269-1325

In Canada

Worldwide Mystery
P.O. Box 609
Fort Erie, Ontario
L2A 5X3

Please specify book title with your order.
Canadian residents add applicable federal and provincial taxes.

WORLDWIDE LIBRARY®

HARDL

The Hour of the Knife

SHARON ZUKOWSKI

First Time in Paperback

A BLAINE STEWART MYSTERY

REST, RELAXATION...AND MURDER

Blaine Stewart found work and self-pity moderately effective ways to cope with her husband's death. Tough, tenacious, burned-out, she was getting on everybody's nerves—including her own. A trip to the Carolina coast was going to give her the chance to tie up a case and then the time to catch some R and R.

But when her client—and friend—was found dead in the marsh, Blaine started asking questions.... Vacations had never agreed with Blaine, anyway, and this one wasn't about to change her mind...especially when it was highly likely it would be her last!

"The fast paced action, assortment of characters and the unsolved death will keep you reading far into the night."
—Polish-American Journal

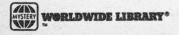

WORLDWIDE LIBRARY®
TM

A TONY AND PAT PRATT MYSTERY

Murder Takes Two

First Time in Paperback

BERNIE LEE

FINAL CUT

An unexpected trip to recording studios in London for advertising writer Tony Pratt and his wife, Pat, sounded fun and exciting—in spite of the rather off-the-wall bunch they'd be dealing with.

The tension was thick as London fog, but there were commercials to be made and sights to be seen. Until the eerie quiet of the studio was shattered by an unusual sound effect—that of a falling corpse—as a murderer began a very personal job of editing.

"One of the more engaging husband-and-wife sleuthing teams."
—*Flint Journal*

WORLDWIDE LIBRARY ®